Sarah, suddenly apprehensive, turned enquiringly to her uncle, who came to her and took one of her hands between both of his own, beginning portentiously, "Sarah, dear..." He hesitated, blushed and looked to Lady Dagley.

"Oh do get on with it, Henry, do!" cried his sister-in-law, with untoward impatience.

"Fact is, m'dear," (a rosy flush engulfed his cheeks) "a deuced delicate matter."

"How vexatious you are, brother. One would think you were inviting her to a funeral! Let me tell her myself, do." And Lady Dagley turned towards her daughter, and, with a theatrical flourish, declared, "My sweet life, we have today received a very flattering and advantageous offer for your hand."

To Be a Fine Lady is Delia Ellis's first novel. Delia Ellis is a qualified teacher, educated at the John Howard School and Keele University. She has a particular interest in Georgian history and would love to live in Bath in order to soak herself in its Regency atmosphere.

To Be a Fine Lady

Delia Ellis

Woman's Weekly Fiction

A Woman's Weekly Paperback
TO BE A FINE LADY

First published in Great Britain 1986
by Malvern Publishing Company Ltd
This edition published 1995
by Woman's Weekly
in association with Mandarin Paperbacks
an imprint of Reed Books Ltd
Michelin House, 81 Fulham Road, London SW3 6RB
and Auckland, Melbourne, Singapore and Toronto

Copyright © Delia Ellis 1986
The author has asserted her moral rights

A CIP catalogue record for this title
is available from the British Library
ISBN 1 86056 095 4

Printed and bound in Great Britain by
BPC Paperbacks Ltd
A member of
The British Printing Company Ltd

CHAPTER 1

The fire shed a dark glow on the occupants of the large shabby drawing room, illuminating softly the five faces gathered around. It was June, but the long settled spell had that morning ended in a sudden storm and the monotonous downpour which followed had lent a chill to the air, quickly felt in the old house, and made the luxury of a fire seem excusable. The family always loved to sit together around a fire in the evenings and were by no means loath to give in to the promptings of the weather, so that dusk found them in their accustomed places, while Sarah read quietly to them in her spirited and melodious voice. She had chosen an old favourite from the shelf, 'Robinson Crusoe': there was little to spare for buying new books now, but in any case, the family loved the old and familiar and young Philip's face glowed expectantly as she retold yet again of Crusoe's agitation at seeing footprints on his island.

"If I'd written this," broke in Hugh, a look of deep concentration puckering his brow, "I'd have made Friday a real man-eating cannibal. Then he could have waited for Crusoe behind a palmtree, captured him and then eaten him all up and boiled his bones to make stew!"

"Really, Hugh, must you be so revolting?" replied Charlotte loftily, at seventeen quite above the ghoulishness that would have delighted her a year before."

"What's so bad in that? Even you will admit that if Crusoe *had* ended up in the pot we wouldn't have to listen to all the boring bits on farming."

"Little booby! How could he write the ending to the story if he was eaten?—and don't call me Charlie!"

"I'm not a booby. Nor am I little. I'm fourteen, in case you've forgotten, as well as being taller than you, and I'll thank you to remember it. You would do as well to remember that you aren't out yet yourself—taking on airs. And if I want to call you Charlie I will," broke in Philip, the youngest and by far most even-tempered of the younger members of the family, "I'm trying to listen." He looked up at his eldest sister from his customary place on a cushion at her feet, snuggled his head against her knee and said sweetly, "Do go on, Sarah, you know this is the part I love best."

"Yes dearest," replied Sarah dryly, "For I can see that the others are quite entranced. So reassuring to know that my reading is stirring enough to have them gripping their chairs with excitement."

On being earnestly convinced that they were indeed listening, however, she turned again to her book and began to read, first moving her hand to adjust the position of her candle so that it shed more light onto her page. Occasionally she raised her eyes to glance at the three youngest members of her family clustered around her, their eyes, bright in the fire's glow, asparkle with excitement at the old tale. At times her attention wandered to her mother, Lady Dagley, reclining languidly on her sofa on the other side of the large pine fireplace, a pleasant, if vacuous expression presented to the world as she held a little handscreen between her face and the heat from the flames, to protect her milky complexion. Sarah smiled contentedly, thinking fleetingly to herself, "If only Kit was here, all would be perfect."

Kit was her brother, Christopher, the Eighth Viscount Dagley, and for some months now, head of their household. He had assumed the title on his father's death some little time before and, although only nineteen, his presence always gave her a comfortable feeling of support, so sensible and far-seeing was he.

Sarah, his elder by five years, had taken upon herself much of the responsibility for her family since her father's death, and, if truth be told, for some time before it as well. Dearly as she had loved her father—for he had been an attractive and witty man—she had to admit that he had been a poor provider. If, when he died, little could be said by his friends on his behalf, it was equally true that little could be held against him by his enemies, save for an

4

unfortunate tendency he had to fritter away the fortune amassed by previous Dagleys over several centuries. Life for the Seventh Viscount had revolved around the tables at Watier's Club in Piccadilly, both gaming and dining, for he had been a man of cards and of good dinners. While his family remained unfashionably at home in the large old house situated near to the town of Newcastle-under-Lyme, he lived most of his time in London, doing nothing worse than gradually discarding the considerable wealth he had inherited some twenty years previously.

Had his wife shared his taste for a fashionable existence, it is possible that she might have exercised some restraint on him, although, in her less optimistic moments, Sarah had to admit to herself that this was unlikely, for her father had been as single-minded as he was charming. But such a scheme was never put to the test. Lady Dagley hated town society as much as her husband loved it and, during the early years of her marriage had used her not infrequent pregnancies to keep her squarely situated at home. Of all things, a sedentary life suited her admirably and, like many another lady of few mental resources, she enjoyed nothing more than lying all day on her sofa, surrounded by those of her children who had survived infancy and remembering those that had not, her vinaigrette nearby to revive her, should she be overcome by her memories. Childbearing days long past, she had found no pressing obligation to remove to the capital, for such a sad invalid as she had become could add little to the general gaiety to be found there.

Although she had had a certain affection for her husband on their marriage, his frequent absences during their life together made their final parting less painful than it might otherwise have been. His sad demise too, prevented him from completing the financial ruin of his family, which was a great blessing, although it must be admitted that he had gone as far along that road as one could reasonably expect him to in only twenty-five years of dedicated self-indulgence.

During her husband's lifetime Lady Dagley, bent on a life of indolence, had given little thought to the smooth running of her household, and, as soon as she became a young lady, the servants turned increasingly to Sarah for their instructions. On her father's death things changed little, for Lady Dagley liked to fancy that she had sustained a further blow to her sensibility and spent the better part of her time in either lying in a darkened room or, on her better days, sitting quietly with her netting on the drawing room sofa. Sarah did not consider herself ill-used at this, for despite her self-imposed ill-health, her daughter knew that Lady Dagley loved her children dearly and was prepared to further their well-being in any way which did not include the expenditure of much personal effort. Sarah recognised fully the nature of her mother's affection, but was very fond of her nonetheless. She was, in any case, of a managing disposition and enjoyed seeing to the household duties at Leighwood, although for some years, the impoverished state of her family had made her familiar with cares from which the other young unmarried women of her acquaintance were carefully guarded. How grateful she was to her uncle for paying Kit's expenses at Oxford, for without his generosity they would be at a standstill. A frown chased briefly across her face. Hugh would be at Eton now had their father made proper provision for him. Instead, their uncle was having to tutor the younger boys himself and there was little chance that either would be able to receive an education befitting his rank. Not for the first time did Sarah thank heaven that her uncle enjoyed a single existence, for had he been encumbered with a wife and family, things might be even worse for them all.

She was not one to dwell long on her difficulties, however, for her disposition tended towards the cheerful, and, shaking off the unfamiliar mood of depression, she was just about to begin reading again when the oak door on the other side of the room opened narrowly to allow entry to a slight lady of uncertain years. Her long grey dress was evidently not a recent acquisition, for it was rather outmoded and a little darned in places, but Miss Nelsworth never forgot, in spite of her lowly calling as governess to the Dagley family, that she was the daughter of a gentleman. As a result, her flushed neck was adorned with a fine lace collar and on her mousy curls rested a cap so lavishly ornamented with point lace that a less indolent employer than Lady Dagley might have been moved to protest at such extravagance. Miss Nelsworth moved from the door into the light spread by the fire and, as she did so, there was a perfunctory movement from the floor just behind Sarah's chair as Bess waved her tail fleetingly to acknowledge her presence.

"My dear Lady Dagley, are you quite certain that you left your needlework in your room? I have searched everywhere I can think of and cannot find it at all," she began in her small, flurried voice.

"Never mind Nelly," replied her mistress languidly, unconsciously calling her by the pet name she scolded the others for using, "It is of no moment after all. I am quite comfortable listening to Sarah."

"I am persuaded, Ma'am," the governess continued, as she fussed around Lady Dagley, plumping up her cushions, "that you have a visitor, for I heard a carriage as I came through the Hall. Who would come to the house so late?"

"My brother-in-law hoped to be home today. But I think he would not venture out so soon after his long journey," said her mistress, the same vanity which would not allow her to continue long in black after her husband's death leading her to put up a hand to adjust the ribbons to her cap in case she was wrong.

The younger members of the family, hoping too that she was mistaken, strained to hear the voice speaking good-humouredly to Jackson, the butler, down in the vestibule. It was *indeed* Uncle Henry, and they waited eagerly for him to come upstairs, not daring to leave their places for fear of their mother's displeasure. Sarah was just as pleased to receive her uncle, though more patient, and smiled calmly as she put her book to one side and encouraged Pip to move onto a footstool next to his Mama's sofa.

Bess, by far the least well-behaved of the family, sprang up at once, almost knocking over the mahogany table upon which Sarah's candle rested in her delight at hearing the familiar voice. She ran quickly over to the door and stood with her nose pressed to the line of the opening, while her long curly tail swished round and round in ever more vigorous circles.

There was nothing distinguished about Bess's lineage. A commonplace black crossbred collie, with a miscellany of additions, Sarah had adopted her as a pup about four years before, when she had rescued her from a group of young tormentors in the village: one look into the eyes of that pathetically shivering scrap and she was lost.

Now, Bess loved all the family with an untiring affection, but she preserved a slavelike devotion for Sarah alone, whom she looked upon as a goddess of all virtues. It would, perhaps, be stretching the truth to say that Bess had ever achieved a high state of perfection in obedience and behaviour, but one word of reproach from her mistress and her ears flattened immediately against her head and her eyes lowered, while she dampIy nuzzled Sarah's hand in an attempt to placate her and be loved again.

Since her puppy days, she had shown a tendency, unnerving for the uninitiated, to remember as a long-lost friend any person to whom she was once introduced so that a boisterous greeting awaited Mr. Dagley when Jackson opened the door for him. As he entered the room, Bess charged at him immediately, encircling him in pure joy, and finally deposited two paws on his chest in an effort to lick the worn features on his face. Luckily, Mr. Dagley was just as much under Bess's spell as were the others and, before even exchanging so much as a word with his late brother's family, he began pulling at the dog's ears absentmindedly, and started a fatuous conversation with her, an exchange not designed to lessen her frantic attempts to be caressed and fondled to her satisfaction.

After attending to the more pressing needs of Bess's welcome, he was at liberty to devote himself to the rest of the family, although Bess stationed herself at his feet in an attempt to ensure that his visit was not curtailed too suddenly. She need not have worried, for Mr. Dagley settled himself comfortably in his elbow chair and answered the family's questions concerning the details of his excursion into Shropshire, while his niece went to pour him a glass of his favourite madeira and Miss Nelsworth hurried to order extra candles to be lit.

Mr. Dagley was, apart from being Reverend of the Parish, the younger brother of the late Viscount, and it must be admitted that the family's fortune would have been better served had he been born the elder, for he was as prudent as his brother had been careless. He had entered the church as a young man, simply because he had had no desire for the alternative military existence rather than for any strong religious conviction, and had, as a result of his brother's patronage, been presented with several good livings in the late Viscount's gift. It had been as much a surprise to himself as to his congregation how well such a life suited him, for his customary bent towards philanthropy made him more concerned for the welfare of his parishioners than many a man with a more obvious vocation might have proved. As he was a thrifty man, he had been able to pay the expenses of his nephew at Oxford, while continuing to ensure the welfare of those members of his congregation who needed his assistance, but he felt a great sense of obligation to the other members of his brother's family, taking on himself all the guilt which the late Viscount should have felt, but had managed so entirely to escape. Viscount Dagley's frequent absences had led his family to rely heavily on his brother, so that it is true to say that he seemed more like a father to the youngest Dagleys than their own had ever been. He had, too, an extreme fondness for his sister-in-law, which made him take up as his own all her troubles and vexations. As a young woman, Lady Dagley had been very much admired, and her brother-in-law had been among those who had considered her the sweetest girl of their acquaintance. In consequence, he had never married and had become wholly devoted to her interests. Now, as always when Lady Dagley spoke, he gave her all his attention.

"I hardly expected to see you today, brother, for we did not think you were returning until late this afternoon," said that lady in her thin, sweet voice, wafting her little handscreen to cool herself.

"Just so m'dear: but I have some news, so I waited only until I had eaten before setting out. Alas, just as I was leaving the house, Jenny Salt arrived to say that her grandfather had taken a turn for the worse and wanted to see me, so I was forced to delay my visit."

"How is poor old Mr. Salt?" asked Sarah, placing her Uncle's madeira carefully on a side table at his elbow. "I took a few items that the family needed down to them yesterday, but they are so shockingly poor that I fear we must try to find a more permanent solution to their problems."

"I do not wish to be unchristian, my child, but I fear that

little can be done for the family while Jenny's father fritters away all the money which comes into the household. How a man can be so improvidential as to ignore the needs of family and squander his money on his own pleasure is indeed beyond me . . ." He broke off suddenly in confusion, "I beg pardon, m'dear!" he looked unhappily towards his sister-in-law. "I didn't mean to cast any stones."

"Of course you didn't brother," she answered placidly, "though it must be admitted that my husband was quite as thoughtless as Mr. Salt—in his own way, of course."

"You said you had some news, uncle," said Sarah hastily, attempting to change the subject. "Not bad news I hope? Not Kit?" as a new worry brought a crease to her forehead.

"Not bad news at all, Sarah my dear, quite the reverse I think, so you need not be afraid. Something, however, that I must first discuss with your mother," and looking enquiringly at Lady Dagley, still reclining lazily at her ease on the sofa, he asked gently, "Do you feel up to moving into the library, m'dear? I really do need to speak with you about this little matter before continuing any further with it, or I should not dream of disturbing you." Like everybody else around her, her brother-in-law upheld the fiction of Lady Dagley's ill-health in the kindest possible way, because he admired her so. Indeed, it was as natural for Mr. Dagley to love her as she herself felt it was to be loved.

Sarah's mother was extremely curious to know what could bring Mr. Dagley out so late and moved far more quickly towards a door situated at the far end of the room than her invalid state might have been felt to allow, pausing only to pick up her vinaigrette and her handkerchief on the way, in case his tidings were designed to pull her down. As the library door closed behind them, the rest of the family were free to discuss with their governess this unexpected turn of events and to speculate on its cause.

"Do you think he might have received a preferment, Nelly?" asked Sarah, "for he is certainly kind enough to get one."

"It can't be that, Sarah," reasoned Hugh. "Why should

he have to discuss that with Mama in private?"

"I only hope that he has not unearthed some new folly committed by Papa," said Charlotte acidly, her down-to-earth streak overcoming for a moment her usual decorum.

"If you cannot speak of your poor dear Papa in a more respectful manner, Charlotte, perhaps you could retire to your room," chided Miss Nelsworth stiffly, a baleful gleam in her pale watery eyes. In spite of her late employer's shortcomings, she would allow no-one to cast aspersions on him or indeed on any member of his family.

Charlotte turned pink with embarrassment, but little could depress her spirits for long and she was soon making guesses, some of them very wild, as to their uncle's business. Hugh even went so far as to listen at the library door to try to hear what was being said. His efforts were in vain, for the door was a thick one, but in a surprisingly short time their mother and uncle returned to the drawing room. To her family's surprise Lady Dagley was exhibiting an unaccustomed animation: indeed she seemed positively glowing. As she advanced into the room, she took one glance at the group seated around the fireplace and exclaimed brightly,

"Why, Nelly, my dear, whatever can you be thinking of in allowing the boys to remain up so long? Off you go to bed now, my loves, you too Charlotte, for I am persuaded you have been looking rather pale of late."

The three younger children attempted to protest, but they recognised, as did their governess, that in this humour she would brook no delay. As the door closed on the noisily departing children, Lady Dagley turned to her daughter and said, in a tone of exultation which Sarah had never heard her use before, "And now, my dearest girl, your uncle has some famous news to tell you!"

Sarah, suddenly apprehensive, turned enquiringly to her uncle, who came to her and took one of her hands between both of his own, beginning portentiously, "Sarah, dear . . ." He hesitated, blushed and looked to Lady Dagley.

"Oh do get on with it, Henry, do!" cried his sister-in-law, with untoward impatience.

"Fact is, m'dear," (a rosy flush engulfed his cheeks) "a deuced delicate matter."

"How vexatious you are, brother. One would think you were inviting her to a funeral! Let me tell her myself, do." And Lady Dagley turned towards her daughter, and, with a theatrical flourish, declared, "My sweet life, we have today received a very flattering and advantageous offer for your hand."

CHAPTER 2

For a fleeting moment the room seemed to slide away from Sarah's field of vision and her eyes first closed and then opened wide in surprise. She heard her voice, as if from a long distance, ask the question, "Who has made this offer Mama?" and was gratified at how calm she sounded.

"My love, you will never guess," cried Lady Dagley, her hands clasped in ecstasy on her bosom, "not if you live to reach your century! Such a triumph for my darling girl! To be able to hold our heads up again! How comfortable that will be to be sure. I declare that no-one knows how I have suffered these past few years from your poor dear Papa's little extravagances. The humiliation of having to give up our carriage and travel in a gig! So depressing. But now, all that is at an end."

"Mama, if you do not tell me who has offered for me, I believe I will have need of your vinaigrette," murmured Sarah faintly, leaning for support on the back of a chair.

"Nonsense, my dearest, you are never ill," replied her mother, "and I have ever been grateful that you have been spared my wretched ill-health. It is a constant . . ."

She was interrupted by her brother-in-law, who had been watching Sarah's face closely and began to fear that she really would have an attack of palpitations if her mother was not halted. "My dear, I have the pleasure to inform you that I, yesterday, received on your behalf, an offer of marriage from Miles St. John Hubert Greville, the Sixth Earl of Wilberton." Sarah's face underwent a transformation, "Uncle Henry, how could you, you hoaxer! I thought you were serious and you have been playing at cat and mouse with me all along."

"I assure you, m'dear, that I speak no more than the truth," he replied, his voice so devoid of expression that

Sarah suddenly knew that this was no joke.

"But why should he choose me?" she asked in a bemused fashion, "He might have anyone he wished. Why seek the hand of a provincial nobody, without a feather to fly with?"

"Really, dearest, such a common expression," protested her mother fastidiously.

"I am sure that he has never even seen me," continued Sarah unabashed, "for I am persuaded that so important a personage would have been pointed out to me had he crossed my path the year I came out."

"I believe, my love, that the year you came out the Earl was still in black gloves for his first wife—killed in a carriage accident in his grounds at Beaumere, you know. Shocking tragedy at the time, I remember.—Anyway, I expect he remained on his estates for a time, which accounts for your never having met him," explained her uncle, adding kindly, "though I am sure that had you met he would have been charmed with you."

"I don't see why he should have been," she replied bluntly. "No-one else was."

As Sarah's debut, five years before, had been crowned with a remarkable lack of success, there was little that either her uncle or her mother could say to this and a brief silence ensued. Lady Dagley refused to be daunted with memories of past misfortunes, however, now that the future looked so bright and began again optimistically, "But what has that to say to anything, love? Indeed, we should be pleased that your hand was not claimed or you could not now have received such a splendid offer. The biggest prize on the marriage mart and you have him!"

"I still do not understand why he should think we should suit," muttered Sarah doubtfully.

"Perhaps I may help to reassure you, niece?" replied her uncle. He hesitated before going on, for he had always understood his niece better than her mother did and knew that Sarah would not be induced to accept simply by his dangling the rank of Countess before her. Other arguments would be needed to persuade her to her duty, and he must certainly make every push to do so, for no-one knew as well as he how imperative it was that she take advantage of this opportunity. He had for some time viewed the Dagley's future with deepest foreboding, but this marriage was the one sure way open to them to bring themselves about. He began his explanation now in the pompous tone he always used on serious occasions, while he picked nervously at the cuticle of his thumbnail, "Of course, you must be wondering how such an offer came to be made, my dear, but I can explain it all very easily to you. While I was in Shropshire, and because of the regard your father had for the late Earl of Wilberton, I felt it only polite, to pay my respects to the new Earl. He has only recently come into the title, his father having survived your own by only a few months, and it seemed to me that common courtesy demanded that I offered my condolences. He is a charming fellow, charming, and asked me to stay at Beaumere while I conducted my business, which, as you may suppose, I was happy to do. During my stay the conversation often centred upon your father and how he left you all at a standstill, so to speak. Wilberton felt it to be a dashed havey-cavey affair and that you had all been abominably ill used,—begging your pardon, m'dear."

He looked apologetically at Lady Dagley, receiving in return a placid nod of understanding, and went on, "When your name came up, Sarah, he expressed great interest, and before I came away he made his offer. It is as simple as that."

"It must be gratifying to you to know that he offers for me out of pity, Uncle," replied his niece acidly, "For we certainly have nothing to give in return."

Her uncle was quick to recognize his niece's expression for her obstinacy was a by-word in the family, and he rapidly sought for the right words to persuade her. "You forget, my love, that although our family is no longer wealthy, it is one of the oldest and most respected in the country. The Earl naturally wishes to ally himself to a family of repute, and a Dagley, you know, can never be despised. The Earl himself is so wealthy that your lack of fortune is of no importance."

"But Uncle, there are many other families equally respected, and, surely such a man would demand a beauty. You must have misled him on the matter. He will take one look at me and regret his impulse," cried Sarah, with all the bluntness for which she was famous.

"You have always under-estimated your charms, my girl, but as you so correctly remind us, Sarah, you have yet to meet, and, should you dislike each other, of course the matter will go no further. But the Earl is not a very young man, you know, he is five and thirty, and he is not on the look-out for a raving beauty. He has made one love-match, in his first marriage, and now looks for a cosy marriage with a conformable woman, who will be willing to raise a family and not expect him to run after her all the time. When he heard how well you look after us all here, my dear, he was struck by the fact that you might be just the girl he is after, and your father's friendship with him would help to seal the match."

Sarah listened to her uncle's words and an unaccountable feeling of gloom descended upon her. She had never considered herself to be of an excessively romantic disposition and, had anyone asked her if she would have been willing to make a marriage of convenience to save the family, she would probably have said that she would. The fact remained, however, that she had never expected to be asked, and it was lowering to find that she was less willing to be cast as heroine than she expected. She was also disturbed that the Earl should have expressed a desire for a 'conformable' wife, for the most optimistic of her friends could not truthfully have described her thus.

"Supposing that, when I meet him, I do not feel that *he* is the man to suit *me*, Uncle, what then?" she asked deliberately.

"Then, my child, you may of course reject his suit, though I trust that you would weigh your actions very carefully beforehand. I am the very last person to wish to remember my late brother's sad management, but on this occasion I feel justified in reminding you how heavily encumbered are the estates. I am glad to be able to afford to pay Kit's expenses at Oxford, but I can see no possibility of raising the blunt for a suitable education for the other two boys. If we are ever to come about, it will take years of careful management and economy, and the estate needs money spent on it *now*. All this is before we consider Charlotte's debut. Heaven knows, you suffered enough

16

when you were presented, and things are even worse now. Who knows how we shall raise enough this time? Wilberton, besides being a matrimonial prize of the first stare, is willing to make a handsome settlement on you, which will enable you to assist your family in just those ways which you would most wish."

He could not have appealed to the girl on any ground more likely to sway her. Before he left, Mr. Dagley had elicited from her a firm promise not only to receive the Earl, but also to accept him should he make the expected offer, unless she felt him to be excessively disagreeable. He knew he might depend on her for good sense and he felt certain that she would make no demur when she had met Wilberton, for he was a fine fellow indeed. So sure had he been of Sarah's complicity once he had explained matters, that he had arranged for the Earl to follow him into Staffordshire in only two days. Today was a Tuesday and on Thursday he would be among them.

After enduring a lengthy and rapturous interview with Lady Dagley Sarah was allowed to seek her bedchamber, for her mother noticed suddenly that she was looking rather pinched and recollected the wisdom of her child's looking her best for her forthcoming interview. As Sarah expected, her bedchamber was not empty when she reached it, for, curled up on her fourposter bed, wrapped in a large Angora shawl, sprawled Charlotte, now to be joined by Bess, who had followed her mistress upstairs. Seated majestically on a chair close by, and just as curious as her young charge, was her governess. Both were startled by Sarah's news and it was impossible to get them to leave her until they had been appraised of every detail.

Miss Nelsworth's partiality became apparent immediately, for she was of the decided opinion that few called to such an exalted sphere could be as worthy of it as her dearest Sarah. Charlotte's comments were less flattering, but rather more to the point, for she was amazed as had been her sister.

"It seems a monstrous notion to me that he should be content to offer for someone to whom he hasn't even been introduced, Sarah, after all, he must meet any number of eligible girls all the time, and any number of beauties, too, though it is certainly the greatest piece of luck for us."

"Uncle Henry says that he does not want a beauty, but I'm sure it is all a hum, for I never yet met a man who, given that he had a choice, would take bread and butter pudding when he might have an iced cake. And then, surely to offer for a stranger argues a cold disposition, do not you think?"

"My dear girls, while I am, of course, a single person myself," broke in Miss Nelsworth, her cheeks pink under her frivolous cap, "I must profess to know a little more of the world than you do and I think you will find that the *beau monde* order their lives rather differently to those in less exalted circles. Marriages of convenience are commonplace, and this is not so surprising when we remember that couples in the best society do not expect to live in each others' pockets. I can assure you, my dear, that your name will be all that is needed to ensure your suitability to the Earl."

Miss Nelsworth sounded as if this should be a matter for congratulation, but to Sarah, brought up on a tradition of literary romance, it seemed only depressing.

"It sounds such a daunting prospect to me, Nelly. I'm not certain that I will be able to go through with it," she said nervously.

"Oh, but you must, Sarah," cried her sister sharply, "You would not be so shabby as to deny us our only chance to *be* somebody again?"

"Really, Charlotte, you must attempt to curb what appears to me to be a distressingly worldly streak," corrected Miss Nelsworth. "Such a proposal must, of course, be favourably received, but not for the reasons you state! You should rather be thinking how happy a thing it will be for our dearest Sarah to be comfortably settled in life with a man of such consequence!"

"Forgive me, Sarah dear. I did not mean to sound selfish, though you must admit that it is not pleasant to be denied all that our friends have. It would be wonderful to be able to have a truly fashionable wardrobe when I come out, and you have often said yourself how agreeable it must be not to have to consider everthing we buy so carefully."

Charlotte's impulsive outburst brought Sarah back to reality. "I am sure you never thought to hear me being so missish!" she said with a shaky laugh. "What a silly goose I must sound. Of course I shall marry him should we suit. I am quite as worldly and materialistic as you can ever be, Charlie."

On this assurance, and seeing her seem more cheerful, the others departed to their room, leaving Sarah a prey to varying emotions, the chief of which was doubt that her acceptance would ever be called for. Examination of herself in the looking glass did little to reassure her, for instead of the dark curls which a recent copy of the Ladies' Magazine had assured her were still all the crack, she saw locks of indifferent light brown, which she was quite aware needed judicious applications of the tongs to persuade them to curl; her mouth, she knew, was considered too generous to be pleasing and her chin exhibited the streak of obstinacy for which she was famous, being rather well-defined. Her only really good feature was a pair of very beautiful, almond-shaped grey eyes, heavy-lidded and fringed by long, thick lashes, but her other less harmonious features obscured their impact and few, on a brief acquaintance, noticed the charm they gave her face. She knew, too, that she was considered too small to be fashionable, although her figure was attractive enough.

Sarah's opinion of herself had been formed several years previously when she had been sent to London for the Season to make her debut. While her father had recognized the need to bring her out, he was as little flush in the pocket as ever and, as a result, little could be spared. But she had gone nonetheless, with high hopes of attracting an eligible alliance, for she was of an optimistic bent and had never, until then, considered herself to be so very plain. Her mother regretted that she was too fragile to make the journey, but she had, instead, been put in the hands of a rather elderly great-aunt, Lady Lydia Chesley, who had agreed to bring her out. It had not taken Sarah long to realize that her aunt was not really *au fait* with the fashionable world, but, since Sarah was tractable, until roused by some obvious injustice, she could not consider it proper to set herself up against Lady Chesley's opinions, given as they were in all kindness, and, as a consequence, had been sent into society in a series of outmoded white gowns, a colour which, however, proper for those just coming out, made poor Sarah appear faded and insignificant. Her father's name and reputation had been enough to secure invitations to all the best of the Season's entertainments, including the highly esteemed weekly balls at Almack's, but she had made little impact on the ton, that very narrow stratum of society to which belonged all those people of fortune or consequence who were either felt to be, or who felt themselves to be, superior to the ordinary run of mankind. She had once even had the misery of overhearing herself described as a "poor little dab of a girl," and, as a consequence, had been more than happy to return home to her family. There and then she had given up all pretences to vanity, resigning herself to remaining single, a future which by no means dismayed her. Now it appeared she was to have her peace overturned for the sake of a stranger. "Supposing he is odious, or cruel!" she panicked, and began to feel abominably ill-used, until she remembered in what a high humour the rest of her family had been cast by her luck. Then she walked determinedly over to her closet to inspect her wardrobe, wishing that, like the rest of her family, she had inherited her mother's chestnut hair and brilliant blue eyes, not to mention her delicate features and tall stately figure. But perhaps the Earl would consider her mouse-like exterior more a sign of conformability and be taken with her?

One look at the contents of her closet brought her back into the glooms. Since her fateful London Season, she had made very few additions to her wardrobe, for she had been the only one of the younger members of the family who had stopped growing and most of her purchases had been made to clothe Charlotte (beginning to be startlingly like her mother) and the boys. As a result, their eldest sister was left with one or two rather dowdy gowns, a year or two out of date, and her old white gowns from five years before, now made over. She looked at them, shook her head miserably and resolutely closed the closet door on them.

"Well," she told Bess, still sitting in the middle of her faded counterpane, head on one side and trying to look intelligent, "He must just take me as he finds me!"

CHAPTER 3

Thursday found Sarah once again with her Mama and her Uncle in the drawing room, awaiting the arrival of her suitor in the greatest trepidation. Charlotte had been allowed to join them in order to lend support to her sister, but the boys were to stay with Miss Nelsworth in the schoolroom, and strict instructions had been received in the kitchen to keep Bess out of the way, "It won't do for him to see that animal prancing about uttering shrieks at the top of her voice. He will think he is in Bedlam" declared Lady Dagley with rare shrewdness, "for I understand from your Uncle that he has extremely nice notions of propriety."

Sarah, for whom this statement represented a touch of doom, had dressed in a high-waisted, straight frock of pale lemon jaconet muslin, at least two years old, for she had refused to comply with her parent's wish that she should rush to have something new made up for the occasion, as Lady Dagley had done. Sarah was by no means sure that anything would come of this meeting and would have felt herself to be behaving most imprudently had she paid out money on such an errand which might be needed later.

Looking around her, she could not help wishing that the house looked less shabby, but she had done her best to furbish it up by ensuring that the old furniture gleamed and by placing huge bowls of early summer flowers in every room.

Leighwood, a rambling, mellow-bricked Tudor mansion, had, alas, been allowed to fall into a sad state of disrepair. It had never been modernised, and to reach the reception rooms it was necessary to climb an ornate pine staircase, which led from the great hall at the front of the house. All the main reception rooms, including the apartment known as the great chamber, but which the family were accustomed to calling the drawing room, led off from a dark hallway at the top of the stairs and each was, regrettably, in as sad a state of neglect as the others. Once-beautiful hangings were faded and worn, and outmoded and shabby furniture had not been replaced. Use had given Sarah a great affection for the old-fashioned house, but she could not help wishing at that moment that it was a bit smarter. She looked once more at the bowl of roses she had set on a side-table by the window in the drawing room, her eyes being inevitably drawn downstairs to the scratches the bowl could not quite conceal, and she shook her head. There was a definite limit to what flowers and beeswax could accomplish.

The family had just partaken of a light luncheon of cold meats and fruit when a carriage was heard coming through the entrance porch into the courtyard. Sarah was almost wholly overset with embarrassment. Her uncle, quick to notice her heightened colour, was shocked to see how hagged she suddenly looked and said kindly to her, "It is of no moment after all, my dear. If you cannot like him we won't tease you to it. Though I am persuaded that you will find him excessively agreeable."

There was no time for him to say more, for steps could be heard on the stairway, and in a few moments the door opened and Jackson announced, "The Earl of Wilberton, my lady."

"Come in my boy, and welcome, welcome," said Mr.Dagley to their guest, showing plainly the easy terms on which the two men stood.

"Thank you sir, I am so happy to be here," replied a gentle, well-modulated voice.

"May I introduce to you my sister, Lady Dagley, m'lord," said the Reverend gentleman, as Sarah's mother graciously stood to shake hands with him, "And my nieces, Miss Dagley and Miss Charlotte Dagley," completing the introductions. Sarah gave him her hand, not daring to look up, while Charlotte curtsied and he professed himself charmed.

When Sarah was quite certain that the Earl was safely engaged in conversation with her mother, she took one look at him and her heart sank, for he was undoubtedly an attractive man by any standards. Tall and slim, yet muscular in just such a way as suggested a peak of physical health and vigour, his handsome features were enhanced by his unaffected manner.

Although he had avoided the extremes of fashion, it was obvious that he was dressed in the first style of elegance, for his formal dress-coat and calf-length pantaloons fitted without a crease. He did not wear the points of his collar so high that, to use the expression of a sporting man, it was big enough to make a white waistcoat, but it was clear that no novice could have achieved the happy result which was the Earl's neckcloth, while his glossy dark hair had been skilfully dishevelled into the style known as the 'Brutus'. All in all, thought Sarah, with increasing agitation, he was perfection, and nowhere could there be a proposed match less equal.

She listened to him now, chatting easily with her Mama, and envied the way he seemed totally unembarrassed by his situation. He and Lady Dagley seemed to be getting on famously: they had already discovered that he was related to the Amberthorpes, Lady Dagley's family, and they were now pleasantly occupied in disentangling the ramification of the line to try to ascertain just how distant was the connection.

"So, your Great Aunt Almeria was married to the Lord Stanham who was my father's cousin," exclaimed Lady Dagley triumphantly. "Well, what a small world, to be sure, and how strange that we have not had occasion to meet until now."

"I am only glad that the omission has now been rectified," he replied gallantly, and with a glance at Sarah, "for it is not every day that one finds oneself able to add such charming ladies to one's circle of friends."

Had such a thing been possible, Lady Dagley would undoubtedly have taken her brother and Charlotte off immediately, to allow the Earl to follow up with Sarah his delightful words, but as this could not be, she contented herself with bestowing on him her most glistening smile and an offer of refreshment, as she questioned him on his enjoyment of the Season. Although too indigent to add to its number, she liked nothing more than hearing of the fashionable circle that flocked to London each year to be amused. She passed a pleasant hour listening as he described the ceaseless round of routs, opera parties, balls and picnics to which the ton had recently subjected itself, while her estimation of him increased every moment as he casually mentioned such exalted figures as the Prince Regent, to whom he carelessly referred as Prinny, and of ambitious hostesses like Lady Jersey and the Princess Esterhazy. As for Lord Wilberton, he found Lady Dagley most agreeable and set out to amuse her with all the details of the latest *on dit* concerning Brummell's removal to the continent. As well, he was able to satisfy in full her curiosity regarding certain details of the marriage, in May, of the Princess Charlotte to her Leopold. His news was told in such a droll way that Lady Dagley was soon treating him as a friend of long standing and she was, as a consequence, not too reticent to ask him for the latest scandal from Melbourne House. Sarah was amused as her mother when he laughing replied,

"Well, Ma'am, society did not at all mind Lady Caroline publishing 'Glenarvon', though they knew quite well that she had allowed herself the impropriety of publishing some of poor old Byron's letters to her as fiction, but when they had the chance to read it for themselves, some of them saw their mistake at once. Apparently she had other scores to settle as well, for, not content with embarrassing Byron, some of her other readers had the felicity of recognising themselves in the most transparent of caricatures. Really, she has the wickedest gift—hit them all off as near as you please. No disguise and certainly no flattery. What then could they do but banish her?"

It was not surprising that Miles found Sarah's mother agreeable, for though a little past her best, enough of her beauty survived for her to be still accounted a very handsome woman. Today, with the added glow of animation unusual to her, she was brilliant. Unlike Sarah, she had spared no pains when preparing herself for this meeting, and Miles found her becomingly arranged on her sofa in her flattering new gown and turban of grey silk, which showed off to a nicety the richness of her chestnut hair and her delicate pale complexion. She had no intention of casting her eldest daughter in the shade, however, and occasionally both she and Wilberton attempted to bring her into the conversation. It was all too much for Sarah, however, and she found it difficult to meet the Earl's eye. She knew herself to be answering him in the stupidest way imagineable and was crossly certain that he must be disgusted by such a sharp contrast to her mother.

The conversation inevitably came around to the proposed length of his visit and Lady Dagley graciously hoped that he was considering a protracted stay. Sarah felt her cheeks burn as, from the corner of her eye, she saw her mother turn her head archly towards her, as if to indicate that Sarah was an interested party in this discussion, and, before she allowed herself to hear the Earl's answer, she told herself, half in hope, half in fear, "I've a notion he won't be staying long now that he has seen me!"

****

Miles would have been surprised had he been able to read Sarah's mind. For his part, he was well content with her, for she seemed a well-conducted young woman, perhaps a trifle shy, and he had been agreeably impressed by her ladylike demeanour. She was certainly no antidote, as he had feared she might be, though it was true that she was no high flyer, either. That did not signify, however, for nobody could ever match up to his first wife, and he had no wish ever to try to replace her in his heart. Yet, however painful the duty, he had a responsibility to his family to produce an heir and this girl would do admirably if, as her uncle had intimated, she was happy with the plan. He was fully conversant with the facts of the Dagley family's financial embarrassment and it had seemed to him, while discussing it with the girl's uncle, that his marriage to Sarah would be a happy solution for both of them.

On her uncle's admission, she had not taken with the ton, although her birth made her unexceptionable as a wife. Safe on his estates in Shropshire, it had seemed a logical step to offer marriage to the unhappy young woman from a family his father had held in such esteem, giving her a creditable establishment in exchange for children to continue his line. His journey into Staffordshire had, however, given him time for further reflection, and he had realised that such a marriage would be folly unless Miss Dagley was aware beforehand that she could expect from him only a degree of affection and not the higher rapture of romantic feeling, all that having been buried with his dead love.

"What a coxcomb I am," he laughed to himself. "She will probably be very pleased to be spared romantic ravings from me." Yet he was determined to make his position known to Sarah and ascertain from her in person that she was indeed content, before making her an offer.

For just that reason, he felt he must make every attempt to get Sarah alone, a scheme endorsed wholeheartedly by her mother and Mr. Dagley, so that, when he expressed an inclination to see the gardens, Lady Dagley replied graciously that she was sure that her "dear Sarah" would not object to showing him round.

Sarah had, however, ideas of her own and had extracted from Charlotte beforehand a solemn promise that she would on no account leave her alone with Wilberton. She was convinced that her mother's sense of propriety would prevent her from flinging her at his head in too obvious a fashion and, if she could only keep Charlotte by her side, was assured of a more comfortable time during his stay. Having now seen him, she was more than ever glad that she had taken such a precaution, for she was certain he could have nothing to say to her and that any enforced tête-à-têtes would only raise false hopes in her mother's breast.

Now she looked speakingly at Charlotte, who, keeping strictly to the letter of her promise, expressed a wish to accompany the Earl and her sister on their ramble. The Earl was too well-bred to betray his consternation, merely saying in his easy fashion that he would be delighted to spare an arm for such a pretty young lady. Charlotte blushed delightfully and ran off quickly to fetch her shawl, wondering as she went if there was any insanity in her family, for surely only a lunatic would try to avoid a proposal from so glorious a gentleman. Sarah stopped only to pick up her parasol and the Misses Dagley were ready. Miles offered an arm to each of them and the trio made its way towards Sarah's shrubbery and flower garden.

Much of the park of Leighwood had been neglected in recent years and now had a wild, unkempt look about it. Because there had been no-one to look after it, the formal gardens—so much a part of the old house—with its box hedges and ornate flower gardens, had had to be dismantled and replaced by lawn, but for her pleasure and that of her mother, Sarah kept a shrubbery and rose gardens at the back of the house.

The storms of the past few days had passed and, as she wandered through the garden with their guest, Sarah felt the sun, warm through the sleeves of her muslin dress, while she watched a bevy of bees buzzing purposefully round a border of bright marigolds struggling bravely once more towards the sun after being flattened by rain. For a time she was able to forget her mother's intrigues while they wandered aimlessly along winding paths meandering through cheerful banks of hollyhocks and lupins. Lord Wilberton knew little of gardening, but his questions and comments were so much those of a person of taste and good sense that they were fast reaching an excellent understanding, Charlotte's artless chatter helping to prevent any embarrassment. The Earl had even managed, by talking first of his own gardens at Beaumere, to introduce the subject of his home to Sarah, as a first step towards discovering whether it was her inclination to share it with him.

Had they been allowed to continue as they were it is most probable that such an understanding might have been reached as to enable Miles to broach the subject which he had travelled so far to undertake. Back in the drawing room, however, Lady Dagley was less than content, for she could see little opportunity for Miles to come to the point while Charlotte was with them.

"I blame myself," insisted Lady Dagley, "for I'm bound to own that I did not think to warn Charlotte not to hang on to their coat tails."

"If you ask me, my dear, Sarah has put her up to it, and who knows, but that it may answer better to let them take their time?"

"Why should they wish to, brother? It seems a nonsensical idea to me, for he has come all this way to propose to her and she is here waiting for him to do so. What can they possibly gain by dragging the whole thing out?"

"Do not you think, my dear, that they may perhaps wish to get to know each other a little before discussing marriage?"

"All the more reason why we should remove Charlotte, for how can they possibly do so with a chit of a girl listening to every word they say to each other? And anyway," (with devastating logic) "there will be plenty of time for them to get to know each other after they are betrothed. He is such a charming young man that I do not wish my poor little Sarah to miss her chance."

Lady Dagley was determined. She would have considered herself to be a strange mother indeed had she not been prepared to make a push for her daughter's happiness, especially too, when her own was so concerned. Even propriety must not stand in the way of so excellent a scheme, and Simpkins, the parlourmaid, was sent to ask Charlotte to return to the drawing room for a moment, as her mother wanted her for "something of a particular nature."

This announcement was enough to destroy Sarah's peace of mind, for so transparent a ploy could only make her ashamed. But she was determined not to be outwitted by her mother and suggested that, "it being so warm," they might all walk back to the house together and take some lemonade. One look at the ludicrous expression on her mother's face as they all walked back into the drawing room together was enough almost to send Sarah into a fit of laughter, a feeling greatly enhanced by her mother's confusion when Charlotte asked innocently, "What was it that you particularly wished to say to me, Mama?"

That the Earl was fully aware of these undercurrents became quickly apparent, for while her mother was trying to extricate herself from the results of her pushy behaviour, Miles smiled at Sarah, his eyes brimming over with amusement, yet so kindly that she immediately felt comfortable again.

By now the afternoon was considerably advanced and it was soon time to dress for dinner as, at Leighwood, they kept country hours. Miles had still found no opportunity for private talk with Sarah.

CHAPTER 4

It had been decided that the children's uncle would remain at Leighwood while the Earl stayed with them, and he occupied his usual rooms just along from the suite known as the Blue Apartment, which had been given to Miles. While her uncle showed their guest the way to his chamber, Sarah, in her determination to avoid being alone with her suitor, waited downstairs until the coast was clear. Before making her way to her dressing room, she first went down to the kitchen to check up on her pet. Bess howled mournfully when she caught sight of her mistress in an attempt to tell her just what she thought of a day spent with only the kitchen boy for company and she set her face into such a pitiful expression that Sarah could not help laughing. She ignored her mother's warning about keeping Bess in the kitchens and allowed the exuberent animal to follow her upstairs to her bedchamber. Here she was to meet with further recriminations for waiting for her were her two youngest brothers, agog with curiosity concerning Sarah's impression of the man who was to rescue the family from all its difficulties. As they were not used to standing on ceremony with Sarah, her entrance found them stationed one on either side of her bed, reaching over it in a desperate pillow fight, her sheets and blankets in a heap on the floor, and feathers flying everywhere. Bess entered immediately into the fray by grabbing a corner of the pillow held by Pip, front legs bent for more leverage, and growling menacingly, causing both boys to collapse with laughter on to the bed as their sister unsuccessfully made an attempt to maintain a prim expression while she scolded them.

As soon as order had been restored, the brothers demanded to know what had been happening downstairs and bemoaned the fact that they had been forced to spend the day inside with "Nelly".

"Miss Nelsworth to you, you little devils," admonished Sarah automatically, while she brushed feathers from her counterpane.

Little was said about Miles, Sarah only acknowledging that he seemed good-natured before settling herself on the wreck of her bed to listen to their complaints.

"It isn't fair that we should have to stay up here, Sarah, just because someone has the good sense to want to marry you," grumbled Hugh. "And anyway, Nelly . . . I mean Miss Nelsworth, well, it isn't as if she's *our* governess, only Charlotte's, so I don't see why we should stay up here with *her*."

"Stop complaining, love, and tell me where Miss Nelsworth is now," coaxed his sister gently, though she had been feeling very guilty about their enforced imprisonment in the upper regions of the house on such a very warm day.

"Helping Charlotte dress for dinner, and she's changing her own gown as well, for Mama says she can bring us down to the drawing room before dinner to make our bows to the Earl," replied Hugh with less heat, until remembering that he had a further grievance, he went on, "And I don't see why we cannot stay down for dinner—at least, I should, after all, I am fourteen and Charlotte is not so much old, besides being not yet out! It is foolish to come down just to make our bows and then have to come back upstairs to eat like the veriest baby!"

"That's why we're dressed up as fine as fivepence, you know, to make our bows," cut in Pip.

"That's why you *were* dressed up as fine as fivepence," corrected Sarah, laughing. "Your little battle doesn't seem to have done much to help."

The boys ran to an old marquetry-framed mirror, which looked out of place hanging on the pannelled wall, and peered at themselves, noting with horror the creases which seemed mysteriously to have appeared from nowhere in nankin pantaloons and jackets well spotted with feathers.

"Oh lor, now we're for it," muttered Pip.

"I think we might repair to our rooms to try and lessen the damage," added his brother with more dignity.

His sister agreed, and as soon as they had gone Sarah went to her closet to take out the dress she had elected to wear that evening—one of the detested white gowns. She had never had a personal maid to wait upon her, but her mother's dresser, Walters, prompted by Lady Dagley, had expressed her willingness to assist Sarah in any way possible at this important time. Since Sarah was used to dressing herself, however, and had, moreover, a knack for arranging her own hair, she had no hesitation in graciously declining such unprecedented condescension.

In an attempt to take away the deadness which white always gave her complexion, Sarah had added some pale pink trimming to her high-waisted gown of tussore silk, and she now threaded a matching riband through her hair in a very simple style. Looking critically at herself in the mirror, she was not certain that the effect of the trimming was entirely happy, for it seemed so much an afterthought that Sarah felt that it might have been better just to look insipid. She was forced to admit that she had very little flair in matters of costume and she found herself wishing that she might be like some ladies of her acquaintance who always managed to appear elegantly turned out, even on a very small income. It was not in her nature, however, to repine long on what could not be helped, so in a remarkably short space of time, her toilet was completed and she was ready to make her way downstairs. She took one last look in her mirror, adjusting deftly her decollété neckline and the little puffed sleeves so as to arrange them to their best advantage, grimacing at the poor picture she made. For one instant she was almost tempted to borrow some of the Portuguese rouge she had once seen on her mother's dressing table, but she resisted and instead added a rose-coloured Norwich silk shawl and matching long gloves to her costume. They did not appear noticeably to help matters, so she picked up her fan and turned resolutely away from her glass.

Calling to Bess to follow, she made her way downstairs again.

* * * * * * * * *

31

Miles's toilet was a far more protracted and leisurely affair. Upon separating from Mr. Dagley at the door of his bedchamber he was met by the imperturbable figure of Jepson, his valet. One look at the unyielding expression on Jepson's face was enough to inform him that all was not well in the opinion of that most fastidious of gentleman's gentleman, though he would, of course, have felt it to be most illbred to utter any complaint. He had been Miles's valet for many years and knew precisely how to accomplish, apparently effortlessly, the feat of sending his master out into the world exquisitely clothed. Unfortunately, Miles had to pay heavily for his expertise, for he had chosen to adopt unto himself much of his master's consequence and was, as a result, easily put out if he found himself quartered in a style which he felt to be beneath him. One look at the reception rooms at Leighwood had been sufficient to inform Miles that this would indeed be such an occasion. He was shrewd enough to guess that he, himself, had been allocated the best suite that the house could offer, and even that was certainly not what he had been used to. The Blue Apartment might well be re-named 'Grey', for the hangings and upholstery, originally probably of peacock, had faded so far as to look merely dingy, while the dark panelling which covered all the walls in both the bedchamber and the dressing room made the suite oppressive to one used to the light walls which were a feature of his own home. He was quick to notice the bowl of marigolds which had been placed on top of a battered old writing table in a corner of the room, however, and his speedy sympathy was excited as he imagined Sarah's vain attempts to make the room more welcoming.

If this was the best the house could offer, he was certain that the room allotted to Jepson would not suit his valet and he prepared himself to heal his servant's lacerated feelings at finding himself in such circumstances.

"Well, Jepson, we seem to be quite settled in here. How have they housed you? Tolerably comfortably, I trust."

Jepson's voice was at its most colourless as he replied, "I make no complaint, my lord, though it is not, of course, what we are used to."

Miles felt his lips twitch, but managed to keep the

amusement from his own voice, remarking a little later, while he was washing, "I collect that you do not approve of Leighwood. You perhaps find it inconvenient?"

"My own convenience is, of course, not a matter for your lordship's concern. It would be strange indeed were I to consider it so, I am sure," replied his servant in top-lofty fashion.

Miles accepted this mild rebuke in amused silence, and, while he was being helped into his evening garments, waited for him to continue, as he felt sure he would.

"I am sure that I will soon become accustomed to having to bring hot water for your lordship up two separate stairways, though I am a little concerned that your lordship may experience some delay at my having to make my way so far from the Servant's Hall to your room, this being situated, as indeed is my own room, in the lower house."

Had his last words been "Hell", they could not have been uttered with more loathing, and Miles judged it to be time for him to soothe Jepson's feelings a little.

"I hope that I am not such a plaguey devil as to refine too much upon such trifles. You have been with me far too long for me not to be aware that any such delay would be caused only by circumstances beyond your control. I am well acquainted with the fact that you are entirely devoted to my interests, I assure you."

Miles's words did not encourage Jepson to unbend noticeably and his master felt that a more direct approach might become necessary. For the moment, however, all conversation had to cease and Jepson held his breath, while Miles completed the tricky maneouvres required in tying his cravat *à la Bergami*. It had been known for as many as half a dozen muslin neckcloths to be ruined before both men were satisfied that Miles had achieved perfection, but this evening all went well, and Miles was free to try to persuade his valet to take a more optimistic view of their lodgings, at least in front of others. He now began, "I am quite certain that you know very well what we are doing here in the middle of nowhere, Jepson, so I will spare my breath and omit any elucidation. I will remind you, however, that it would distress me greatly to hear that any member of my household had allowed himself the liberty of openly criticizing anything which we may find at

Leighwood. Collect, if you can, how embarrassing it might be to find that one had been guilty of a want of conduct towards one's new mistress or her family."

These words were gently spoken, but Jepson was in no doubt how to take them knowing only too well that, although at most times, the Earl had a sweet nature and was well-known for his amiable disposition, he was too, as a result of always having been the heir to an Earldom, used to having his own way without question and more than one person had been surprised to find themselves confronted, on occasion, by a certain intractibility, perhaps even a little ruthlessness. He had been brought up to consider carefully the feelings of anybody with whom he came into contact, for the late Earl had detested the cavalier treatment many of his contemporaries meted out to servants and had encouraged Miles always to be as courteous in his demands to servants as he was in his treatment of friends. While this might then encourage some of them to think he was an easy touch, any attempt to take advantage proved just how misleading his affability could be, for he could crush pretension as easily as he might step on a spider, a fact quickly comprehended by those in his employ. At the same time, however, those who served him well found him the best and most appreciative of employers, which had the happy effect of making them double their efforts to please him!

Jepson had served his master both long and well, and was excessively insulted at his master's hint that he might gossip in the lower regions of the house, considering any such behaviour beneath the exalted position he held, but he knew better than to say so when Miles used that particular tone of voice, contenting himself with assuming his most bland expression and replying in an impassive voice, "Of course, my lord."

Nothing more was said while Miles slipped on his evening pumps and repaired some slight disordering of his dark gleaming curls, declaring himself then ready to be eased by Jepson into his coat. He was not sure how formally the family would dress for dinner and had taken no chances in his choice of evening wear, so that they would find him in a plain dark blue tail coat of exquisite fit, worn over a white marcella waistcoat, snowy-white shirt and cravat and cream-coloured, kerseymere breeches.

Pausing only to fix a solitaire pin into his cravat and slip a gold ring on his finger, he dismissed his servant and made his leisurely way downstairs.

He was a little early in descending, but he excused this breach of etiquette without hesitation, since he had been bidden by Lady Dagley to stand on no ceremony with them. He hoped that he might have a chance for some private conversation with Miss Dagley before the family were assembled, for he guessed that she would be more comfortable in a tête-à-tête arising naturally rather than one contrived by her mother.

He was by no means discouraged at her reluctance to be alone with him, correctly attributing this to a natural disinclination to be the centre of heavy plotting rather than to any actual aversion to himself, and he looked forward to taking advantage of any opportunity which might present itself during the evening to become further acquainted with her. From his conversation with her that afternoon, he had seen nothing to give him a disgust of her, and while she was clearly not quite as modish as many ladies of his acquaintance, such details concerned him little and he felt her to be well enough. His slight knowledge of her led him to believe her to be just a little wanting in dash, but this must surely be held an advantage in a wife, however insipid in other ladies of one's circle. It would not do, after all, for his Countess to have any but the nicest notions of propriety.

These were the Earl's musings as he came down the central stairway, so it came as rather a shock to him to be met in the drawing room, not by the model of propriety he had conjured up for himself, but by the startling vision of a lady in full evening dress of white, trimmed with pink, lying almost flat out on the floor and apparently speaking to a large old bureau in a corner of the huge chamber!

He coughed softly, which brought the crimson-faced lady to her feet more speedily than elegantly, almost tripping over a chair as she raised herself, and was satisfied to confirm that he was indeed, as he had suspected, in the presence of his bride-to-be. Somewhere in the region of his brain the comfortable picture he had been building up for himself disintegrated in an instant, while he waited, eyes sparkling, for an explanation which he felt sure must soon be forthcoming.

"Why, Lord Wilberton! What a start you gave me," cried Sarah, "I had not thought anyone else down yet."

"I rather suspected that you might not," he replied gently.

"What a very pleasant evening it is to be sure," she began, cooling herself with her fan and hoping that he might not have noticed her peculiar behaviour, "and how much less fatiguing now that the heat of the afternoon has gone."

"Yes, I can see you are cooler," he remarked dryly, taking the fan and wafting it for her. "And now, I must say, I suppose, that it is a pity it looks like rain, or some such thing?"

"Why, whatever can you mean, sir?" (momentarily diverted), "I am sure that it does not."

"I mean that, if you are quite determined not to let me in on the reason for the singular position in which I found you on my entrance, I suppose we must speak of less interesting matters."

"Ah! You saw then?"

"I am afraid that, yes, I did."

Her spirits were quite overborne by the realisation that he was laughing at her. Could anything be so vexatious as that he should find her at such a disadvantage?

Deciding that, rather than allow him to think her a sad romp, she had better make a clean breast of it, she began, "You see, it's Bess."

"Of course: Bess," he replied, making every effort to compose his features. "I'm afraid I don't . . ."

"My dog, you know," she went on hurriedly, in an attempt to clarify the matter. "You see, Bess can be, well, rather awkward, so Mama said that she should be confined in the kitchens while you were staying. We are all familiar with her odd little habits, but Mama felt that, well, you might not be amused by them."

"How poor-spirited she must think me, to be sure," murmured Miles, *sotto voce*.

"Well! I am glad you should say so, sir, for I'm bound to own that it did seem nonsensical. Mama would have it so, however, and poor Bess spent the whole of the day down there as a result, when she is used to spending all of her days with me."

"A blow!" said Miles, encouragingly.

"Indeed," replied Sarah, relieved at finding him so sympathetic. "Naturally, as soon as it was time to dress for dinner I went down to her, but she was so miserable that I simply had to chance Mama's anger and allow her to come upstairs while I changed."

"Naturally!"

"Unfortunately, when we came down and she realised that she was being taken back to the kitchens, she ran straight back up here before I could catch her, and hid behind the bureau—you see, it is just far enough away from the wall for her to squeeze into the gap. I could not manage to pull her out from behind, so I was, er, lying down in an attempt to pull her out from underneath it. That was when you discovered me, I'm afraid."

"All is now perfectly clear," said Miles smiling, "but we still seem to have a problem. Your dog. Would you like me to get her out for you?"

"How very kind you are," replied Sarah with real gratitude, "For Mama will be so vexed if she is still here when she comes down. It will not do, however, for I am afraid that Bess does not respond well to people outside the family and will not come to you." She added unnecessarily, "She is not really the most obedient of animals."

Miles crouched down by the bureau and began to coax Bess in a firm voice, telling her to come out at once like a good girl. As if determined to make Sarah look ridiculous, she came out of her hiding place at his first word, and began fawning on Miles in the most speaking way.

Miles looked at Sarah nonplussed. "It is the fatal Wilberton charm," he said, "no females can resist it."

Instead of taking Bess back to the kitchens, Miles promised to ask Lady Dagley if she could stay. He was so friendly that Sarah managed to forget to be embarrassed by his presence and they were so far becoming friends that Miles decided to broach the matter of their betrothal. He had gone so far as to say, "My dear Miss Dagley . . .," when he was interrupted by the noise of the drawing room door opening and an entrance being made by a fussily nervous Miss Nelsworth: in her wake the three youngest Dagleys.

CHAPTER 5

That evening passed in unexpected enjoyment for Miles, although he still found no opportunity for private talk with Sarah. When he had realised, on arrival at Leighwood, that he was to be the Dagley's only guest, he had been horrified, for though he understood that extravagant entertainments were out of the question, he really had no experience of what it could mean to be in such straitened circumstances as his hosts. It was incomprehensible to him, therefore, that they could consider inviting him without making any provision for his amusement, but such was the case—no fellow guests were to be seen and he had slowly realised during the afternoon, with increasing gloom, that it was not even their intention to increase their covers for dinner in his honour. It was not, therefore, with any real expectation of pleasure that he left the sanctity of his dressing room that evening, and had anyone foretold that he would enjoy himself immensely, he would have considered them a serious candidate for Bedlam: yet so it proved.

Much of his enjoyment had arisen as a result of a generous impulse of his own, for he had no sooner seen the misery on the faces of the two youngest Dagleys on being instructed to return to the schoolroom, than he begged their Mama's permission for them to join the rest of the party for dinner.

Lady Dagley was all compliance and so, some small shufflings of china occurred in the dining room and the two, along with Miss Nelsworth, were allowed to take part in the boys' first grown-up dinner. All Lady Dagley's children were well-behaved, but their manners had not been achieved at cost to their spirit and the boys were certainly not tongue-tied at finding themselves in company with an Earl. From their conversation, it became clear that not all of that afternoon had been wasted up in the schoolroom with Miss Nelsworth. They had visited the stables and had discovered that Miles had travelled to Leighwood in his own sporting curricle, drawn by four matching greys which Hugh had no hesitation in guessing were the sweetest goers possible. Pip had somehow managed to pry from one of the Earl's grooms the information that Miles was a notable whip and a member of that august society which called itself The Four-in-Hand Club, and Miles was kept fully occupied in answering the many questions which occurred to boys who, on their own admission, were uncommonly fond of horses.

"Is it really true that you wear striped waistcoats *and* spotted cravats?" asked Pip incredulously, "Don't they clash a bit?"

"Will it sink me beyond reproach if I admit that we do?" replied the Earl, grinning engagingly. "You see, it is the insignia of the club, and nobody who is not willing to look a little foolish is allowed to join."

Hugh, who had rather a leaning towards dandyism, looked misty-eyed, and said it sounded all the crack.

His brother snorted his disgust, although both boys were young enough to be equally impressed at the Earl's descriptions of the princely dinners served to club members at the Windmill on Salt Hill. It only needed Miles's generous offer that, if Lady Dagley and their uncle had no objections, he would take them up in his curricle next day and even allow them to tool the ribbons themselves if they behaved, for them to declare him to be the best of good fellows.

Mr. Dagley and the Earl spent little time over the port and, as soon as they moved back into the drawing room to join the others, Pip recommended Speculation, shrewd enough to realise that his mother would be less likely to send him off to bed if he was in the middle of a game. Sarah was sure that nothing would bore their guest more thoroughly and suggested whist instead, but Miles was no great card player, and, in any case, had not failed to detect Pip's disappointment. He made the astonishing announcement that he had never before played at

Speculations, but assured them all that he would be happy to join in if Pip could teach him.

Pip felt all the responsibility necessary for the Earl's game and, at first, spent much of his time cheating himself to ensure that Miles won enough fish. He was soon able to leave the Earl to his own devices, however, since he was quickly making intelligent bids for himself. Miles had never known the simple pleasure of being part of a large family, his only sister being some years his junior, and he found the gleeful spirits engendered by the foolish game highly infectious.

Charlotte, who had been quiet during dinner in her determination not to be classed with her brothers as a childish chatterbox, now became quite as excited as they, joining in the usual heated discussions as to whether or not Hugh was playing fair, and Sarah found her eyes constantly meeting the twinkling ones of their guest in shared amusement.

When Lady Dagley finally decided that the children must retire, Sarah was just congratulating herself on how well-behaved they had been, when she was put to the blush by Pip innocently asking on his way out, "I say, sir, when you marry Sarah do you think I might have my own pony?"

For a brief moment, all conversation was suspended, then Miles was spared the necessity of answering by Hugh's loud condemnation of Pip as a "great gudgeon" and by the combined efforts of Lady Dagley, her brother-in-law and Miss Nelsworth to disguise this tactless remark in a welter of small talk. But Sarah was mortified.

As Miss Nelsworth led away her young charges, their sister was left to feel that she would never be easy again while the Earl continued under their roof.

To gloss over this unfortunate incident, Lady Dagley had the good sense to suggest that they might have a little music. All the Dagleys were musical and she knew Sarah to be extremely well taught—indeed, it was the only thing in which Miss Nelsworth was really proficient and she had passed both her technique and her excellent taste on to her eldest pupil.

Sarah was at first unwilling to perform. Not only did she still feel hot after her brother's words, she was also sure that the Earl must find her performance wanting, being used to the society of those taught by the most superior of masters. Yet Miles expressed so warm a desire to hear her, that it would have been rudeness to refuse and she made her way to the old mahogany pianoforte, situated near to the fireplace, feeling like a horse being inspected for good points by a prospective buyer. All went better than she could have hoped, however, for, as she played and sang her mother's favourite, "The Yellow Haired Laddie", she had the satisfaction of hearing her performance described, more truthfully than was often the case, as 'delightful'. She was soon persuaded to join with Miles in a duet and it seemed a cause for satisfaction to them both to find that their voices blended perfectly and that they had an inclination for very similar types of music.

Under the soothing influence of music, Sarah forgot to be shy and the rest of the evening passed so quickly that, before they thought it could possibly be time, the tea tray had arrived. Long before it was time to say goodnight to his hosts, Miles had decided not only that Sarah would make him a very suitable wife, but that he would enjoy of all things being part of such a lively family, and he made plans accordingly to ensure that not one more day should pass before he knew if Sarah was of his mind or not.

****

It was at no very advanced hour that Miles made his way downstairs next morning and he deliberately by-passed the door which led from the hall into the small breakfast parlour, moving instead down a back stairway to the gardens. He felt almost certain that the solitary figure he had espied from his window was Miss Dagley and he now set off to seek her out in the rose garden, where he had last caught sight of her. He was determined to say his piece before breakfast, for he wished to avoid giving her any more cause for embarrassment and he could by no means feel confident that one or other of her brothers might not make such another blunder as had upset her on the previous evening.

Sarah was always up early, for she hated to waste the day by lying in bed, and today the effort was more than usually rewarded, for the garden looked and smelled so fresh. There had been a heavy dew and drops of moisture lay sparkling on flowers and leaves in the early sunshine. A few steps away from her, she watched a thrush trying to break a snail's shell on an anvil stone and she smiled to see Bess crouching down in the wet grass and watching it intently, not daring to move closer and chance her mistress's anger.

Sarah made a sufficiently pretty picture that morning in a long-sleeved day dress of printed cotton and plain straw bonnet, tied to one side with blue ribbons. Over her arm she carried a large basket for collecting new blooms to replace one or two wilted flowers in the house. She had just cut a rosebud of the palest of pink tints, lifting it to her face to enhale its fragrance, when, as she added the flower to her basket, she noticed Bess running to greet someone exuberantly. Looking up, she knew her worst fears realised as she saw their guest bearing down on her in a purposeful way. She was realistic enough to know that such a confrontation was inevitable, however, and decided that her own best interests would be served by hearing him out and so getting it all over with as quickly as possible.

Consequently, she waited for him almost to reach her and then called, in a calm voice which betrayed none of the distress she felt, "Good morning, my lord. What an early riser you are, to be sure. I do trust it is not a lumpy matress which has chased you so soon from your bed."

"Indeed no, I cannot remember when I slept more comfortably, Ma'am, but I always like to be up and about early. I am surprised to see you though. I thought ladies liked to spend a more leisurely time in the mornings."

"Ah, but you forget that we are in the country, sir. We retire so early, as you had an opportunity to note last night, that we really have no excuse to dally in the mornings," replied Sarah, happy to keep the conversation at such a general level.

Miles was not to be deflected from his plan, however, and he took Sarah's basket from her arm, to lead her purposefully over to a rustic-looking bench which had been conveniently placed in the shade of a huge old cedar tree. Sarah obediently sat at one end of the bench, Bess at her feet, leaving plenty of room to allow Miles to share it with her if he so desired, but he did not immediately join her, suddenly finding it more difficult to begin his proposal than he had anticipated. She too was ill at ease and pretended to be intent on following closely the progress of a cabbage butterfly, which had wafted early into the garden while she waited for him to embark on the explanation she knew must follow. After what seemed an age, Miles sat at the other end of the bench and turned towards Sarah, smiling ruefully to himself at his lack of poise. He remembered the last proposal he had made and how much easier it had been, in the rapture of his love for Caroline, to simply take her into his arms and pour out his wishes. It was very different to have to do the thing in cold blood! Realising that Sarah might mistake his reticence for lack of willingness, however, he hurriedly began, "My dear Miss Dagley, you are too sensible a lady for it to be necessary for me to pretend that you do not know why I am here at Leighwood. I hope, therefore, that you will not consider me insensitive if I waste no time in speaking to you about the matter, for it is only because I think we must both be more comfortable once it is in the open that I rush, pellmell, into it in this rather graceless fashion."

Sarah felt her colour rising, but, as Miles had opened the subject, she was in honour bound to assist him. She agreed, therefore, that some kind of discussion should be attempted, and then settled back, like a sensible woman, to hear what else he had to say. Unfortunately, he seemed to be at a standstill, so Sarah, in her forthright way, decided to take a hand, saying,

"While I am, of course, fully sensible of the honour you have done my family and myself in seeking this alliance, my lord, you must forgive me if I say that it seems a little, shall we say, unusual, to offer marriage to a comparative stranger, and especially to one who can give little or nothing in return."

Miles was shocked at Sarah's plain speech, but grateful too, as it gave him an opportunity to make clear to her exactly how things stood with him. He explained to her now, more fully, what her uncle had already told her: how, when his first wife Caroline had been killed, a part of his own life had gone with her, a part which he never would recover, nor indeed would ever wish to, so precious was her memory to him.

"It is important to me, Miss Dagley, that you understand the exact nature of my offer. You see this contract as an unequal one and I agree with you, but whereas you feel it to be me who gives most, I feel most decidedly that any sacrifice would be yours. It would give me the greatest pleasure to bestow on you my wealth and position in society, for our short acquaintance has been enough to assure me of your great good nature and leads me to believe that you would make any man an admirable wife. Since I do not set as much store by wealth and rank as others might, it seems to me that I offer you very little in exchange for those personal attributes you so obviously possess in abundance. You, on the other hand, would have to leave your home and a family that I can see you love very much, to come and live with a man who, on his own admission, can give you only a degree of affection. These past few hours have given me already a great regard for you and have convinced me that you are just the sort of wife I have been looking for and would be an excellent mother to any children with whom our union might be blessed. Indeed, this brief time has convinced me that we might deal very comfortably together, but I feel I would be less than just if I did not point out to you that you can never expect from me what you might have in a love match. Only your uncle's assurance that you have no previous attachment has allowed me to take the liberty of continuing thus far with my proposals, but should he be in any way mistaken, I will, of course, withdraw my offer immediately."

Sarah listened carefully and in silence to all he had to say, and for quite a few moments after he had finished she found that she could not speak. It was true that she had known all this beforehand, but then she had not heard the bleakness in his voice insisting that, along with his first wife, had gone all that had made life worth living for him. His habitual demeanour was so cheerful that she had had no idea that he still longed for Caroline so much and she felt the understanding they had been reaching crumble beneath the weight of his grief. She was disturbed, too, by his coolness when he spoke of their coming union. It seemed harsh to be seen only as a prospective mother when she wanted to be valued for herself. Almost she refused to accept him. Only the realisation of what she owed her own family gave her the courage to agree to the match and before they left the gardens, the bargain was sealed with the Earl's chaste kiss on her pale cheek.

CHAPTER 6

Every member of the Dagley household, excepting the one most concerned, looked on Sarah's betrothal with unalloyed delight and even Sarah found compensations in being so creditably settled. As soon as the news became generally known in the district, a continuous stream of calls began from neighbours, eager to know just how it was that such a mousey creature as Sarah, should have received such a brilliant offer. Sarah was human enough frankly to revel in their envy. Just to allow them one glimpse of her betrothed was sufficient, for his handsome features and careful solicitude for his future wife convinced them all that she was the luckiest woman alive. He was far too careful of Sarah's feelings to exhibit any sign that he was not the happiest of mortals, and Sarah had the doubtful felicity of knowing that only she guessed the true state of things.

Miles had presented his future bride with a beautiful ring of sapphires and diamonds, and his betrothal gift was a splendid necklace in matching gems. Sarah acknowledged to herself with typical honesty that sapphires suited her better than other, more flashy gems might have done, but always at the back of her mind she found herself speculating as to the jewels he had presented to the beautiful first Countess. It was foolish, she knew, to keep comparing herself to Caroline, for this was no love match on either side, yet it was difficult to contemplate marriage knowing that she could never hope to be of first consequence with her future husband, however kindly disposed he was towards her and her family. That he *was* kind to her family could never be called into question, for he was at all times generous and considerate, and he seemed to enjoy nothing more than bestowing gifts on them all, taking great delight in assuring Charlotte gravely that she might have an unlimited wardrobe when she came

47

out, and that he would certainly open his London home in Berkeley Square for the occasion. Sarah would have seen all this with delight could she have been certain that the gifts and promises were not made by him only to disguise from his future bride how little happiness he felt at their proposed match, but though she tried to concentrate her thoughts on her family's joy, her mind could not rid itself of a picture of Miles's bleak face when he had proposed.

It had been decided that the wedding should take place in the middle of August and, although Sarah well knew that few fashionable people married in church, she wanted her uncle to preside at her nuptuals and she wished very much to be married at the little church in the village. Miles, the easiest of men in such matters, readily agreed and he agreed, too, to her preference for a very quiet wedding, understanding quite well Sarah's unspoken wish not to have exposed for his wealthy relations the shabbiness which reigned at Leighwood. Much as he valued his own family, Miles could not but agree that one or two of them might indeed look askance if asked to put up in such poor surroundings: on his side, therefore, it was arranged that only his sister, Amabel, and his best man, would journey into Staffordshire for the occasion, although this meant that Sarah would need to visit Beaumere, the Earl's country seat, before the wedding, in order to make the acquaintance of some of the more important members of his family.

Sarah had expected to have to make this journey alone, but surprisingly, Lady Dagley felt it to be encumbent on herself to accompany her daughter, and her uncle decided as well to accept Miles's kind invitation. Not only they were to make the journey with Sarah, however, for it was tacitly acknowledged by all the Dagleys that, if she was not to be considered as more than just a trifle beneath the Earl's touch, Sarah had at least to be provided with a lady's maid. Lady Dagley, recognising that their new family connection now made economy all but unnecessary, wished to send to one of the fashionable London agencies to acquire an experienced dresser for Sarah, advising sagely, "Depend on it, my love, you will be living with just such a set of people who will despise you if you are not well turned out and an experienced dresser will be able to guide you in just how to go on. You are not very stylish, you know, my dearest!"

Sarah knew it only too well, but had other ideas, for

here was an opportunity to solve a problem which she had long puzzled her head over. Quietly she said, "Mama, if you do not mind very much, I would far rather ask Jenny Salt to be my maid."

"Jenny Salt! My poor foolish Sarah, what a nonsensical notion! Why, I am sure that we must all wish to do as much for the Salts as we can—indeed, with such a father how could we not? But to be ruining the impression you make on the Earl's family will not do. No indeed, it will not do at all."

"But Mama, I am sure that if you asked Walters to instruct Jenny in everything she needs to know all would be well. Jenny is an intelligent girl and she would certainly learn quickly enough."

Jenny Salt was not nor had she ever been, a lady's maid. Rather, she was a maid-of-all-work. The Salts were so poor and their father's constant state of intoxication made their poverty such a continual ill, that she had always to turn her hand to any work which offered in an attempt to ensure that her large family was fed. Her mother worked when she could, but was so often either giving birth, or waiting to do so that she could do less than she wished, so whenever any casual help had been required at the Hall, Sarah had made it a point to send for Jenny. About the same age as Sarah, or perhaps a little older, she was a very plain young woman, whom no-one had ever wished to marry—which was just as well for her family, for what they would have done without the money she earned, Sarah could not imagine. Always valuing Jenny as she deserved, Sarah realised that, as the Countess of Wilberton, she would be in a position to pay her a very generous wage and so temper permanently the wretched situation endured by her mother and the little ones. Moreover, she felt that to have a friendly face about her at Beaumere would be welcome indeed.

Lady Dagley was aghast at her daughter's suggestion and not at all swayed by her reasons, remonstrating in failing tones, "My dearest, it takes years to learn all that is necessary in a good lady's maid—and you will be moving in the first circles." She had already noted uneasily, however, Sarah's jutting chin and the obstinate expression which had descended onto her usually mild features and knew herself defeated. In due course, then, the happy Jenny was informed of the honour which awaited her and a less enthusiastic Walters was begged by an overwrought Lady Dagley to play her part as best she could. Walters, though sincerely attached to her mistress, was furious to be asked to teach Jenny, considering it a gross impertinence, but once her mistress had explained Sarah's determination—and, incidentally, presented her with a charming necklace which she had always coveted—she recognised that only she, Walters, could prevent the Dagleys from being exposed to the Earl's connections as not quite the thing. She could not bear to think that any family to whom she had deigned to offer her services might be seen in such a light and set to work immediately to try to evince in Jenny a miraculous transformation.

Sarah's new maid was soon housed in the lower regions of the house, along with the rest of Leighwood's retainers, her exalted rank ensuring her a room of her own. She learned quickly all that Walters had to teach and in a few days was able to ensure her mistress's comfort in many ways. But to say that she became at once a first-rate lady's maid would be less than honest, for it was the melancholy truth that, although Walters gave herself airs, she had never herself worked in a really superior establishment and Lady Dagley had shunned society for so many years that both she and Walters had fallen sadly into country ways. Lady Dagley's natural beauty ensured that she always appeared to advantage and it had not been necessary for her dresser to acquaint herself with artful means to aid her mistress. As she had never had to work on a less inspiring subject, she was unable to instruct her young protégée in any tricks to help improve the future Countess, so that, however pleasant Sarah found it to be to have warm water prepared for her in the mornings or to have her hair brushed before retiring, little had been achieved to make her stylish. Jenny became at once chief confidante and staunch ally to her mistress, but was unable to help her towards becoming a dashing leader of fashion.

Had Lady Dagley been allowed her way and sent to London for an accomplished maid for Sarah, it is possible that that person might have been able to make suitable suggestions for Sarah's trousseau; instead, Sarah was subjected to the tender ministrations of Lady Dagley's own dressmaker, Mrs. Weaver, who owned a small establishment near to Market Street in nearby Newcastle under Lyme. Mrs. Weaver had, of course, heard all about Sarah's astounding luck and knew only too well that whoever was fortunate enough to be honoured with her patronage would be assured of a comfortable living for some time to come, since, certainly all the local ladies of fashion would wish to use the same dressmaker as the new Countess. She found herself wishing that she had been less speedy in the past to dun Sarah's mother for a few paltry pounds for it seemed unlikely that this would be overlooked in the family's new affluence. She had, however, reckoned without the lack of perception which characterised Lady Dagley and which helped her not only to overlook Mrs. Weaver's transgressions, but which had also ensured that she had not noticed them when they had occurred.

As Lady Dagley and her daughter stepped in through her door the costumier could hardly believe her eyes, and nothing could have been more fulsome than the compliments she paid them, so different from the usual indifference she had invariably shown them on previous occasions. Sarah, unlike her mother, was quick to recognise Mrs. Weaver's hypocrisy, but could not help feeling how much more comfortable it was to accept than her barely repressed insolence had been.

Calling quickly to two of her assistants to arrange chairs for her esteemed clients, Mrs. Weaver gushed, "My dear Lady Dagley, what a great pleasure to see you, to be sure, and what an unconscionable time since we were honoured with your presence—and that of your so charming daughter." She looked archly at Sarah and murmured, "Would it be indelicate to offer my felicitations, dear Miss Dagley, at this happy time?"

Miss Dagley barely inclined her head, but if anything, this only increased the extravagance of Mrs. Weaver's prose, for, in her experience, this was just how the rich and famous always behaved. Sarah listened to her mother informing the dressmaker of her desire that her daughter be provided with clothes in which she would not be out of place in the society of the *haut ton* and could hardly prevent her lip from curling as Mrs. Weaver replied, "Of course, my lady. Just leave everything to me and you will soon see how exquisitely we can turn her out. Why, with her natural advantages, she will be a regular out-and-outer."

Sarah was fairly certain that Mrs. Weaver's optimism was not matched by any flair, an opinion soon confirmed as the ladies were shown one indifferent gown after another, being assured by their designer that they were 'all the crack." When she heard Mrs. Weaver asserting knowledgeably that only white, or "perhaps the palest of pale creams" could possibly be acceptable for bride clothes, she felt it to be unreasonable to expect her to take any further interest in the proceedings and resigned herself stoically to yet another period during which she would not show to advantage.

Mrs. Weaver did not quite know how it came about, but Sarah left her premises having placed a far smaller order than could possibly have been anticipated. Wilberton's future wife knew that the Earl was to foot the bill for her bride clothes and had felt from the start that to order a huge quantity would show a degree of voracity which she was disinclined to exhibit, but when she realised that those dresses she did order had to be made either in white or insipid cream, she felt it to be no sacrifice to cut down even further—after all, it would be no worse to appear in old frocks which did not suit her than new ones. In spite of her mother's warnings that Miles's family would consider her to be "not up to snuff" if she did not have a completely new wardrobe, including the requisite number of walking dresses, carriage frocks and ball gowns, she contented herself with ordering, as well as her wedding dress, just a few of the modiste's less fussy gowns, with some pelisses to match and one or two hats which she did not altogether despise. She spent rather more than she had intended, however, on nightgowns and undergarments and mentally blushed to think what a lack of delicacy this displayed.

In what seemed to be a remarkably short time her new wardrobe had been assembled and all the arrangements made for her journey into Shropshire. Miles had sent to Beaumere for his commodious travelling coach to ensure that his future bride might travel to his home in comfort and a fine morning in late June found Charlotte, Hugh and Pip gathered together at the front of the house to wave goodbye, while Miss Nelsworth fluttered around assuring

Lady Dagley that she need have no fears for the family in her absence.

Sarah felt very sad to have to leave them all, more so because she suddenly realised that this was only a rehearsal for the more complete separation which would soon take place. Almost as difficult was having to leave Bess behind, although she recognised her mother's wisdom in insisting that she should do so—soon enough for Beaumere to accept Bess when it had accepted her mistress. Bess, of course, saw only that Sarah was off somewhere and, as the steps of the coach were let down and the door opened, jumped confidently into the luxurious vehicle with her before anybody realised her intention. Her look of dismay when she was kindly, yet forcibly removed by Hugh was ludicrous to behold and her wails of protest travelled with Sarah in her mind for some distance, preventing her from immediately appreciating the comfortable cushioned seating and soft rug which her betrothed had himself spread over her lap before mounting his horse.

Miles and her uncle travelled on horseback, the day being so fine, leaving room in the coach for Lady Dagley and Sarah as well as for Walters and Jenny. The party began its journey early in order to ensure that they need not stay more than one night on the road and in spite of her sadness at leaving behind some of her loved ones, Sarah soon found herself to be in the highest of spirits, for the landscapes they passed as the carriage bowled along were so green and iridescent it was impossible to feel downcast.

She was still in spirits next day as, after a comfortable night's rest and a sumptuous breakfast, they left the Victoria in Newport on the final stage of their journey. The sun continued to shine, which seemed to augur well for her visit. Suddenly, as the coach encountered a rough stretch of road, Sarah clung tightly with one hand to the leather strap which hung from its wall, vowing to herself that she would make every effort to love her new connections and be loved in return.

CHAPTER 7

Could Sarah have heard a conversation taking place at that moment in the breakfast parlour at Beaumere, she might have felt rather less optimistic. Seated at the round satinwood breakfasting table were two ladies, a rare sight in that room so early in the day, since at Beaumere, ladies invariably breakfasted in their own bedchambers. This was, however, no ordinary day, for today Miles was bringing home his future bride and neither lady could bear to stay long in bed when they might gossip together about this extraordinary event.

At first glance, the two fair occupants of the room did not appear to bear any resemblance to each other. One had hair of the deepest auburn, worn in heavy swathes reaching down her neck to nestle against her beautiful sloping shoulders in an unusual fashion she had created for herself, striking enough on its own, but lying as it did against milky skin and contrasting with bewitching green eyes, it would be a very particular person who did not find her beautiful. Had she been standing, it might have been seen, too, that she was a fashionably tall, statuesque lady, with a shape which showed off to perfection her stylish silk dress in her favourite pale green, which she had had made up with a low front, but with a small collar and pelerine attached to give an impression of modesty.

Her companion must also have been accounted a beauty, with her silver-blonde hair and delicate pale complexion, being spared from insipidity by the possession of a pair of violet eyes, fringed with thick dark lashes, over which arched fine brows, and which, together with her small straight nose and rosebud mouth, combined to produce a countenance of extraordinary sweetness, invariably matched by her disposition. Her figure was less intrusive than her cousin's, for she was smaller and more slender.

Indeed, she had often been likened to Lady Caroline Lamb, and she revelled in the admiration she could command, especially when some of her admirers created extravagant names for her, such as 'Divine Elf' or 'Sylvan Nymph', just as they had done for that lady before her disgraceful behaviour with Lord Byron. Today she would certainly have inspired the more inventive of her followers, for she looked enchanting in a white muslin morning dress, flounced at the hem and having a high lace ruff which emphasized her graceful neck and the pretty set of her shoulders.

While a casual onlooker would see little resemblance between the two, a more lengthy observation might reward the perceptive by revealing a likeness, although it was rather to be glimpsed in an occasional expression or action than in any feature, accounted for by the nature of their connection.

At the very moment that Sarah was making her vow and wondering what her new relations would be like, they in turn were conversing animatedly about her. It was astonishing that they still had anything to say for they had first heard the news of Miles's betrothal more than a week before when his sister, Amabel, the lady in white, had received a missive from him to inform her that she would soon have a new sister-in-law and she had done little in the time which followed but discuss the surprising news with her cousin Elizabeth, at present her guest at Beaumere. Now Elizabeth was saying for about the hundredth time, "I really do not know what can have possessed Miles to run off and do such a rackety thing. Really, it is the outside of enough that we went without informing you of his purpose, but to spring it on you in a letter and then to bring her here without so much as a 'by your leave', it is more than I can understand."

"Oh Lizzie, you are funny! He hardly needs my leave to bring home his fiancée. Beaumere does belong to him, you know."

"Yes, but you are his sister and have been used to being the first lady of consequence here since your Mama died. I should have thought that common courtesy would have made him tell you his news in person. It would, after all, be enough to swallow for anyone."

"Miles knows only too well," replied Amabel gently, "that if he is happy then I will be too. Since Caroline died I have feared that he might never be happy again. Outwardly he has always appeared to be his usual self, but I know so well how hard her death had been for him to bear. I was only a young girl when they became betrothed, but even I could see that to him she was as no other. Surely no man was ever more in love."

She did not notice the hardening of expression on her cousin's face and went on, "I remember so well her beauty, but she had more than just looks. She seemed to be the embodiment of everything that women seek to acquire. She was the most graceful of creatures, she played and sang to perfection, painted well and looked as though she had been born riding a horse. She was the most brilliant of all the girls who came out that Season—no-one else could hold a candle to her."

With a curling lip, Elizabeth interrupted her, saying, "Since I came out during the same year as Caro, I can only say 'thank you', Coz."

Amabel raised rueful eyes to her cousin's face and held out a hand to squeeze her arm, "Oh Lizzie, you are far too sure of your own beauty for me to need to apologize to you. You have enough admirers not to begrudge poor Caroline her brief hour. When she agreed to marry Miles, it seemed the promise of a new and brilliant era for the family, but all her accomplishments could not help her to survive."

"Well," replied her cousin, waspishly, "it is no good thinking back on all that. We have other problems to worry us now. How Miles could ally himself with a Dagley when he might have taken his pick from the ton I cannot comprehend."

"Come now, Lizzie, the Dagleys are a very old and respected family."

"Oh, of course, very respected! And I suppose you will be saying next that before his death Miss Dagley's papa did not sport his blunt in every gaming club he could find, nor did he fritter away his family's fortune. No indeed, he has left them all in high fettle has he not?"

"It is true that he was not as prudent as he should have been, but his daughter can hardly be blamed for that, can

56

she?" replied Amabel fairly.

"Oh, I don't really blame *her* for anything, it is Miles that I blame, for foisting an unfashionable nobody onto the family when he might have taken anybody he wished. Certainly nobody would blame *her* for jumping at an opportunity to become the Countess of Wilberton, but Miles owed it to the family to be particular in his choice."

"We do not know for certain that she is unfashionable, Lizzie. Surely we should not judge her before we've even seen her."

"But I told you, Ami, Lady Denbridge said that she distinctly remembers Sarah Dagley. She was in London for a Season four or five years since and she said that the girl had to go home in disgrace because she simply did not take, such a mousey little creature as she was, with no style. It is too bad of Miles to subject us to this."

"I wouldn't mind what she looked like if I was sure she would make him happy, but I am almost certain that he had never seen her until he went into Staffordshire recently and I am afraid that, far from being a case of love at first sight, he is making a marriage of convenience for the sake of an heir. I was afraid how it would be when Miss Dagley's uncle stayed here, for I could see that Miles was much struck by Mr. Dagley's description of her good sense and clever management. I wish he had discussed his intentions with me before making a decision, for I am sure that I might have been able to persuade him of the folly of making such a match. When I think of how he loved Caro, I feel this marriage is doomed to failure, for no woman could live up to my brother's memories. Even a beautiful woman would encounter difficulty, but if she is as plain as you say . . ."

Amabel left her sentence hanging in mid-air, for at that moment a footman opened the door of the breakfast parlour to admit entry to an elderly lady. Dressed in clothes from an earlier period, the newcomer appeared to have given up any pretence to fashion some time during the last quarter of the previous century, for she wore wide skirts to her green brocade dress and a full bodice, deeply décolleté, but filled in with a neckerchief, a style which she was able to carry, since she was well above average height. She still wore her hair powdered for great occasions, but today she used no powder and her iron-grey hair was covered by a morning cornette of muslin and lace. As she came into the room she could be seen to be leaning heavily on a black cane, but this frailty was belied by her forceful expression and a pair of probing, clear dark eyes. The two younger ladies looked up at her entry, and she immediately began to speak.

"What are you gels doing about so early? In my day ladies breakfasted in their rooms when they were in the country. They didn't show themselves round the house before noon. The morning's not for women; it belongs to the men. They don't want to see a pack of females at the breakfast table. Put's 'em off their food."

"What are you doing here then, Aunt?" replied Elizabeth saucily, "Are not you as much a woman as we?"

"Impudent minx," murmured Lady Stanham, for such was the old lady's name, "Why, I'm past the age when I need concern myself with such nonsense. I go where I please. When you get to be as old as Methuselah, like me, men don't have to make up to you any more, so it's of no concern to 'em if I appear at breakfast or not. With you young things it's different. Why, then they have to start all this shilly-shallying about—and believe me, they don't take at all kindly to it so early. Where are they, anyway?"

"Out riding," replied Amabel, laughingly, "and not expected back until luncheon, so they are quite safe Aunt."

"Thank the Lord for that, at least we can have some peace for a time. And what were you two gossiping about when I came in, eh? Your brother's foolishness, I'll be bound, Ami."

"I've just been saying, Aunt Almeria, that for cousin Miles to marry a Dagley is the most infamous thing imaginable. For all we know, she may be just like her father and run us all into debt before we can turn round," put in Elizabeth before Amabel had a chance to answer.

"How you do run on, gel, and what a spiteful tongue you've got! It's a constant surprise to me that you managed to make such a good match with a tongue like yours, and even more surprising that you are able to keep such a pack of dim-witted creatures dangling after you as they do. Still, there's no accounting for taste, is there? Just the same, I marvel that you should get yourself all in a pucker over such a trifle. You don't throw away a cartload of apples because one gets a worm in it! Every family has its black sheep—it don't mean the rest of 'em aint whiter than white. The Dagleys have always been an unexceptionable family—why I'm connected with them myself. And I daresay they will be able to live down the foolish antics of one of their members." Then, staring hard at Elizabeth, she went on, "Heaven knows, we have enough in our family to make allowance for!"

Having disposed of Elizabeth, the old lady returned her attention to Amabel, and said sharply, "Well, gel, suppose it's too much to expect you to remember that you promised to write some letters for me today?"

"Of course I remember, Aunt," she replied good-humouredly, "And I have just this minute finished breakfasting, so would now suit you? The Library is empty so we could move in there and not be disturbed."

Her Aunt volunteered no reply, but simply moved in her stately fashion towards a door which led from the small breakfast room into the Library. Lady Stanham was angry at herself at being coerced into championship of her future relative, for she was quite as put out as the rest of the family by Miles's cavalier behaviour in choosing a wife without any consultation, but, as always, Elizabeth had managed to annoy her and she knew that she would now be obliged to declare herself Miss Dagley's friend, a course which did not greatly recommend itself to her.

Amabel cast an amused glance at Elizabeth and began to follow her Great Aunt out of the room, pausing only to ask her cousin if she would be joining them.

"I rather think not," replied Elizabeth pettishly, "It's too early in the morning to spar with Aunt Almeria, and anyway, I am still hungry. Thompson can bring me some more toast." As she spoke, she moved gracefully towards a bell pull which hung next to the large mahogany sideboard on which reposed the chafing dishes for breakfast, and she tugged the cord impatiently. Almost immediately, Thompson appeared and she quickly gave her orders, returning to the table, where she seated herself once more in one of the comfortable upholstered armchairs. Her expression was not pleasant, showing only too plainly some of the turmoil in her mind, for she was deeply unhappy. Since she was now alone, she abandoned her usual elegant pose and allowed her elbows to rest on the table, her chin cupped in her hands, and frowned heavily as she gazed blankly before her in an attitude of despair, wondering, not for the first time, why fate had been so perverse as to make it possible for her to fall in love only with her cousin Miles of all the men she had known. Almost every other man she had met had responded to her in no uncertain way, so why did it have to be only for him that she cared? In the quiet of the breakfast room, she found herself unable to resist thinking back to how it had been when she was growing up under Miles's eye, their mothers hoping for a match even though he and Elizabeth were first cousins. She remembered now, a slight smile touching her lips, how he had teased her as she grew towards womanhood, running tame around the grounds of Beaumere, Miles teaching her to ride and hunt, letting her tag along when he went fishing with his friends. How she had worshipped him, nearly ten years her senior and more handsome than she felt any man had a right to be. He had not married and she just knew that he was waiting for her. All would have been well had it not been for Caro! As she thought of her cousin's first wife, her fists clenched instinctively until her knuckles stood out and her nails made sharp crescents in her palms. It was all Caro's fault; he would have loved her, Elizabeth, had he never seen Caroline Manders.

She remembered as if it were yesterday the alfresco party at which Miles and his wife had first been introduced. Elizabeth had gone, escorted by Miles, and she could still hear in her mind his lazy voice complimenting her on her good looks as they made their way in his curricle to join their friends. It had been a perfect spring morning and she had been in the highest of spirits, for she had only lately come out, her entry into society a triumph. Everyone was predicting a brilliant match for her, not a few even going so far as to name Miles as the man who would win her, and life had never seemed sweeter. All that was at an end the moment Miles laid eyes on Caroline, for he needed no more than a brief glance at her to want her for his wife. She had been seated on a blanket under a large chestnut tree, surrounded by men, when they first saw her and, thought Elizabeth bitterly, that was how she seemed to be ever afterwards, for men swarmed round her like bees round a hive. On that morning she had been wearing nothing more dashing than a prim white muslin gown, high at the neck and long in the sleeve, but its delicate fabric could not disguise the swell of her firm figure or hide her tiny waist. Beautiful as had been Elizabeth, she was, as Ami had said, nothing to Caro, with her heavy raven hair, contrasting so dramatically with ice-blue eyes and each of her features complimenting further the others, from her small straight nose and sensual mouth to the dimple in her cheek. Every young single man in their set, it seemed, wanted her, but it took only a few days for Caroline to make up her mind that only Miles, Elizabeth's Miles, would do for her.

Looking back, Elizabeth was never sure how she had lived through those days. Every time she had to see them together was torture and in between she had had to listen to Miles's earnest confidences about his new-found passion. Even now, when she thought of his wedding day, her face began to feel hot and clammy. The year of Miles's marriage had been a nightmare, for she had had too much pride to allow anyone, especially Miles, to guess at her misery and humiliation, and she had had to go through a seemingly endless round of entertainments with her head held high as if she had not a care in the world. Once Caroline was claimed, Elizabeth had become the most sought after girl of the season, receiving one proposal after another and refusing them all, to her poor mother's consternation It had seemed as if fate was indeed laughing at her when Caroline had died only two months after Elizabeth had finally married one of Miles's closest friends, Lord Blissworth, in a futile attempt to make Miles aware of what he had thrown away. Of course, her marriage had not hurt him in the least; only she and her husband had suffered by it, for, although she had been able to keep her secret from others, Jeremy had been too fond of her not to realise where his wife's affections really lay. He had set himself to win her love in the early weeks of their marriage, but when Caroline had died and he had seen the hope revitalized in Elizabeth he had given up the unequal struggle and contented himself with watching, cynically amused, his wife's attempts at winning her cousin's attention.

After Caroline's death, Elizabeth's tortured mind had known some respite, for, although she knew that Miles still longed for his dead wife, at least *she* did not have to think of him physically sharing his life with anyone. Vaguely at the back of her mind Elizabeth had always imagined that 'something' would happen to allow her to marry Miles and now all her hopes were to come to nothing once again since he was to make this second marriage. It just was not fair! The thought that an insignificant little creature was to share Miles's bed with him made her feel sick. "She probably doesn't even want him!" she whispered desperately to herself. "No doubt she will be one of those prissy creatures who think of their duty before they submit to their husbands. If only I could be his wife, I would know how to wipe the memory of Caroline from his mind! Why should Sarah Dagley have him? She has not spent half a lifetime longing for him as I have." As she focussed her mind on Sarah, her eyes glistened with an unnatural brilliance and she began to wonder how she could make her pay for stealing Miles from her. If Elizabeth had her way, Sarah's matrimonial voyage would be a stormy one indeed. The more she thought of Miles with his new bride, the more her resolution hardened.

CHAPTER 8

Sarah caught her first glimpse of Beaumere late on the afternoon following her departure from Leighwood. Miles had arranged in advance for his own horses to be stationed at appropriate coaching inns so that no broken-winded nags were harnessed to his elegant vehicle to slow them down and they travelled the Postcoach route, making their way first through Newcastle under Lyme and Trentham to Eccleshall, and then Newport, where they had stayed the night in fine style at the Victoria. The next day saw the party move off early, travelling on through Hay-Gate and making a final stop at the Lion in Shrewsbury before setting off for Beaumere, situated to the north of the city.

It had been discovered that unfortunately Jenny suffered from coaching sickness and her tolerant mistress could not bear to ignore her sufferings as Walters suggested, causing Miles to have his vehicle stop at the side of the road whenever necessary to alleviate the poor girl's sufferings. So, although the horses were high steppers, it was not until five before the house came into sight.

At first glance, Sarah was conscious of a little feeling of disappointment, for, elegant though it appeared, Beaumere was by no means as large a house as her imagination had led her to expect, nor was it so very old, having been built as late as the middle of the eighteenth century. All Sarah's expectations of gothic mansions evaporated, for the house was quite square, built in unpretentious local grey stone, the family apartments situated to the west side of the house, while those rooms used for entertaining were on the other side of an ornate central staircase, a single porticoed entrance hall serving both. Miles had recently added a separate servant's block to the house, next to the private apartments, and a large conservatory almost the entire length of the back of the house, yet with all these additions, the house seemed scarcely more imposing than Sarah's own home.

The park in which it stood, however, found high favour with its future mistress for she admired the way the gardens sloped down from the house and around a small natural lake situated a little way from it. The beautiful aspect was enlivened still further by a pretty little pagoda, which could be more easily seen, she supposed, from a bridge she glimpsed built across a part of the narrow end of the lake and which served to make continuous a path around the gardens.

Miles and her uncle had ridden on ahead a little so that, by the time the travelling coach drew up at the front of the house, their horses had been led away by waiting grooms and the two men were themselves able to hand the tired ladies down from their vehicle.

Sarah, used as she was to a very modest establishment, suddenly felt that she was being overwhelmed by servants. They seemed to be everywhere, in great numbers, some removing luggage from the coach, others apparently waiting just for the pleasure of greeting their master, most of the male servants wearing the Earl's blue and silver livery. Miles's guests were led through the front entrance hall, having received a greeting on behalf of the servants from the butler, Stebbings, and Sarah received a vague impression of two endless lines of hirelings, their costumes dark against the pale-coloured walls of the hall.

Noticing Sarah's fatigue, Miles suggested that his guests might like to be shown straight to their rooms, since the rest of the household were clearly making themselves ready for the evening. He added kindly that he would arrange for some tea to be sent to their apartments and delay dinner until they had rested. Sarah could only be grateful for his consideration. Jenny was still feeling sadly knocked up, so she knew that she could depend on little or no assistance from her—it was more likely that she would have to minister to Jenny instead, and probably unpack for herself as well.

Miles himself showed Sarah's uncle to his rooms, while a respectable-looking housekeeper, Mrs. Pride, but whom Miles familiarly called Pridey, escorted the ladies upstairs.

Looking around her in wonder, Sarah thought she had never seen anything as pretty as her room, with its elegant satinwood furniture and sumptuous tent bed, hung in charming blue chintz to match the curtains at the long windows and was more aware than ever how shabby her own home must have appeared to Miles.

Sarah's predictions proved only too true and she had indeed not only to get herself decently prepared for the evening ahead and unpack her things, but also to minister to Jenny as best she could. As she prepared a few drops of laudanum in water for the girl and tried to persuade her to swallow a mouthful of the tea so thoughtfully provided, Sarah could not help smiling to herself to think how angry her mother would be to see her.

When the last of her clothing had been put away and she had despatched Jenny off to her own quarters to lie down, she realised that she had left herself very little time to get ready, so she had a very speedy wash and quickly dressed in the first of her new gowns that came to hand, a pretty frock of white crêpe over a sarsnet slip. Sarah was certain that on most girls it could not fail to be admired; on her, it looked nothing. She was painfully aware, too, that she had overcrimped her hair in her hurry and the more she combed it the more frizzy it seemed to get, but since it was too late to do anything about it, she collected together her comb and handkerchief, deposited them in the little pocket she wore round her waist inside her petticoat, feeling herself now as ready as ever she would be to go downstairs.

Beside her sapphire necklace, she had decided on the addition of a pale lilac shawl, a recent present from her fiancé, and gloves she had bought at home to match, but she could not convince herself that they produced the desired effect for she still looked as insignificant as ever.

Miles had been thoughtful enough to send a housemaid to guide his betrothed and her mother to the large drawing room in the East Wing and together they made their way there, exchanging with each other information about the elegance of their quarters, and Sarah telling her mother of Jenny's continued indisposition.

"I knew how it would be, my love, murmured Lady Dagley under her breath, "The girl just does not know how to go on. Had you taken your Mama's advice and furnished yourself with a superior dresser like Walters you must have been more comfortable."

Lady Dagley as ever looked admirable, although Sarah was certain her excellent appearance owed far more to her natural beauty than to any of Walters' efforts. In her favourite dark purple silk, with matching turban, she managed to look perfectly charming, although Sarah knew that her dress was not in the first stare of fashion. If only she too might be allowed to wear deeper colours. She had only time to whisper back to her mother that poor Jenny considered herself to be quite as wicked as could be wished for, when she heard herself being announced at the door of a large apartment, within which were assembled a number of people.

As they entered the room, Miles moved forward to greet them, while an unnatural hush descended on the rest of the company. Sarah soon caught sight of her uncle, already seated contentedly in a comfortable armchair near to the handsome fireplace, speaking to a very pretty young lady and she expressed a wish to join him, for she had become uneasily aware that she was being stared at in a rather ill-bred fashion by almost all of the occupants of the room.

"I was just going to take you over, my dear," replied Miles, "for he is with my sister, Miss Greville, who is longing to meet you."

They made their way over to Amabel, and Miles quickly completed the introductions, at which Amabel impulsively stood up, holding out both hands to Sarah and saying sweetly, "Oh my dear Miss Dagley, I cannot tell you how happy I am to meet you! Miles has been telling me all about you and about your younger brothers and sisters too! I am sure that we will become the greatest of friends, for it will be so pleasant for me to have a sister. And how comfortable that you will be able to chaperone me to all the balls and parties. I know it will be the greatest of fun!"

Amabel's brother had indeed been telling his sister about Sarah and explaining to her how his betrothal had come about. She had listened to him avidly, hoping to have some indication that Miss Dagley had stolen his heart. In growing consternation she heard, instead, how kind she was to her young brothers and sisters and what an unconscionably hard time she had had of things in past years. Her heart sank, for she was sure that a man who had lived, however, briefly, in a romantic dream with Caroline, could not be content with such prosaic commonplaces. As Sarah entered the drawing room and she was brought face to face with the reality that her brother had betrothed himself to a complete dowd, her generous heart went out to Sarah, causing her to make her pretty gesture and to determine to do all in her power to ensure her new sister's comfort.

****

It was quite late when Sarah returned to her room that evening and she was relieved that before going downstairs she had told Jenny to take herself off to bed, for she now felt that if she had to speak to anyone at all she would succumb to a hearty bout of tears. She stepped out of her dress and washed quickly, pausing only to brush her hair out of its stiff style and put on one of her pretty new frilled nightgowns and caps before stepping into bed. She wished that she was back home in her own room at Leighwood, for she would have liked to draw her bed curtains closely around her bed to blot out the world while she indulged herself in a fit of misery.

All had seemed to be going so well when she had first gone down. When she had time to look round more carefully she had seen that the party was not really so large, for besides the Dagleys, Miles and his sister, only the Blissworths, together with two other young couples, Lord and Lady Mountjoy and Mr. and Mrs. McBride were present, the party being completed by Lady Almeria, and by two young single gentlemen, Viscount Stephen Anstey and Miles's second cousin, the Honourable Freddy Middleton.

She saw at once that the young ladies present were by far more fashionable than she was herself, but when Amabel had shown herself determined to be pleased, she had felt that they might scrape through pretty well.

Even her presentation to Lady Stanham had passed off happily. Miles had forewarned Sarah that that lady was known on occasion to be difficult and when Amabel and her brother took her and Mrs. Dagley over to be introduced she had known a brief moment of panic for she knew that Miles set great store by his Aunt's opinion. Her trepidation, however, proved ill-founded.

Lady Stanham had been for many years the terror of her family, not to mention her numerous servants and indeed almost everyone with whom she came into contact. A widow of many years standing she had once been as stunning as either of her great-nieces and her face was still a remarkably fine one considering her age. Nearly eighty, she showed no signs of approaching senility and had a way of disconcerting visitors by her forthright manner, scathingly mocking the manners and customs of a generation younger than her own. Although most of her family lived in dread of her acid tongue, they were all very attached to her and Sarah was in no doubt that this audience might make or mar her comfort. They moved over towards the high-back mahogany armchair on which was seated the old lady, in her stiff full skirts and powdered wig, but before her nephew had a chance to introduce his guests, she said to him peevishly, "So, you've come back have you? What do you think you've been up to, running about the countryside willy nilly, without so much as a by your leave? You invite me to stay and then go off without a word to anyone, leaving me to scratch amusements as I can. It won't do, my boy, won't do at all!"

"And I am delighted to see you again too, dearest Aunt," replied Miles at his most urbane, holding her hand up to his lips to be kissed and then planting a gentle kiss on her flushed cheek in a flagrant effort at toad-eating, as she had no dissatisfaction in informing him.

"There's no need to try turning me up sweet m'boy, save it for your flirts!" She looked shrewdly at Sarah, "I suppose this is the chit that all the fuss is about. Well, you may introduce me—though I have no hesitation in pointing out that in my day it was considered polite to acquaint one's family with projected matches before they took place—and especially to acquaint the senior members of one's family! But that's the trouble with so-called *modern* young people; no sense of occasion. Well, what can you expect," she continued, now fully launched on her theme, "when gels go around in frocks which look more like nightgowns than is decent. It was obvious where it would all end when they started to tax powder! And as for you young gentlemen, though what you are supposed to have done to earn the title I do not know, well, I can only say that I'm speechless."

That this was very much an untruth became apparent almost immediately, for she went on, "Next thing we know, you'll *all* be in these silly thingummybobs, what're they called? Trowsers, or some such mamby pamby name. It's bad enough that you've all taken to wearing enough starch round your necks to keep a washerwoman happy for a year, though why you should want to stop yourself from being able to move your head is beyond me. But trowsers! Pooh, it puts me out of all patience.—Well, my dear, you may kiss me."

Sarah, rather mesmorised by all this eloquence, was not at first certain that Lady Stanham was speaking to her, but seeing that lady turn her cheek towards her, she realised that she was indeed being so condescending and quickly obliged her. Miles then introduced Lady Dagley to his venerable relation and that lady had the doubtful felicity of hearing Sarah's future relation reflecting, "It's a pity the chit ain't got more of her mother's looks, for then she might go on very well."

Lady Dagley was moved to defend her daughter, "We at home feel Sarah to have a sweet face," she protested.

"No-one's saying it ain't sweet," replied her adversary fairly, "just that she ain't a diamond of the first water."

"Perhaps beauty is a matter for opinion," replied Lady Dagley spiritedly.

"Ay, and mine says she ain't one," explained the old lady, battle now fairly joined.

Sarah judged it wise to interfere at this point, for Miles and his sister were overcome with embarrassment at the old harridan's straightforward speech and so could not be relied on to intervene. She began in an amused voice, "Indeed, Ma'am, you really must allow Lady Dagley to champion me, for though I have to admit to being a rather frowsy creature, a mother's partiality, you know, must not be denied."

"Oh, so you've a tongue in your head, have you? And something to say for yourself too if I don't mistake the matter. I'm glad to hear it for these sickly silent gels are what I've no patience with."

"I too am not fond of reticence, Ma'am," replied Sarah, her eyes sparkling in appreciation of the old woman's performance, "so we should certainly deal admirably together."

"Hm, a little cat—with claws too, I shouldn't wonder."

Great Aunt Almeria turned to the three witnesses to their conversation saying, "All of you, make yourselves scarce. I want a word in private with the chit."

Even Lady Dagley dare not argue and, as they all three moved away, Miles with a rueful look on his face which betokened his appreciation of the scene, Lady Stanham patted the empty chair next to hers and bade Sarah sit down, saying, as soon as she was settled, "Now tell me in truth what you think of this proposed match of yours. I suppose you are in high croak about it? I collect that you think that m'nephew is every young gel's dream and that you will live happy ever after."

"I am not so very young, Lady Stanham," replied Sarah laughing.

"Don't try bamming me, my girl. It cannot have escaped your notice that you might have some rough ground coming up."

Sarah preserved a rigid silence, for even she was a little taken aback by the old lady's forthright way of coming to the point.

"No need to be stiff-rumped about it gel. I like you and I'm glad to see that Miles had the wit not to choose one of your simpering misses, but I don't want you to be running willy nilly into what you don't understand."

"You are speaking, Ma'am, about his first wife. It would be idle to deny that his continued regard for Caroline's memory, deep as it is, has given me food for thought, but I believe I can make him comfortable and mean to try."

"Well, m'girl, I'd as lief have you trying as any other, but a word of warning. There's more to life than comfort and there may come a time when Miles is not content to settle for a well-ordered house and good dinners on the table. Mark me when I say that memories might be the least of your problems. The living always have an advantage over the dead (which should be some comfort to you m'girl), but Miles knows many women who are very much alive, which is something to bear in mind. I do not hesitate to drop a word in your ear, for it's plain as a pig's trotter that you're not pudding-hearted. I like you gel—yes I do!"

"Thank you, Ma'am. I'm obliged to you," replied Sarah, amused at her forthright speech.

"Go off and make yourself agreeable to the others now or m'nephew will accuse me of keeping you to myself."

At that, a rather thoughtful Sarah was given to understand that her audience was at an end and she was free to return to her mother's side.

The other guests had to wait to be introduced to her, since at that moment dinner was announced and she was taken on Miles's arm into a large dining room, where she was seated on his right hand, with Lord Blissworth on her left.

She had a considerable time to make her judgment of Lady Blissworth's husband as they made their way through a gargantuan meal, which included such delicacies as semelles of carp, removed with a loin of veal and a raised pie, a lobster served in a sauce which, Miles assured her, was made to a recipe known only to his French cook, and a broiled fowl served in mushrooms.

Lord Blissworth, like Miles, seemed determined to put Sarah at her ease and, as he had a dry sense of humour which matched her own, she was soon happily engaged in a laughing conversation with him.

Sarah thought him a very pleasing man to look at, for while he was not in the strictest sense of the word handsome, he had great charm of countenance, since his very open, boyish looks were unclouded by any appearance of ill-humour and he had a smile which crinkled his eyes at the corner mischievously and lit his face impishly. Not as tall as Miles, he was yet tall enough for the hackneyed phrase 'a fine figure of a man' to be frequently applied to him, and his broad shoulders could not be disguised by his well-fitting tail-coat.

While he would never have been pronounced clever, (he was too lazy for that) he had a great deal of discrimination and a degree of native quickness which made him at once a sensible and a witty companion.

When he had married Elizabeth, it was with all the ardour of which he was possessed, but finding that his wife's affections were already engaged elsewhere had not soured him. Hurt as he had been, he was yet determined that life should continue sweet for him and, if occasionally, when he saw the naked lust in Lizzie's eyes as she looked at her cousin, he felt that his soul was being torn apart, for the most part he was able to live quite comfortably, even if that comfort was earned by the rather dubious expedient of deliberately turning a blind eye to what he preferred not to notice. He was, however, shrewd enough to guess that Elizabeth would do her utmost to make Sarah's stay uncomfortable and was eager to let Sarah see that she had one friend at least in that company. For her part, seldom had she been better entertained and they were soon chatting together as amiably as if they had known each other for ever.

By the time the ladies left the table they were on the way to becoming fast friends and Sarah was beginning to feel that she had worried too much about these new acquaintances.

The next hour was to prove her wrong.

CHAPTER 9

After dinner, Amabel led the ladies back to the drawing room, while the men settled down to a serious study of the port. Sarah had had little opportunity to look about her before dinner, but was now at leisure to note that the room they had returned to was furnished in the first cry. Fashionable eau de nil walls were enhanced by draperies of deeper green at the long windows and around several mirrors hung along the wall facing them. Rich dark rosewood furniture was placed elegantly *dérangé*, some chairs being set round a handsome grand piano, and others in groups near to the windows, to enable the occupants of the drawing room to enjoy the beautiful view down to the lake and the gardens. Sarah thought most of it vastly pretty, letting her mind wander idly on one or two trifles she might consider altering when she was mistress there.

She was not left very long to ponder her improvements, however, for now it was Amabel's duty to introduce her to the other ladies of the party.

Lady Blissworth had been delighted to see that Sarah was quite as dowdy as she had been led to believe, but this in no way disposed her more kindly towards her and when she gave Sarah her hand to shake, Sarah was aware of a disquieting sense of antagonism, only partially concealed by Elizabeth's company manners.

The two ladies not yet introduced, Lady Mountjoy and Mrs. McBride, were the type of women that Sarah had endured in droves during her London Season, empty-headed, vapid, insipid creatures of little beauty and less sense: their conversation was all of fashion and of the fashionable and they enjoyed nothing more than a comfortable cose, tearing to shreds the reputation of a lady with whom they had dined on excellent terms the night before. Lady Mountjoy, large, plump and raven-haired, gushed that she was "delighted to meet Miss Dagley under such very auspicious circumstances," while Mrs. McBride, a tall, shapelessly thin creature with frizzy mousey hair and protruding hazel eyes, joined her in her congratulations, adding, "We must certainly stick together you and I Miss Dagley, for I must tell you that I have only recently become a bride myself—to my dearest Georgie, you know. Of course, being a bride, I ought to have claimed precedence this evening on going into dinner," she exclaimed archly, "but naturally, I waived the privilege in your favour on such an important occasion."

Sarah was highly amused by her speech and found herself wondering whether its purpose was to ensure that Amabel did not allow this breach in etiquette to continue, or simply to boast about her married status to a girl as yet only betrothed.

Amabel served tea and, while Lady Dagley and Lady Stanham, their earlier disagreement forgotten in the pleasure of talking over old acquaintances, Sarah was left to try to strike up a friendship with the others. This was more easily said than done, however, for Elizabeth had decided to waste little time in beginning her attack on Sarah, and she was particularly safe to do so while her Great Aunt was fully occupied with Sarah's Mama.

"Well, Miss Dagley," she now began, "and what do you think of us?"

Thinking this rather an absurd question, Sarah replied, "I hardly know how to answer you, Lady Blissworth, for if I say I am vastly taken with you all, you must think me a foolish creature for making up my mind on such a brief acquaintance, but if I say I am not, then I must appear extremely rude, must I not?"

"Really, Miss Dagley, I hardly think my question to have warranted prevarication, or perhaps you think me impertinent to have asked it?" wondered that lady in her sweetest tone, a smile forced to her lips.

"Not impertinent, Lady Blissworth,—perhaps just a little precipitate? I find I must take a little longer to make up my mind," replied Sarah, now laughing audibly.

"Really?" questioned Elizabeth tartly, "I should not have thought it so difficult."

Amabel, quick to sense an atmosphere, judiciously applied herself to healing the breach by offering tea and macaroons to everyone, but it would not do, for her cousin had decided that such a pretentious little upstart as Miss Dagley needed a lesson. Seating herself very close to Sarah, therefore, and smiling in an odiously insincere fashion, she said confidentially, "Miss Dagley, or may I call you Sarah? We are to be related soon, you know, and it would give me such great pleasure . . .?"

Sarah nodded her agreement and Elizabeth went on, "well, Miss Dagley . . . Sarah . . . now that we are apart from the gentlemen, shall you think it the greatest cheek if I say that we are simply agog for details of your betrothal and how it came about? Such a romance as it must have been! Why, we had no idea that Miles knew you, did we Ami? Tell us all, dearest Sarah, how it happened. Did he meet you at a ball and sweep you off your feet, or see you at an assembly and write a sonnet to your beautiful eyes? Do tell, Miss Dagley, for I declare I am breathless in anticipation. We were so envious of you for being the subject of so much masculine ardour, were we not Amabel?"

As Amabel stared at her cousin in horror, Sarah suddenly remembered Aunt Almeria's earlier warning. She was shrewd enough to comprehend that Elizabeth knew exactly how her betrothal to the Earl had occurred and she could not, therefore, embroider the truth in any way. Only by refusing to be drawn into lies could she retain even some of her dignity, so calmly she folded her hands before her and gently replied, "Well, I assure you, Lady Blissworth, that there is little in our meeting to awaken envy in the heart of any romantic. You must know that Miles spoke to my Uncle before seeing me at all."

That Elizabeth must have received great satisfaction in hearing her confirm what she already well knew, Sarah could be in no doubt, but no professional actress could have more convincingly feigned surprise than she did now, for she lifted her hands as if thoroughly distressed to have caused such embarrassment. "Oh, my dearest Miss Dagley . . . Sarah . . . forgive me, I pray! That *I* should have been, however, innocently, the cause of bringing up what you must have most wished to forget! I can never forgive myself, indeed I cannot!"

"It does not signify," replied her victim, placidly, "for I am not ashamed of it in the least."

Amabel, blazingly angry at her cousin, knew her duty and quickly intervened saying in her kindest manner, "Of course not, Sarah, and indeed, how should you be? Miles has been telling me that as soon as you met he knew that you were just the woman to suit him," and Lady Mountjoy and Mrs. McBride murmured soothingly, "Just so, just so," although it was quite clear from the sly looks they exchanged, that they were enjoying the scene immensely and that they even shared Elizaeth's pleasure to see Sarah distressed, probably because she was about to make an alliance superior to their own.

When she had finished taking tea, Sarah walked over towards the canterbury placed near to the piano and looked through the store of music it held, determined to stay away from Elizabeth and so give her as little opportunity to attack as possible.

Elizabeth, however, had by no means finished with Sarah for that evening. Muttering something under her breath to Lady Mountjoy and Mrs. McBride, seated side by side on a sofa, she made her way over to Sarah once more.

"Why, Miss Dagley, I noticed that you do not have your reticule with you. Can it be that you have misplaced it in the Dining Room?" She looked expressively at the attractive little bag, made to match her own expensive evening apparel and which dangled from her wrist, as if to ensure that Sarah did not mistake her meaning. Sarah, thinking that perhaps she had been mistaken after all and that Elizabeth wanted to be friends, replied amiably,

"Indeed I have not, Lady Blissworth, though I thank you for your concern. I do not use one, you see, but prefer to use a pocket," and she reached through the slit in her gown to bring out her handkerchief as if in confirmation.

"Why, how quaint!" replied Elizabeth, looking down at her gown, "I declare I have not seen a *lady* using a pocket for, well, simply aeons, have you?"and then she turned her head towards the sofa.

Too late Sarah saw the amused exchange between Elizabeth and her friends and another point was lost. Elizabeth knew her friends well. Nothing could more surely earn their contempt than a failure to cut a dash.

Anyone still old-fashioned enough to wear a pocket would certainly be considered fair game. Now Amabel's cousin turned away from Sarah and began to play with her curls, an expression of scorn on her face. What a pity the chit didn't offer more sport. "Really, it is too simple," she thought to herself languidly, "She is hardly worthy of my pains."

****

Not long afterwards, to Sarah's relief, the gentlemen returned to the drawing room. She was certain that Elizabeth would be too clever to attempt to discomfit her in Miles's presence and she was right, for nothing could have been more proper than her behaviour towards his betrothed in his presence, indeed, she spent much of the evening hanging onto Sarah's arm in an affectionate and playful manner and praising Miles for his good taste in brides.

When it was time for music Sarah was happy to be able to plead fatigue and remain a spectator and it was Elizabeth alone, now in her element, who was able to delight the company since Amabel's duties as hostess kept her busy and the other ladies professed to have given up music since their marriages. Mrs. McBride assured the company that her reason for so doing was "not one of choice, I do protest, such a pleasure as it was to me," while her friend, Lady Mountjoy, agreed with her, adding archly, "Indeed it seems like boasting but before my marriage, friends were wont to say to me, Alice . . . my name you know, . . . Alice, they would say, no-one has your taste! But, alas, it has all had to be given up with the cares of married life."

Since it was well understood that the only cares known to either lady concerned whether pink or blue suited them best, or the difficult business of having to decide between the relative merits of a rouleaux trimming or one of quilling, little notice was taken of their protestations and the company settled down to be amused by Lady Blissworth.

Predictably, Elizabeth played and sang well: she had been taught by a master and had applied herself so diligently that she had in time become accomplished enough to echo his style almost perfectly. But she had little natural taste and Sarah found herself thinking how much more enjoyable her performance must have been had she made an attempt to interpret the music in a more simple style of her own. Her singing was more to Sarah's taste, for although her voice was less trained, she had a clear contralto, which she used to great effect in the popular ballads requested by her audience. Sarah noticed in surprise that in spite of her own presence, Miles pleaded most earnestly, almost flirtatiously, with Lizzie to sing and he entreated her most especially for his particular favourite, *Under the Greenwood Tree*. It seemed most *particular* indeed to Sarah, brought up as she had been, out of society!

As she watched, Elizabeth turned purposefully to Miles, saying, "Well, my bold cousin, I will agree happily to your desires, but you shall not escape, for I will only sing if you will agree to a duet."

She spoke slowly, lingering over the word 'desires' in such a coquettish manner that Sarah's face burned with indignation.

Miles, at first, seemed unwilling to oblige the lady, but the weight of Lady Mountjoy and Mrs. McBride's entreaties added to hers persuaded him and he strolled casually over to the piano, giving his betrothed a brief smile and shrug, which seemed to indicate that he only agreed in order to have some peace, although, to Sarah, this by no means appeared the case.

Their performance came as something of a surprise to Sarah, for it soon became apparent that they must have sung very often together and recently too, their voices blended so perfectly and the harmony produced was so faultlessly practised. This was not the only surprise for Sarah either, for now, for the first time, she was in a position to observe Elizabeth's face as she looked at Miles. Lady Blissworth was by nature a flirtatious creature and Sarah had already had occasion to notice of her that she preserved a saucy demeanour when speaking to any gentleman. When she looked at Miles, though, she was transformed, her beautiful face showing only too clearly her hunger for him. As an engaged woman, Sarah might not be thrilled at Elizabeth's overt flirting with her betrothed, but she was woman enough to admit that any man might be delighted to receive those speaking glances and certainly Miles did not seem at all loth to do so.

She found herself peeping covertly at Lord Blissworth's face to see how he was affected by this display and for an instant she was shocked at the naked misery she saw there. Before she had a chance to turn her head away, however, she saw his usual amused expression descend once more to hide what she had seen.

Sarah was not sure what all this meant, but as the entertainment was brought to an end and she saw Elizabeth and Miles, heads together as they put away the music, she knew a sudden pang of fear. Surely Miles had not betrothed himself to her to disguise an illicit affair with his cousin? Almost she refused to entertain the thought: Miles was too kind for such shabby behaviour! But she had to admit that every time she looked at her future husband, he seemed to be sharing in some banter with that lady, which made it difficult for Sarah to be certain. She could not remove from her thoughts the memory of the pain she had surprised on Lord Blissworth's face, remembering at the same time how much greater had been his opportunity to observe them together.

As she moved over towards the tea tray just placed before Amabel, she passed Great Aunt Almeria, who spoke under her breath to her, saying, "Hm, a very affecting little performance, wasn't it? Gel always was an alley-cat!"

So, she was not the only one to notice! Sarah was furious, but as always her obstinacy came to her aid. They might notice, but Sarah was quite determined that no-one should realise how upset she was. She stayed close to her mother for the rest of the evening, until it was time for the gentlemen to present the ladies with their candles for bed. She refused to be drawn into any but the smallest of small talk with her betrothed, thanking him only with a dignified word as he put her candlestick into her trembling hand and wished politely that she might sleep as well at Beaumere as he had at Leighwood. For just a moment she felt that she must have been mistaken, and was about to be more friendly when she noticed that he had turned to pick up another candlestick, handing it to his cousin and saying, "Here you are, my little nightingale. For such a sprite as you it should really be a glow-worm, but this will have to do."

Although Sarah could see that her mother was almost bursting with vexation at such a scene, she managed, as they went upstairs, to fob her off with stories of a headache, so reaching her bedroom alone without having to bare her soul.

As she lay in bed, the tears streamed down her face. She could not decide whether she was more miserable or more angry at what she had seen. She only knew that she wished she had never heard of her uncle's precious Miles St. John Hubert Greville. Too late now for that, however, but no-one should be given a chance to say that the future countess was not up to playing the kind of games that seemed so common in that house. If Miles wished to flirt, so be it. For her part, she would show him just how good a bargain he had made by refusing to notice it in the least. At least he should learn what good manners were! His Lordship wanted a conformable wife did he? Well, it was stunningly obvious now why! He would have what he had paid for, then. Whatever happened, whatever she saw, she would not give him the satisfaction of knowing that he had the power to hurt her in any way.

CHAPTER 10

In later years Sarah could never remember her introduction to Beaumere without a shudder, so successful had Elizabeth been in undermining her peace of mind there. It seemed to Sarah that her ingenuity knew no bounds: she seemed able to conceive of any number of spiteful little schemes to make Sarah look foolish. The one which for ever remained in Sarah's memory as her most hateful occurred on the second evening of her stay.

She had not particularly enjoyed the day, for after Miles's behaviour towards Elizabeth she wanted nothing less than to be forced into a tête-à-tête with him and so had studiously avoided being alone in his company all day, preferring rather to pursue instead her promising friendship with Lord Blissworth. Lord Blissworth walked with her in the park around the house, showed her the best views Beaumere had to offer and gave her a guided tour of the family treasures, while of Miles she saw nothing, for he was too busy being regally entertained by his cousin to notice her absence.

When the party collected together that evening to await dinner, Elizabeth, in high spirits after a day spent exactly as she liked best, suggested that after dinner they should play charades. Sarah noticed a wicked gleam in her eye, but put this down to a wish to show off again and readily joined her voice to those who liked the scheme.

Amabel declined to take part, wishing to concentrate on the comfort of those guests wanting to play whist. Thus, Sarah, Mrs. McBride, Miles and Freddy were left to match their skills against the Mountjoys, Viscount Anstey and Elizabeth.

From her long association there, Elizabeth was quite at home and had organized everything to her satisfaction, making available a great number of props enclosed in a large chest brought down from the storerooms by some manservants. Sarah was surprised to see Elizabeth, before the game began, speaking in undertones not only to Lady Mountjoy, on her own side, but also to Mrs. McBride, and remembering the affair of the reticule, began for the first time to feel a little apprehensive. It soon became apparent that her caution had been well advised.

Few words had been guessed before Lady Mountjoy came forward to announce that her side had chosen for their new charade a single word only. The whole word was to be acted out in one scene. Only a short pause occurred before Elizabeth walked in from another room, her hair slightly dishevelled, and wearing a dress which, if not identical to the one Sarah had worn on the previous evening, so similar as to be able to pass for it. Sarah watched as one in a trance as Elizabeth walked further into the room and stopped by a mirror, putting her hands up in feigned horror at seeing her disarranged locks and then, *reaching through a slit in her skirt*, pulled out a comb and began to comb her tumbled curls with it, returning it, when she had done *to a pocket* hidden under her overskirt.

Needless to say, the gentlemen were totally in the dark as to what the word could be and there were many minutes of "By crikey, could it be?" and "I wonder if it might be" before Mrs. McBride, as if inspired, cried out, "I know what it is. The word must be 'dowd', indeed it must!"–and so it proved.

Of course, the gentlemen were little wiser when the word had been 'guessed', being frankly puzzled as to how Elizabeth's act could possibly signify the chosen word. And indeed, how should they when they had not been present when Elizabeth had made her original attack on Sarah. They were equally puzzled as to why Elizabeth and her two malicious friends were so obviously highly amused, but being too uninterested to question, they moved on to the next word, leaving Elizabeth with a pleasant feeling of having triumphed again over her rival and Sarah to bear all the chagrin of having been made to look absurd by three very ill-bred young women. It is true that Mr. Middleton, though heard to murmur, "Lor', Lizzie, at least stick to the possible, won't you," and to insist that she choose words which even a mere male might reach for, seemed to have an inkling of what was going on, but the other men were completely in the dark—and from this Sarah had to take what comfort she could.

During her stay, whenever they were not visiting family members and friends or being visited by them in return, Sarah did her best to remain within her own comfortable circle. Good manners, however, made it impossible to stay with her mother or Amabel all the time and she was forced to make her way with the others as best she could. Lord Blissworth she continued to find quite charming: in him she saw none of the pretensions exhibited by some of her other fellow guests. He was never above being pleased, falling in easily with whatever plans were made for his entertainment and always apparently in high good humour. But she could never be easy with his wife, and Lady Mountjoy and Mrs. McBride continued to take their lead from her, so there was little chance for friendship there. Since Lord Mountjoy and Mr. McBride were concerned only with the quality of their sport, cards and dinner, and indeed, Viscount Anstey seemed not much different, she found herself often thrown into the company of the Honourable Freddy Middleton, Miles and Amabel's second cousin. In him, Sarah found the most comfortable of companions, for he seemed far less complicated than the other guests. In some ways he reminded her of her brother Kit and she spent many hours with him in amicable conversation.

Mr. Middleton was equally pleased with Sarah and he swiftly came to the conclusion that it would be in the interests of each to develop their friendship. Having quite early in life decided that a bachelor existence suited him in every way, he knew that if he was to conform to the highest rules of the ton, it would do him no harm at all to be thought to be the hopeless admirer of some lady of rank. In that way no-one would think of pressing him towards the altar. To be quite candid, a countess fitted the bill perfectly, especially one so unassuming. True, it would have been better had she been more beautiful, and even more so had she been more fashionable—he really hoped that she might quickly acquire some town bronze after her marriage, or even he might not be able to help her pass muster—but he had to admit that she was by far the most restful to be with of all the ladies of his acquaintance, for she never went into a miff if he forgot to flirt with her, nor did she expect him to run after her in the exhausting way that some spoilt beauties did. She seemed to be perfectly happy to hear his anecdotes of larks he had got up to with chums, or of how he had been to watch the sparring at the Fives Court in St. Martin's Street, where he had had the great good luck to see the great ex-champion of England, Gentleman Jackson in an exhibition bout with an up and coming new man, nor did she mind either, when he accidentally dropped into boxing cant, for, as she told him confidentially, she had a brother, now at Oxford, also madly interested in the art of fisticuffs and whose greatest ambition was to see a match of the Fancy at Moulsey Hurst. Yes indeed, Sarah would suit his purpose admirably if she could just smarten herself up a bit and anyway, he liked her. Dashed if he didn't.

And their friendship was not to be only for his benefit: in return he knew a hundred and one ways to smooth her path into society, for strange as it had always been to him, most of his friends seemed to trust his judgment in matters of ton. He never could get over his surprise at this, but so it was!

However modest Mr. Middleton was, and few could have equalled that gentleman so far as a lack of personal vanity was concerned, it is not so surprising that he was considered as an arbiter of taste amongst the more discerning of the ton since he always dressed in the most precise way, never joining the ranks of those whose starched shirt points rose to monstrous heights or whose cravats were tied so high as to prevent them from looking down. Nor did he ever make himself look foolish by appearing in a wasp-waisted jacket with huge lapels and massive silver buttons, or even the Cossack trowsers some young bloods affected. Always neatness and propriety epitomised both his costume and manner. His watchword was moderation. Not a *very* wealthy man, his fortune was nonetheless as respectable as his birth. The son of a viscount, he had a nice little property not too far from Beaumere on which many a mother of a promising young girl cast an envious eye and, although not precisely handsome, he was pronounced by all to be well-looking. His good nature was a by-word and made all who knew him declare him to be the best of good fellows and even dragons like Lady Stanham could find little fault with him.

As he was also known to be very nice in his notions of decorum, he knew that if he was seen to approve of Sarah, it was unlikely that she would be shunned by certain members of society who might otherwise declare her to be a frump, nor would there be any chance that she would be denied vouchers for any of the important events of the Season, especially Almack's weekly ball. Freddy was a good-hearted soul and had quickly realised on meeting his cousin's intended that she would need considerable assistance if she was to make her way successfully through the maze into which her marriage to Miles would thrust her, and he had soon made up his mind that it would be to their mutual advantage if he tried to clear her way.

He would have liked to suggest to Sarah even then that she might try to be a little more in the mode, but that would be impolite knowing her so slightly. Why did she insist on wearing white, he asked himself wonderingly? Anybody could see that the girl needed some colour. And hadn't she noticed that dresses were a little shorter now and that they didn't hang straight any more? Really, he was astonished that someone who seemed to have a good headpiece on her had so little idea in matters of dress. "I'd like to have the dressing of her," he muttered to himself one day, when watching her walking with her Mama in yet another unfashionable morning dress and spencer. "She's no beauty—never will be—but she don't need to look like a rag!"

Mr. Middleton might not have been equipped with the brainpower of some of his contemporaries, but he was shrewd enough in his own way and had been quick to see that his cousin Elizabeth was doing her utmost to make things hot for the new little bride-to-be, though his intuition would not run so far as to tell him why. He was determined if he could, to let Sarah know that he was a friend, and, as a result, he offered after luncheon that day to drive Sarah out for an hour or so to see some of the countryside about. Although Miles seemed rather non-plussed when she seemed to prefer Freddy's company to his own, she readily agreed to go with him, for she found it difficult to prevent herself from watching her fiancé all the time to see how much attention he was paying his cousin.

Mr. Middleton drove a curricle, not as dashing as the Earl's but smart and comfortable and drawn by two neatish bays which Sarah did not hesitate to say were "just the thing". He was a good driver and for some while Sarah was content just to sit quietly, lost in admiration at his expert handling of the reins. After a while she was moved to say, "What a smooth ride you are giving me, to be sure Mr. Middleton. Surely you must be a veritable whip?"

Freddy hesitated before answering her, for he did not want her to feel that he was poking his nose into business not his concern, but decided to take the plunge, replying "I could wish that you were having a less bumpy ride at Beaumere, if you do not think it the greatest impertinence for me to say so, Ma'am."

Sarah was touched at his thoughtfulness as much as by his tactful way of introducing her problems into the conversation and said in her unaffectedly friendly way, "How kind of you to have noticed, sir, and indeed it is true that there have been times in my life when I have been made to feel more welcome! Of course, Lady Greville has been perfectly charming to me and even Lady Stanham does not make me afraid, but I do rather seem to have fallen foul of Lady Blissworth, do I not? Can you possibly know why?"

"She's always been a spoilt brat you know and likes to rule the roost. Practically brought up at Beaumere, of course, and Amabel lets her have her head in all. Miles too . . . Thinks of her as a sister, don't you know?" he explained hastily, to reassure her.

But Sarah was not reassured. If even Freddy had noticed then Miles's behaviour must be obvious indeed. Once again pride came to her assistance. Freddy and everyone else would just have to know that she did very well without their concern.

"It is very good of you, Mr. Middleton, to try to make me feel less daunted," she replied in a playful manner, "but I should explain that my marriage to Miles is one of convenience—for both of us! I do not expect him to hang on to my skirts and pretend to be a lover, for he does not feel that way about me, nor I about him! I would most certainly not dream of making such demands on him: it would embarrass me greatly. If he wishes to engage in, shall we say 'dalliance', with other ladies, he is free to do so."

Freddy, finding himself in hot water, hastily said that as far as he knew there had never been anything like that between the two, "After all," he reasoned brightly, "had he liked her that much he could have married *her* instead of Caroline, you know? Mothers liked the match and all that. No-one to stand in the way. No, take my word for it, all a hum. Just Liz playing her usual games—girl likes to think herself a siren or some such thing. Vixen if you ask me." He seemed much struck by the thought. "Come to think of it, Miles has often been troubled by that type!"

On this enigmatic phrase, he refused to say more and they finished the drive companionably discussing the beauties of the countryside as they bowled along. Freddy was more than ever determined to do his best for Sarah and Sarah felt that she had gained a valuable champion in this friendly and undemanding young man.

****

The rest of her brief time at Beaumere was spent in getting to know her pretty new sister-in-law and the house she was to share with her and her brother in the near future. She was happy enough wandering round the grounds, learning the names of the plants new to her, or peering into endless succession houses, while the proud Head Gardener boasted of the excellence of his produce. If it seemed rather as if she was taking stock of her new possessions, it was too bad. At least it kept her busy and helped to avoid the necessity for intimate conversation with Miles, which suited her nicely. If he was indeed marrying her to lend countenance to his relationship with Lady Blissworth, she preferred not to know about it and kept her mind on other things. She began to understand quite well why the lady's husband turned a blind eye as he did, and did not see why she should allow herself to be any more torn in two than he.

Miles, hurt by her obvious reluctance to be alone with him, but not understanding the reason, left her often with Amabel, glad at least that the two were fast developing an excellent understanding. He, in turn, devoted himself to entertaining Lady Dagley and Sarah's uncle, both enjoying hugely the unaccustomed luxury of the estate, but there were times when he began to wonder at the wisdom of marrying someone who seemed to have little inclination for his company.

All too soon it was time for Sarah to leave Beaumere and return home. Miles was to remain behind to have certain alterations put in hand, and he and Amabel would not be at Leighwood until the day before the wedding. On the evening before Sarah's departure, Miles found an opportunity to take her for a walk around the grounds alone, and, as they made their way through the French windows of the drawing room, down the sloping lawns to the lakeside Miles bent his head to look searchingly at Sarah, a worried frown on his face. When they reached the little bridge at the end of the lake, they leaned against the parapet, looking across to where the moonlight touched the little pagoda on the other side. For a long time neither spoke.

Eventually Miles said to Sarah, "Miss Dagley . . . Sarah, my dear, you seem unhappy. I had hoped that your stay here would be a pleasant one, but that does not appear to have been the case. Will you tell me what has made you miserable? Is it something I have done? Or is it Beaumere that you dislike?"

"Why my lord, I am sure I cannot tell what you mean. Who could fail to be charmed here?"

"Then it is with me that you are angry. Won't you tell me why?"

When she did not answer him, he took one of her hands between both his own, turned it over and kissed her palm gently. As he did so, she trembled as an unaccustomed feeling of excitement went through her, and, as Miles felt it too, he put his arms round her, pulling her to him ardently. His mouth came down on hers, not in a chaste kiss as at their betrothal, but hard and searching. To her chagrin, Sarah found herself responding and was furious that her body should betray her so. She hated him for making her look absurd with Elizabeth, she told herself, and, as she felt his lips moving down to her throat, she pulled herself hard away from him, afraid at the new sensations rising inside her. She was determined that he would never see how his kiss had sent that strange warmth through her limbs. He might be capable of carrying on romantic interludes with two ladies at once, but he would not have the satisfaction of knowing that he moved her in that humiliating way.

"Indeed, my lord, you are quite out! Why, I am perfectly content," she lied, her voice shaking, "I think, however, that perhaps we should go in. With so many servants about it would not do to be seen."

Miles, still breathing heavily from their encounter, looked at her in disbelief. He had been sure that she had found as much pleasure in their embrace as he had and thought he might have vanquished from her eyes the little frown he had seen there for the past few days. When she pushed him away, he felt as if she had slapped him and he did not know what to think.

She had begun to walk quickly back to the house, and he caught up with her, saying nothing, simply taking her arm. As they were walking, she spoke of everyday matters to avoid being drawn into any more personal discussion, while he was not yet enough in command of himself to speak at all.

That was the last chance Miles had to see her alone. The next morning his travelling carriage bore her home to prepare for their marriage.

CHAPTER 11

Nothing occurred to postpone the Earl's wedding and he married Miss Dagley in the little church at Chetley on a sizzling August day, with the whole village looking interestedly on.

After some days spent in seclusion at his family's little hunting lodge in the Dane Valley, the new bridegroom carried his bride off to honeymoon in Italy. Sarah's husband had not made the Grand Tour through Europe as a young man, Napoleon's activities having interrupted such travelling for some years. He had, however, found opportunities to visit many parts of the Continent in his adult life, though it was not until he had cause to visit Italy that he had really understood why such a tour was high on the list of priorities for an earlier generation. Here the reason was brought home to him in no uncertain way, for he was mesmerised by all he saw. It was gratifying for him to realise now that Sarah was overtaken by that same enchantment.

The two made their way amicably from Venice on to Florence and then headed inevitably towards Rome, with all its glories from the past. Then down towards the Bay of Naples, chasing the sun and, as they travelled, taking in any of the smaller towns and villages that took their fancy along their route, towns like Lucca and Siena, their histories so inextricably linked with that of Florence, and other places, like Ravenna and Perugia, the poetry of their names alone being enough to tempt the travellers to make any necessary detours so that they could be overawed by incomparable Byzantine monuments or enchanted by the tiniest of churches discovered down winding narrow streets. Much of their travelling was done on horseback, for the Earl had discovered, to his delight, that Sarah had an excellent seat and she laughed to scorn his suggestion that, for her better comfort, they should travel by coach.

To any onlookers, the Earl and his new wife seemed blessed with the greatest felicity, having apparently a propensity for enjoyment in the same sights and experiences, yet all was not completely happy between the two. However harmoniously spent their days, their nights were less satisfying to both of them.

Miles had expected some awkwardness to attach itself to his wedding night and had been determined to make all as easy for Sarah as he could. The fact that he was not carried away by desire, he told himself, could only help to ensure that her sensibilities were unbruised and he had made up his mind beforehand that no attempt on his part should be made to rush her into receiving his embraces until she had grown used to him. To be honest, Miles had not envisaged how ticklish the whole affair could be! Whenever he had chanced to think of them married, he had imagined them comfortably esconced at the dining room table or walking around the park at Beaumere in amicable conversation, perhaps with one or two little Grevilles tagging along behind them, not allowing his mind to dwell on the problems of getting them there. It was not until a few days before the wedding that he suddenly realised how awkward it could be to be expected to make love to a woman who did not care for you. True, he had had several Cyprians in his keeping since his sainted Caroline had passed on, sweet little things too, he remembered reminiscently, and the most optimistic of his friends had never implied that even one of them had harboured for him any of the more tender feelings. Surely then it should be easy enough to manage the thing perfectly well? Regrettably, however, he was forced to admit that this was rather different: with those little *affaires* each knew his part and played it to a nicety, no-one getting hurt in the process, the little love-birds moving on to another stricken admirer in due course, considerably plumper in the pocket and leaving behind no hard feelings. It wasn't the same at all with Sarah. Although she wasn't in the first blush of youth he knew that she was as innocent as a new-born lamb.

He began to wonder if he had made the right decision in marrying Sarah, for he suddenly realised how embarrassing it might be for both of them if he found he could not perform his part in this marriage. True he had agreed to

91

make few demands of her, but she might well be surprised if he made none!

It was with no great feeling of confidence, therefore, that Miles made his way from his dressing room to join his new wife on that warm August evening. He was used to sleeping naked, but Jepson, a custodian of the niceties of life, had insisted that he should dress with propriety on that night of all nights so that Sarah, sitting in solitary splendour to one side of the rather ornate fourposter boasted by the Lodge's master bedroom, saw him enter the room magnificently attired in a full length silk dressing gown, highly patterned and frogged down the front and on the sleeves, while underneath this awe-inspiring garment, she could just see peeping out a plain white linen nightshirt with a high folding collar.

She herself was dressed in the prettiest of the expensive muslin nightgowns bought at Mrs. Weaver's establishment, through which her comely shape was seen to its best advantage, and Jenny had refused to allow her to wear a nightcap or indeed to put up her hair, saying that, as a bride, she must leave it hanging loose. Sarah had often suspected Jenny of having a romantic disposition and her suspicions were proved in full on that day, for while they were waiting for Miles to appear, as well as brushing her mistress's hair until it shone, she insisted on rubbing Sarah's skin with lavender water, giving it as her reason that her lady would feel more comfortable in that heat, though, since the summer had all but passed without her once suggesting such a thing before, Sarah was amusedly certain that she had a more inspired notion.

As Miles came into the room, Jenny bobbed a quick curtsey and left, while the two main characters in this little drama took stock of each other.

Miles was quite frankly astounded at how different Sarah looked wearing the provocative nightgown, her hair loose and shining around her shoulders, and he suddenly became uncomfortably aware that he had little need to fear any inability to play his required part in the night's proceedings. He became convinced, at about the same time, too, that his intention not to rush Sarah into accepting his embraces too quickly was perhaps a rather foolish idea!

Sarah was determined not to be discomposed by her

situation and, as he came over and sat on the bed besides her, she observed in her most playful manner, "Well, my lord, and how splendid you look to be sure: What a fine dressing gown that is—almost fine enough for some Eastern potentate."

"You must thank Jepson, my love, for allowing you such a gaudy sight, for he would not give me leave to come to you until I was dressed in my full glory. I think he never can have heard that clothes maketh not man, you know?"

"My maid Jenny has been quite as absurd my lord, brushing my hair like one demented, though I tried to explain to her that one cannot make a kingfisher from a mere sparrow."

Hearing her words, Miles took her hand in his and looked at her very deliberately, allowing his glance to roam over her pretty half-exposed shoulders and those charms displayed so becomingly by the thin nightgown. "Her efforts have obviously been crowned with far more success than Jepson's, poor fellow, but then she had more promising material to work with," and, as once before, he lifted her hand to his lips and kissed her palm. Once again, he felt the answering tremor pass through her and all thoughts disintegrated in his mind of allowing his bride time to get to know him before pressing his claims. It was suddenly a matter of the utmost urgency that she become his without delay, and he began to pull at the laces which tied her flimsy nightgown with trembling fingers and an almost indecent appearance of haste.

As she felt her body responding treacherously beneath his fingers, Sarah reminded herself fiercely that this man was apparently quite capable of taking one woman to wife while his heart belonged to another, and that other not a respectably dead wife as she had been led to believe, but the very much alive wife of one of his best friends. She was determined to remain cool no matter what.

But, as her husband's hands began their journey of exploration, she quickly realised that it was one thing to tell herself that she would remain aloof from the proceedings and another to accomplish such a feat. As she felt his lips now, first in her hair and then at her breasts and heard him groan with emotion as their firmness betrayed the nature of her feelings, she knew that she had lost that first battle for indifference, and gave up, for a time, the unequal struggle.

****

It was considerably later before Miles realised that anything might be wrong, in fact, for some time he was of the opinion, not only that he had made a particularly happy bargain, but also that he was the luckiest of all men, for his Sarah seemed to respond in the most gratifying way to his love-making. It was not until his immediate hunger had been assuaged and he was lying lazily beside her, one arm resting lovingly across her firm body, that he had a first inkling that she was not at one with him in thinking the world new-made by love. Stroking his hand gently across the slight swell of her stomach, he started to tell her, with little love sayings and foolish phrases, how fortunate he felt in having made her his own, when, to his amazement, instead of the affectionate reply he expected to hear, she observed coolly, "I am very happy that you find no cause for complaint, my lord."

"Complaint?"

"Why certainly, sir. I would not have you other than satisfied with our bargain," replied Sarah, determined to show no weakness.

It was just as on that day at Beaumere when he had kissed her and she had turned from him and, once again, he felt as if the earth tilted slightly on its axis. He just could not understand the woman. A moment before, she had been an exciting, passionate creature, possessed as he was with a need for their mutual gratification, and now, a lifeless doll.

It had been Miles's intention, when they had rested for a while, to continue what he had felt to be their mutually satisfying familiarisation with each other. Now, at her remarks, the nature of their alliance was too clearly visible for comfort and, instead, he bade her a polite goodnight, turned over and fell into a deep and troubled sleep.

For her part, Sarah could not even find comfort in slumber for she had never been so torn by emotion before. Never in her life had she felt such joy as she had in her husband's arms and never such misery at the thought that he might be using their marriage to cover a sordid intrigue.

It had taken every ounce of her not inconsiderable obstinacy to make her answer Miles as she had, for she wanted nothing more than to be allowed to lie in his arms and have him make love to her so deliciously.

After that, Miles found that each time he shared her bed his wife was submissive to his wishes, indeed, happy to share with him those moments of intimacy which somehow made him feel like the Eastern potentate she had once jokingly called him. But always, when the edge had been taken from their desire, he felt her remove herself mentally from his reach and he began to wonder if she really enjoyed his lovemaking at all, or if she was merely a remarkable actress and he somehow disappointed her.

On their wedding trip through Italy, he found her to be an amusing companion and a dutiful wife, sharing in full his pleasure in all they saw, and making his life comfortable in a dozen ways by her housekeeping skills, but she never hung on to his shirt tails as other newly-wed women seemed wont to do, and he always felt that she was as happy out of his sight as she was with him, a feeling which gave him little pleasure. True, their bargain had included an implicit understanding that they would not be forever in each others' pockets, but surely she was just a little too complaisant when he was needed elsewhere.

By the time the couple returned to Leighwood, where they were to spend Christmas with Sarah's family, Miles was already in the habit of spending some of his nights in his own little dressing room rather than having to listen to the cold, dutiful words which invariably ended their intimacy, not knowing that on those nights his new bride cried herself to sleep.

CHAPTER 12

It was of some comfort to Sarah that no-one could guess from her husband's demeanour at the slight estrangement which had occurred almost imperceptibly between the two. His manners were so exquisite that is was perfectly natural for him to put Sarah's comfort before his own at all times, and it was not surprising, therefore, that during the couple's stay at Leighwood, Lady Dagley and her brother-in-law spent much time in mutual congratulations at having brought the match off.

The Earl and his new countess stayed for the whole of the festive season and for several weeks afterwards and, in spite of his feelings of inadequacy concerning Sarah, it was one of the happiest Christmas times that Miles could ever remember having spent. Since his mother's death some years before, Beaumere had been closed at Christmas, those remaining members of the family joining friends elsewhere, so that it was long since Miles had passed that season as part of a close family circle, and he had forgotten the simple pleasure that children's excitement brings to any household as the great day draws near.

For their part, the young Dagleys were quite as enthusiastic concerning their new brother-in-law, for it had been some time since Christmas had been celebrated in the lush way that their sister's marriage now allowed. Although always a happy time for them, this year it exceeded all their expectations. Overjoyed at having their elder sister back with them again, as well as their brother Kit for the holidays, the youngsters were in the highest of spirits, and Hugh, especially, was determined to make this a holiday to beat all others, for, immediately afterwards, he was off to Eton to begin school in earnest. Now he persisted in making up parties of all those willing to scour nearby forestland for huge armfuls of holly and mistletoe with which to adorn the hall, and he soon discovered that no-one was more willing than Miles to be hauled off for such purposes; no-one happier to climb up to decorate those high places the others could not reach, or to watch, fascinated, as the girls made decorations of oranges and apples spiked with cloves, some to flavour bowls of punch for visiting carolsingers from the village and others, tied round with red or green ribbons, to add colour and scent to the hall.

The days leading up to Christmas seemed full of forgotten pleasures: helping to stir the Christmas puddings; joining Sarah and Charlotte in setting up the crib in the church for Uncle Henry; helping to choose the Carols for the Carol Service; even joining the boys in hot pursuit when Bess stole a spiced ham from the kitchens and chased off with it through the shrubbery.

By the time they had to leave, Sarah was amused and happy to realise that Miles had become a firm favourite with all and that they had loved having him share the festivities at Leighwood almost as much as they had enjoyed having her home again. Their private relationship might have its awkward moments, but Sarah was glad that her family and Miles shared a mutual affection which seemed daily to increase.

Only one cause for disharmony had arisen during their stay, for Charlotte, quick to scent her opportunity, was determined that she should be allowed to have her coming-out a year early now that her sister was so prominently settled. Miles was all affability and readily promised to have a ball for her at his home in Berkeley Square, provided her Mama agreed to it—but there was the rub! Her Mama did not agree! Lady Dagley was appealed to in vain, for she had already given the matter considerable thought. Remembering that Amabel had only come out the year before and had not yet, from all her crowd of admirers, decided on whom to bestow her hand, heart and not inconsiderable fortune, Charlotte's Mama did not think it suitable to bring her youngest daughter out just now. She was afraid that it would be asking rather too much to expect Sarah to chaperone two young ladies into Society when she was hardly up to snuff herself, a state of affairs which Lady Dagley sincerely trusted was only a temporary one. With luck, the coming Season would both settle

Amabel's future and give Sarah a little self-assurance, enabling Sarah to give her complete attention to her sister's coming-out the following year, which would naturally mean that Lady Dagley herself need not be called upon to stir herself, a course which greatly recommended itself to that indolent lady. It was decided, therefore, much to Charlotte's disgust, that Lady Dagley's second daughter should come out not one moment sooner than was usual. However easy it was for Charlotte to coax her new brother to accede to her requests, she found her mother adamant, and the newlyweds left Leighwood, with only Bess to keep them company.

Miles and Sarah were then called upon to begin the expected round of bride's visits to important members of their respective families, their number so extensive that it was not too much in advance of the London Season when the couple found themselves making their way to that city to open up the family residence in preparation for Sarah's entrance into fashionable society.

As a new countess, it would be necessary for Sarah to be received at Court, and it would be thought odd indeed if Miles did not plan a series of grand entertainments during the season to celebrate his marriage.

It had been agreed that Amabel should join them in Berkeley Square, and Sarah had greatly looked forward to renewing her relationship with Miles's gracious young sister. She was less happy, on their arrival, to find that Lady Blissworth had accompanied her.

****

The house in Berkeley Square seemed very grand to Sarah. It was a fine, solid building of Portland Stone, with the fashionable stucco finish covering its front elevations. In the late Lord Wilberton's lifetime, the interiors had been redesigned by Adam. He it was who had been responsible for the pastel ceilings with small painted panels still seen in the house, and no-one had cared, either, to remove his beautiful chimneypieces, decorated finely with ormolu, which had graced the rooms for a previous generation. In the reception areas pastel walls ornamented in delicate low relief were much in evidence, for Miles loved the spacious feeling they gave the house, though he had followed the fashion and introduced wallpapers into some of the bedrooms.

However few alterations Miles had made to the essential decoration of the house, he had shown no such reticence with regard to furniture, for here everything was fashionable, much of it in the Greek style, he having decided that the Egyptian was too heavy for his taste. Sarah was moved to congratulate him, for all was just as she would have wished had she designed it for herself. She was especially pleased with her own suite, for, as a surprise Miles had had the rooms traditionally used by the Countess redecorated for her. Remembering how she had liked the Eau de Nil colouring in the drawing room at Beaumere, he had put in hand plans for her bedchamber and dressing room to be redesigned around a similar scheme. The new bride found her suite charming, with its pale green ceilings, silk hung walls, and floors of polished oak, laid with sumptuous carpets patterned to echo the ceiling. As she stroked her hand across the silk coverlet which covered the magnificent fourposter dominating the bedchamber, Sarah wondered if she could possibly be mistaken about Miles.

"Surely no-one could be more thoughtful," she said to herself. "Could he really be so deceitful? I must be wrong." But then she remembered that almost the first person she had come face to face with in her new home had been Elizabeth and her doubts raised themselves once more.

"Thank heaven she isn't actually staying here," thought Sarah gratefully, "I don't think I could have borne that!"

It was not necessary for her to do so, however, for Lord Blissworth and his beautiful wife had a house of their own, not far away in Mount Street, to which Lizzie made her way shortly after Sarah's arrival so that Miles and his new wife could settle in after their long journey.

Amabel had been staying with Elizabeth and her husband at Lord Blissworth's country seat while Miles was on his wedding trip and on her return they had travelled up to London with her in order, or so Lady Blissworth declared, to supervise preparations for opening their own house for the Season. It must be observed that Elizabeth had never before shown the slightest inclination to concern herself with such housewifely duties, preferring to leave it to her higly skilled and efficient housekeeper, but if her husband felt there to be a more sinister reason, he did not allow it to annoy him and the three made their way comfortably together to the capital in Lord Blissworth's elegant chaise.

It had not taken long for the Ton to hear that Miles and his new Countess were opening their home in Berkeley Square and, though London was still rather thin of company, cards and invitations were already awaiting their arrival. Miles's first inclination was to consign them all to the waste basket until they had had time to settle in, but his eye fell on a rather ornate card printed with gold lettering, which chanced to be near to the top of the pile and proved to be from his Aunt Almeria. The card very properly requested the pleasure of the company of the Earl and his Countess at a small dinner party to be held that very evening, but he ruefully admitted to Sarah that it was tantamount to a royal command and he felt that they and Amabel must attend. Sarah was quite happy to oblige him in this and, at an hour long past the dinner time to which they had become accustomed in the country, the three stepped into Miles's carriage to make their way to their Aunt's house in Grosvenor Square.

If anything, Lady Stanham's house was even grander than their own and it looked especially so that evening, with all its lights ablaze to welcome guests. Had she not been forewarned, Sarah could have been startled at the number of visitors arriving, for her notion of a small dinner party differed greatly from her new aunt's. Despite her age, Great Aunt Almeria insisted on greeting her guests in person, and was stationed, as was proper, at the head of the magnificent stairway, the only allowance made for her years being that she was seated. She was clearly glad to see them, but had time for little more than a brief word of welcome before the press of new arrivals carried them forward.

A quick survey of Lady Stanham's old-fashioned drawing room was sufficient to confirm Sarah's worst fear, for there in one corner of the room, beautiful and animated as ever in the flickering candlelight, stood Elizabeth.

She had earlier thought that nobody could possibly outshine her pretty sister-in-law that evening for she had, as she had confided confidentially to Sarah, decided to remind her old admirers what they had been missing while she was away from town by appearing in a particularly ravishing dress of white crepe, its bodice ornamented with deep vandykes of white silk and blue beading. Sarah, feeling very faded, had been certain that Amabel would be the prettiest girl at the dinner party, but she had not then reckoned with Elizabeth.

Elizabeth made it a rule never to give any other females in her company a chance to outshine her and that evening she honoured them all by appearing in a deceptively simple dinner dress of twilled sarsnet, made in a deep shade of lemony cream which showed off to a nicety her striking colouring. It was deeply décolleté, very short in the waist and tightly fitted in the body. Her magnificent figure shown off to the full drew all eyes, some disapproving, some admiring, others, like the lady's husbands', simply amused. She had set cream silk roses in her hair, the colour of which exactly matched her dress and accentuated the auburn of her wonderful curls and the result made every other woman in the room feel plain.

As soon as she saw Miles she excused herself to the sprightly old viscount with whom she had been beguiling the time in mild flirtation and made her way, as if drawn by an invisible thread, to where they stood. Sarah could hardly fail to notice the appreciative look on Miles's face as he caught sight of his cousin and indeed Sarah had to admit that any man would need to be made of stone not to be moved by such opulent charms. What a contrast I must be to her, thought Sarah. She knew that nowhere in her wardrobe was there a dress which could bring that look to her husband's face.

As soon as Elizabeth reached them, Miles lifted her hand to his lips in tribute.

"Well, Lizzie my love," Sarah heard him say, "I must congratulate you, for almost every lady in the room is ready to slander you in that . . . ah . . . modest little gown. I should not leave the room unless you wish your ears to burn a little."

"Ah but Miles, my charmer, can you tell me what the men are ready to do, that is ʋy far more important?" replied his cousin audaciously, glancing shamelessly up at him from under her lashes while he took full advantage of his lofty position to drink in all he could of her loveliness.

"I think you do not need me to tell you that, you little rogue. You have sufficient admirers ready to swoon at your feet without needing to add me to the number," he replied lightly, suddenly remembering guiltily that his newly-acquired status did not allow agreeable little flirtations with Lizzie any more, certainly not while Sarah was looking on at any rate!

Elizabeth was not so foolish as to antagonise Miles by continuing to ignore Sarah now that he had obviously recollected her presence and turned to her to say sweetly,

"How charming you look this evening, Countess. Is not that the gown I admired so much at Beaumere?"

Sarah gritted her teeth in fury at this flagrant impertinence, only too aware that her words had been couched in just such a way as to make it impossible for Sarah to reply, and that Miles, completely unaware, was looking on complacently at them both. She forced herself to answer in the placid voice she always returned to Elizabeth's goading, that it was indeed just that gown, or so she believed.

Elizabeth curled her lip in contempt at such poor sport and would have continued to bait her, but at that moment Lady Almeria's butler threw open the double doors leading to the dining room and announced dinner.

Sarah had become too accustomed, since her betrothal, to fine dinners and was not as impressed as she would once have been by a meal which stretched itself across several hours. It was not, therefore, with much reluctance that she heard Lady Stanham ask the ladies to withdraw. Had she known what the rest of that evening was to bring, she must rather have wanted to stay in the dining room for ever.

CHAPTER 13

The gentlemen returned, the company were invited by their hostess to choose their entertainments. In one of the salons leading off from the main drawing room she had had set up several tables, each with its new packs of cards ready to be split by those who considered no evening complete without a rubber of bridge or of whist. The tables were quickly filled, mainly by the older members of the party, only too eager to lose a few pounds in such select company. For most of the rest, music was the order of the evening and Sarah settled down to listen to some very superior performances.

Most of the people in the room were strangers to her, but between performances, she was delighted to renew her acquaintance with Lord Blissworth, who asked her how Bess was in the most friendly way and, on being told that she had now joined the happy couple in Berkeley Square, professed himself eager to see this *canine paragon* for himself. They chatted together with the ease of old friends for a few minutes until he was called away autocratically by Lady Stanham to help set up yet another card table.

Left once more on her own, Sarah was relieved to see Mr. Middleton making his way towards her, for Miles was missing from his place at her side and she was embarrassed at being deserted.

As Freddy moved across to where she was sitting, Sarah was struck as always with his wonderful elegance. Beside him every man in the room looked either a trifle over-dressed or a little shabby. Even Miles did not manage to attain quite the perfection that Freddy achieved, she decided, though she was the first to admit that her husband was more handsome. That evening saw Freddy clothed quite formally in a very dark green dress-coat, which fitted so exactly to his form that Sarah found herself wondering how many of his servants had been needed to ease him into it. With this wonderful garment he wore light-sage green kerseymere pantaloons, with a watered-silk waistcoat of exactly the same shade, over a spotless shirt and a cravat tied in the Oriental style. His hair was closely cropped in a layered style à la Titus, designed to look carelessly windswept, but no-one privileged to see his person, perfect from his dark green evening pumps to his uppermost curl, could seriously suspect that he had allowed so much as a draught to ruffle his handiwork. As he reached her, he made her the most exquisite bow she had ever seen. Surely nowhere was there anyone more practised in the social graces!

Freddy's thoughts on seeing Sarah were rather different. Good Lord, he thought, the chit ain't still wearing that abominable gown! It's a wonder Miles allows himself to be seen with her! Then he noticed the warmly welcoming look in her eyes and he was immediately guilt-ridden. Gal just wasn't up to snuff. Not her fault, just needed a nudge in the right direction. Nothing there that couldn't be put right. And what was Miles about allowing the sweet little thing to wander about making a cake of herself? Always thought he was a downey one. And where was Miles anyway? Come to think of it, where was Lizzie? Surely he'd seen her before dinner in that abominable dress? Freddy had never been accounted more than a slow-top by his family, but by the time he had made his way through the gathering to Sarah, he had added two and two together and he hadn't made five. "Something wrong here," he muttered to himself, "Simple thing for Miles to give her a new touch. Why hasn't he?" She needed help. Have to see she got it!

"Lady Wil, how delightful to see you. Had no idea until I arrived here this evening that you and the Earl were in town, or I'd have certainly left m'card."

"Well, we only arrived in Berkeley Square today," she explained, "and of course you must call on us. You must be sure to stand on no ceremony, for I count you a particular friend."

"Most obliging of your ladyship, I'm sure. Certainly would like to see something of you. Been a long time. Wedding day, wasn't it?"

"Yes indeed, though I must confess I was so nervous I hardly knew who *was* there," replied Sarah laughing.

"Assure you, Ma'am, I was there to see the knot tied all

right and tight. Best man and all that! And how's that pretty little sister of yours? Fetching little thing, aint she?"

Gratified by his praise of Charlotte, for she knew that Freddy was accounted something of an expert in his opinion on the fair sex, Sarah would have told him so, but before she had a chance to open her mouth, they were joined by Lady Stanham. Sarah had not seen her since she had stayed at Beaumere before her wedding, but she felt herself to be something of a favourite with the *grande dame* and the two ladies and Freddy were soon deep in pleasant conversation.

After her polite enquiries about Sarah's family and other generalities, their conversation turned to Italy. Freddy knew the country well and loved it as Sarah did, and she found it very agreeable to be able to describe to a sympathetic listener some of the sights she had seen on her wedding trip. Aunt Almeria, too, was very knowledgeable about parts of that country having, she said, travelled extensively there with her late husband over forty years before. They were pleasantly entertained during the intervals in the music in exchanging anecdotes, when Lady Stanham suddenly declared to Sarah, "I've a journal which might interest you, m'girl. I kept a record of our travels, you know: usual stuff, diary, etchings, a few watercolours, you know the style of thing. Might like to see it one of these days. Only if you're interested, mind!"

"I should love to see it," Sarah replied earnestly, "It would, of all things, interest me!"

Surprisingly, Freddy too expressed interest in the journal and their aunt, gratified by their transparent enthusiasm, said that they might take a peep at it that evening if they wished.

"It is in the library, Freddy; on the shelf where I keep all the travelogues. You know! Quite near to the door as you go in, to the left. You cannot mistake it, for it is a very large book covered in dark red leather. Why don't you take Sarah along now before that dashed Pomfrey woman starts singing. You won't get the chance when once she begins, for it's the devil's own job to stop her again. I wouldn't mind if she had a voice! Doesn't, of course. Sounds like a sick tomcat! Take my word for it, be off while you've still got the chance. Good mind to come with you. I can't, of course. Hostess and all that," she recollected miserably.

Since Sarah and Freddy were both genuinely interested in seeing the journal and had both, in any case heard enough singing for one night, they needed no second invitation. The library was on the same floor as the drawing room, but to reach it the two were obliged to pass by several other rooms, including the games room, where Sarah noticed that one or two of the ladies and gentlemen were enjoying a game of billiards. The door to that room being open, she looked in briefly as she passed to see if she could catch a sight of her husband, in case he too was interested in the journal, but he was not there either.

"Ah, here we are," said her companion, as they came to the last door, near the end of the gallery. "I hope we can find it."

As he pushed the large oak door to the library and stood aside for Sarah to enter, it opened very quietly, for the catch had not been properly fixed. On the thick carpet, the movement of the door made little sound and did not disturb the two occupants of the room brought suddenly into full view. As Sarah began to walk into the room, her movements were suddenly arrested at the sight of the two figures, a man and a woman, locked together. The man stood looking down at his fair companion, an expression of great tenderness on his face, while the woman, her head very close to his and her arms entwined possessively around his neck, whispered clearly enough for Sarah to hear,

"You do care for me darling Miles, don't you?"

Sarah waited only to hear her husband reply, "Of course I care for you, dearest little Lizzie," before she hurriedly closed the door on them.

One look at Freddy's horrified expression was enough to tell her that he had seen it all, but she could not, in any case, have hidden her distress from him had she tried. Try as she would to quench them, tears sprang to her eyes and she began to shake violently. Freddy, fearing a scene of all things, quickly ushered her to the very end of the gallery, where there was a small divan placed in a shadowy embrasure. For some while he said nothing, while Sarah, taking deep breaths, made every attempt to stop her shuddering. There was little he could say anyway! That

Miles should do such a thing, and in his Aunt's house too! Miles, of all people! He's known some loose fish in his time, but he would have sworn that his cousin wasn't one of them! Dashed if he didn't feel like tipping him a settler! Probably couldn't do it, of course. Miles known to be a Corinthian at fisticuffs, but dashed if he wouldn't like to try it!

Sarah felt as if her legs had been swept from under her when she saw Miles with his cousin that way, but it was so much a part of her nature to allow herself no histrionics that within a surprisingly short time, to Freddy's admiration, she had herself under control. Turning a rather damp face towards her friend she smiled at him, saying, "Oh Mr. Middleton, how absurd that you should find yourself caught up in this. It really must be the most embarrassing situation for you. I apologise to you with all my heart. What an idiot I must seem to you, making a fuss about a trifle in such a way, for you know full well that Miles and I have an understanding not to interfere in each others' lives. I think I must just be a little tired, with the journey you know, and then having to come out on our first evening. Certainly nothing has occurred to which I should take exception and I shall be mortified if you imagine that I am unhappy!"

"Tosh, Lady Wil! Of course you are unhappy. Do you take me for a complete flat? What's more, you have every right to be unhappy. Never thought to have to say so of m'cousin, but I'm dashed well ashamed for him, so I am! Dashed loose screw if you ask me!"

"You won't say anything to him, though, will you, Mr. Middleton?" cried Sarah in anguish, tearing at her handkerchief. "Indeed you must not. Please promise me that you won't, for I think I could not bear for him to know that I had seen them."

"What *will* you do then? Can you possibly continue just as if nothing has happened?"

"What else can I do? This is my own fault. I knew the risks in marrying without affection, but you know what my family's situation was. I have made my bargain and I fully intend to keep it. I have no option. Miles has kept his promises to my family and he never professed to love me, after all. What else can I do but ignore what happened

107

tonight if there is to be any dignity in our lives at all?" she asked, looking up at him with large, trusting eyes.

Freddy hesitated before answering her. He wanted very much to help her, but it was such a delicate situation. After all, it was a social solecism to criticise a lady in any way! Perhaps he'd best say nothing. Yet seeing her all awry in an alien world tugged so at his sympathies that he knew he must.

"My dear Lady Wilberton," he said, "being sure that what I am about to say is the greatest breach of etiquette, I am trusting to my instinct in thinking you will not be offended."

Sarah's moist face looked up at him again, surprise overriding, for a moment, her intense misery. "What is it you wish to say to me? Please, Mr. Middleton, I won't be offended, really I won't. You have shown yourself too much my friend."

"Well, here goes then. It just occurs to me to wonder if you have not given Elizabeth her head by making things so easy for her, that is all."

"Why? What have I done? I think I have tried to be a good wife to Miles," she replied, her brow wrinkling in an effort to remember any occasion when she had failed to consider his comfort.

"No-one could doubt that for a moment," replied Freddy gallantly, "but . . . forgive me if this sounds ill-bred and pompous . . . I wonder if you have, perhaps, not given full consideration to the status you now hold. Miles asked you to marry him and you told me yourself that yours was to be a marriage of convenience. Can it be that you feel, therefore, that no attempt need be made on your part to be attractive to him? Have you forgotten that you are his countess as well as his wife?"

They both blushed equally deeply at his candour, but Sarah replied with her usual unruffled calm, "My dear Mr. Middleton, I am enough a woman to wish to both attract him, as you say, and to make him proud of me as his countess, but I fear it would take more than a dowdy creature like me to manage it. As you have seen tonight, competition is rather fierce!"

"Have you never wondered if it might be worth the

attempt? You may not be the *most* beautiful woman in London, but you are well enough. It should not be impossible."

"You may not think so," laughed Sarah shakily, "but I *do* try. If only I knew how," she added humbly, "I assure you that I would be more than happy to do whatever was necessary. But I have no natural aptitude for fashion. It is hopeless. I see women in clothes which look beautiful and try to have something made up to look similar, but by the time it transfers to me, it just looks, well, unbecoming."

"No need for it to happen, Lady Wil. No need at all! If you will allow me, I would consider it an honour to be allowed to serve you in this. Matter of pride you know. No wish to see you unhappy. Think I can help. I may be a slow-top in most things, but you can't live on the town for as long as I have without picking up one or two tricks. Miles is used to the ladies of the house cutting a dash. No reason for you to be different. You don't yet know how to go on that's all. Nothing unusual in that. How would it be if I came round to see you tomorrow? Ask Miles if we can go on a shopping spree? I can tell you just how to go on— did the same for m'sisters, you know! Lord, you've no idea what a sight m'sister Knaresby looked before I took her in hand. No need to give Lizzie and her kind a free run. No need at all!"

"Oh Mr. Middleton, would you really be kind enough to do that for me? I would be so very grateful if you could help me at all. I know I will never be a "diamond of the first water" as your Aunt would say, but if only you could help me not to be such a drab! Of course, I quite see that it will be difficult and shall not at all blame you if you cannot succeed!"

Freddy, almost unmanned by her humility, replied kindly, "Now don't you fret, Lady Wil. Soon have you looking more the thing. Simplest thing in the world. You leave it all to old Freddy."

With that, Sarah had to be content and they returned to the drawing room, making their excuse to Aunt Almeria for not being able to locate the journal.

The rest of the evening passed in a haze of misery for Sarah, her mind fixed on the memory of her husband, Elizabeth's arms clasped firmly about his neck. When he returned to the drawing room some time afterwards, looking flushed, Elizabeth was not at his side. They were obviously quite expert at playing the game. Sarah immediately pleaded a headache and, Amabel having no objection, they made their way home, with Miles, to Sarah's acute discomfort, all solicitude. On the way, her imaginary headache was enough to excuse her while Miles and his sister made the usual small-talk of tired people and, as soon as they arrived at Berkeley Square, Sarah made her apologies and went to her room.

For the first time in her marriage, when Miles came to her room that night she pretended to be asleep.

CHAPTER 14

When Freddy set himself down in Berkeley Square rather early the next morning, the first person he saw, on entering the small morning parlour at Wilberton House, was his cousin Amabel. Anyone listening to their conversation would be in no doubt as to the long-term nature of their connection, for Freddy kissed her lightly on the cheek, saying saucily, "Hello Squab! You're about early. All this country living getting you into bad habits?"

"I could say much the same about you, Freddy, and I do wish you would not call me by that silly name now that I am out!"

"Used to like it when you were a little dab of a thing!" he protested.

"Well, I'm *not* a little dab of a thing now!"

"Oh I don't know! Still only just reach m'shoulder. Shouldn't think you'd grow any more now. Have to give up any ambitions to be a Long Meg I imagine!"

"What makes you think I wish to be any taller?" replied his cousin, tossing her head in the most bewitching manner. "I'll have you know that Viscount Anstey thinks me *perfect*." A gurgle of laughter escaped her and the glint in her eye showed that she had, at the back of her mind, a very satisfying recollection indeed as she went on to explain, "He said that if I were to grow any taller it would destroy his peace of mind entirely."

"Just the sort of misleading thing he would say. M'self, I don't think an inch or two could have done anything but good!"

Amabel stamped her little foot in vexation at Freddy's refusal to flirt with her. He had known her for ever, it was true, but it was very annoying that he showed no inclination to languish at her feet like so many other young gentlemen of her acquaintance. She wished, not for the first time, that she could bring him to heel.

"Really, Freddy, you are the most provoking man imaginable! And why did you come to see me if you wished only to make yourself disagreeable?"

"Didn't come to see you at all, you little shrew. Came to see Lady Wil!"

At this his cousin's demeanour underwent a strange alteration for instead of the playfulness she had shown up until then, her shoulders stiffened suddenly and she turned on him a glittering, though rather brittle smile, saying in a voice which trembled slightly, "Indeed! Why, I had no idea that you were such an admirer of my sister-in-law, Mr. Middleton!"

"Oh don't make a cake of yourself, Ami," replied her cousin, "You can't grudge the poor little soul one caller, surely?"

Recognising quickly that this was no lover-like language, Amabel was immediately contrite. "Oh Freddy, I'm sorry. No of course I don't. It is just like you to wish to make her comfortable."

"Good girl. I knew I might rely on you. And I could certainly do with some assistance if you are so inclined."

Again his cousin was suspicious. "Tell me what you mean first. Assistance with what?"

"Fact is, Squab, that she just ain't up to snuff. You will be the first to admit it. Don't like to see her looking such a dab do you? Family pride and all that. Mean to make a push to help her. Duty, you know, to bring her into the picture."

"Dear me, Freddy. Yes! She really is the most frightful dowd isn't she? I have wanted to drop a word in her ear any time past, but it seemed such an impertinence, her being my senior as she is. She has no idea at all. Those awful dresses! And white is *not* her colour! While she has been in the country I have allowed myself to be easy, but I must say that I have been in a quake knowing she was opening Wilberton House for the Season. Yet surely it is for Miles to drop a hint, not you or me?"

"That's just it! He hasn't, has he? Dashed queer behaviour if you ask me. Shouldn't be surprised to hear something wrong there. Stands to reason. Easiest thing in the world for him to guide her into the right pike if all was right and tight. Hasn't though. Someone's got to do it for him. Nice thing it would be to have her parading herself in Bond Street in one of her awful get-ups."

Much struck by this possibility, Amabel asked him how he meant to achieve his admirable ambition and was surprised to hear that he had already successfully broached the subject with Sarah. "No Freddy! However did you dare to bring it up?"

Freddy had no intention of telling his young cousin what had occurred to force him to do so, merely saying vaguely, "No problem at all. Seemed to think just as she should on the matter. Persuadable little thing you know. She's twigged that she's not running true to form at present, just doesn't know how to do the thing. Happy to have my assistance if only we can get Miles to like it."

"Well, Miles is no problem. He will be the first to admit that you have more taste even than he has."

"Yes, but will he like me escorting Lady Wil all over town on a shopping expedition?"

"Oh Freddy! Sometimes you are truly gothic. You cannot suppose that Miles would be so stuffy as to disapprove! Why, even Aunt Almeria could see nothing wrong in a lady accepting a gentleman's escort on such an errand—especially one so nearly related!"

Freddy was still doubtful, but Amabel's intuition proved true. When he bowed himself into the breakfasting parlour where Miles and Sarah were still completing their repast, he explained to Miles that Sarah had asked for his escort. Miles seemed a little surprised that she preferred his cousin's company to his own, but it was here that Amabel came to Sarah's aid, for she clapped her hands delightedly, crying in her silvery little voice, "Lord, that's a put-down for you, Miles! But there's no denying that Freddy's the truly *tonnish* member of the family and it's very clever of Sarah to have seen it. Anyway, people would think you most unfashionable should it be said that you two lived in each other's pockets. Cousin Lizzie, you know, will never allow Bliss to shop with her, for fear of them both being termed provincial! No, Freddy is just the thing."

Sarah had been concerned that she had hurt her

husband's feelings, but mention of Elizabeth hardened her resolve and she said mildly, "I should so like an opportunity to indulge myself, my lord, and since Mr. Middleton so kindly offered his services, I thought it would save you from having to tease yourself. I feel that now we are among all the smarts I must refurbish my wardrobe."

Since Miles could do no more than agree with her, he made no demur, merely remarking, "A put-down indeed, Ami, as you say. I see it has all been arranged, so will not put on my husbandly look of disapproval. But it seems I must smarten myself up if my wife is to trust to my judgment in future."

Surprised that they had brushed through with so little trouble, Sarah made no delay in fetching her pelisse and bonnet.

Amabel had good-naturedly offered to accompany them, but, as Freddy knew that she would spend more time looking for things for herself than in helping Sarah, her offer was rejected, and Sarah soon found herself alone with Freddy, bowling down Bruton Street towards Bond Street, only a groom in attendance.

Since Freddy was quick to tell her that she need not fear to be overheard, as Josh had been with him "for ever", they were soon comfortably discussing her problem. It was immediately apparent to Freddy that he had taken on rather more than he bargained for, for Sarah shyly confided to him that she would, of all things, love to purchase just such a gown as Cousin Elizabeth had been wearing on the previous evening. The severe shock this gave his system was enough to take his mind off his horses for a moment and slacken his control, causing them to rear their heads and move, as Josh would have been the first to acknowledge, "quite nohow" along the cobbled streets in an ungainly fashion quite foreign to his usual precise handling.

"Well, if that don't beat all," he exclaimed in a peeved voice, as he skilfully brought his horses back into line. "If that aint the outside of enough!"

"What have I said, Mr. Middleton?" asked Sarah anxiously.

"What have you said? You tell me you want to be brought slap up to the mark one day and then the next you say you want to look like Lizzie! There's no understanding females!"

"But I thought she *was* all the crack!"

"Crikey, Lady Wil, you've even more to learn that I thought! Tell you what, it's obviously too soon to start laying out your blunt. Need to talk first so you don't let every modiste in Bond Street know you ain't up to the marker yet. Take a breather first! Go back to Gunther's, have a little tongue-wag before we start handing over any dibs!"

Sarah, only too glad to trust Freddy's judgment, soon found herself cosily ensconced in Gunther's, the most celebrated of all the London pastrycooks and haunt of the ton. Although Freddy immediately saw several of his acquaintances, he knew to a nicety just how to prevent them from joining him without putting up their backs and he and Sarah were soon happily drinking their coffee and commencing Sarah's education.

"First thing you have to realise is that there's a world of difference between being tonnish and putting friends to the blush!"

"Oh I should not wish to do that, Middleton," replied Sarah earnestly.

"Of course you would not. Stands to reason, don't it? You want Miles to be proud of you. Fact is, m'cousin Lizzie, bit of a lightskirt! Not something to bandy about mind! But you are family, so no harm done telling you. Not saying she ain't popular; not saying either that she would go so far as to risk her reputation. Only saying that the way she dresses is more in the Cyprian style. Not saying, you understand, that she would ever accept a touch on the shoulder, but that's only because she knows her way about. Knows how to refuse anything in that line. Up to every rig and row in town, our Lizzie. You ain't, so can't afford to chance it! Fact is that that dress she had on her back last night was outside the line. If you want m'cousin to be proud of you, you don't want to take Lizzie as your pattern card, get me?"

Sarah, though not understanding quite all his references, thought she was beginning to understand, but was still a little puzzled. Hesitantly she began, "I think I see, Mr. Middleton, but, forgive me if I appear a little dense, it did

115

seem to me that Miles rather liked Lizzie's appearance!"

"Lord, there's nothing in that! No man alive wouldn't be affected by such a display. Still don't want his wife looking like a straw damsel, that you can be sure of. Felt sorry for poor old Blissworth, upon my word I did! No, my dear, take my advice and steer a straight course. By the by, won't you call me Freddy? Our relationship allows it, you know."

"Yes indeed Mr. Mid . . . Freddy. I should be proud to do so and you may call me Sarah, if you wish, though I must admit that Lady Wil sounds delightfully friendly!"

"Lady Wil it is, then. Now let's get busy shall we? First things first . . . You must immediately stop wearing white! Hope you don't mind me saying so but it makes you look a perfect fright."

"Oh Freddy I know! But I thought it was *de rigeur* for newly-married ladies. Mama's dressmaker assured me I should simply have to wear white and then when I was at Beaumere I noticed that Mrs. McBride always did so and she was just married you know."

"Stupid woman thought it suited her, that is why. Seen her often enough in other colours though. Thing is, Lady Wil, never wear anything which puts you at a disadvantage. True that many newly-married ladies wear white for a time, but not when it don't suit 'em."

"You cannot imagine what a relief it would be for me to discard those awful dresses! It was bad enough when I had my come-out and I had always to wear that appalling colour, but when Mrs. Weaver declared I must have my bride clothes in white, I felt ready to sink."

"Poor little thing, I can imagine you might. Mind, it is rather different with a come-out. Most girls wear white during their first season, though even then, if it didn't suit you, you should have insisted on something which made you show to advantage. Could have managed with a soft pink, or perhaps a pale lavender. Still, that's all in the past: it is now we must think of and I must say that it is not only the colour that is wrong. You wear your dresses too long to be in the pink of fashion, and they cling too much in the skirt. Latest thing is for the skirt to stand away a little at the hem—haven't you noticed?"

"I did notice, Freddy, but only after I had had my brides-clothes made. Then I felt that it was hardly worth having the frocks altered or having new ones made until I could come out of white, which you may imagine, I intended just as soon as could be."

"Lord, what a mess you've got yourself into, poor little kitten. Still, time to change all that. Now, about colour! We don't want anything too livid with your delicate colouring—none of your puces or purples remember. And because you are petite, make sure you stick to one colour, don't break up the line. If you wish to wear two colours you may wear one colour for the slip and another for the overdress. For heaven's sake, none of those dresses with a different coloured bodice to the skirt, for they will not do at all for you. Just do as I say and take my word for it: it will give you extra height. Always wear a small heel to your shoes and boots—these flat pumps and sandals are alright if you're a maypole, but not for you. Not too high a heel, of course, or you will teeter!"

Once launched into his subject, Freddy seemed set to go on for ever about the do's and dont's of fashion. To Sarah, he seemed the fount of all wisdom, for there was nothing he did not know about any item of clothing, from the various merits of having half-boots to match one's outfit to the reason why a reticule really was superior to a pocket! Eventually, however, he declared himself satisfied that he had imparted enough knowledge that she should not make a complete widgeon of herself and the two were ready to descend on an unsuspecting Bond Street.

CHAPTER 15

That day passed for Sarah in a frenzied orgy of spending. Never had she imagined that she could so effortlessly become a lady of fashion, but with Freddie's help it was easy—more, it was the greatest of fun. Never in her life had she been beguiled by such a display of walking dresses, carriage dresses, dinner dresses, ball gowns, hats, pelisses, spencers, shoes, half-boots, gloves, bonnets, caps, turbans and every other type of fashionable trifle. Never before had she had the pleasure of knowing that she might buy any of them which took her fancy or that she could depend on choosing only those which suited her.

As he put her down at Wilberton House much later that day, Sarah thanked Freddy heartily, saying, "Now that I have all I need, I shall know just how to go on."

"All you need?" replied Freddy incredulously, "Lord defend us! Why, we've only just started; though I must say we've done a good day's work. We can't attempt much more today—perhaps just see about your hair. Amabel will be just the person to go to about that. Her dresser, Miss Bidmore, fine woman. Have to persuade her to take an interest in you. Come to think of it, you need your own dresser! Know just the person to ask to look out for one for you. My Aunt Stanham—up to all the tricks. All the best connections. Be pleased to do it for you I shouldn't wonder."

"But Freddy, I already have a maid. She came with me from home. She would be hurt if I sent her back."

"No good to you in Town, little one. Don't know how to help you, does she? No problem anyway. No need to send her home. Have two maids! No-one's counting, not with Miles's fortune. Plenty of ladies of fashion have more than one personal maid. Just set 'em different duties. Say your new position demands it, or some such thing. Lord gal, you're the mistress you know! First rule—never let servants get the upper hand—fatal. You pay 'em don't you?"

Freddy managed to persuade Sarah that she owed it to Miles to get herself a good London dresser of the first stare and what with interviewing the several applicants Lady Stanham sent along for her pleasure, having her hair layered into a new and dashing style which, Miss Bidmore assured her would draw attention to her eyes, her best feature, and visiting any number of tiny shops and large cloth warehouses around Piccadilly, the next three days quickly passed for the new countess.

On the third day the first dresses began to arrive from the fashionable Bond Street dressmaker to which Freddy had escorted her, so the following morning found Sarah dressed, since she had arranged to go shopping with Amabel, in a lavender zephyrine walking dress which Freddy had assured her would suit her to admiration. Sarah had to admit that he had been quite right and was delighted with everything about the dress, from its long narrow sleeve topped by a charming half-sleeve of gros de Naples and zephyrine to its skirt, in the new shorter length with a pretty trimming of lavender-coloured gauze and satin.

Sarah's new dresser was Miss Langley, and Jenny, far from showing any pique at being considered less than adequate, fully entered into the spirit of the whole adventure, thinking it very suitable indeed that her beloved mistress should employ someone of the first stare. "For it's plain as pudding I can't turn you out as she does, Ma'am," she admitted with devastating honesty.

Miss Langley certainly knew her business, for that morning she had, with no effort at all, coaxed Sarah's hair into its new style. Parted in the centre, her hair had been arranged to the sides in clusters of small curls, while the rest was twisted into a large knot at the back of her head, seeming to give her extra height. Miss Langley's skills did not end here, however, for she recommended to Sarah that perhaps a little colour to her face might be felt an advantage. "Not that I mean for you to paint your face like a hussey, Ma'am, dear me no," she comforted, seeing the doubting look which had quickly shown itself on Sarah's face, "None of my young ladies leave my hands but are dressed with propriety. Yet all young ladies of fashion allow themselves just a little, a very little assistance, when it is needed. If you cannot like it, Ma'am, we can always wash it off you know. It seems criminal not to take such advantages as we can, do not you think so?"

Sarah found herself being persuaded to allow Miss Langley to have her way and apply just the merest hint of rouge in her cheeks, which she powdered over so that it almost disappeared. Enough remained, however, to make Sarah's skin appear to glow and Sarah admired it so much that she did not feel moved to protest when Langley followed this with a touch of lip-salve. Both mistress and maid professed themselves highly pleased with the result and with more than usual confidence and a fair measure of guilt, Sarah made her way to the breakfast parlour.

If she had expected her husband to fall in love with her on the spot, however, or to throw up his hands in amazement and delight, she was doomed to disappointment, for apart from remarking, on looking up from his newspaper, that Town air seemed to agree with her, he did not so much as mention her transformation.

CHAPTER 16

Her sister-in-law was a far more satisfactory audience to Sarah's gratifying triumph over Nature, professing it quite wondrous that the countess could look so well and generously confiding, to Sarah's secret amusement, that now she would not be ashamed to be seen anywhere in her company. "Indeed," she went on seriously, "it would not greatly surprise me if you manage to attach some admirers now that you are dressed so becomingly. No, I think I may be bold enough to say that it would not be asking too much at all."

Since Sarah humbly felt her chances to be quite as modest as did Amabel, she found no fault with her artless prattling and the two were soon busily absorbed in choosing which, from an absolute mountain of invitations, would be honoured with their acceptances. It was, after all, a considerable step upwards to be thinking in terms of *possible* admirers after so many years of considering oneself to be past hope.

Although Amabel continued to assure her that London was still very thin of company and informed her knowledgeably that, when everyone had arrived, they would be much gayer, Sarah did not know how they could conceivably be so, for, as she wrote to tell Lady Dagley and the family, every possible waking moment appeared, to the untutored eye, to be filled with pleasure. It seemed to Sarah that each hostess vied with every other to provide the most lavish of entertainments for those fortunate enough to have begun the Season early. True, it was too cold yet for such delights as ridottos or breakfast parties, al-fresco or water-parties, or, indeed, any of the outdoor pleasures with which the ton chose to beguile their time, but these deprivations were more than made up for in the number of musical assemblies, balls and suppers they attended and that was without taking into consideration the delights of an evening spent visiting the Opera at His Majesty's Theatre in the Haymarket, or at the Wednesday Assemblies at Almack's Rooms, the inner temple of exclusivism: not to mention a dress party at Carlton House, to which Sarah had gone in great trepidation.

When Sarah had had her earlier London Season, it was at Almack's that she had suffered most. Almack's had another name, The Marriage Mart, for it was here that the rich and well-born collected each week of the Season to see and be seen by other members of the ton and it was here that marriages were arranged within the beau-monde. No-one not first vetted by its patronesses would be granted vouchers for the assembly, and without those much prized vouchers, it was impossible, either to pass through those hallowed portals, or to enter the cream of society. In spite of its tame entertainments and its rather meagre refreshments, nobody could afford to neglect Almack's for very long, for even the highest born might find himself ostracized should he offer any affront to the powerful ladies who busied themselves in its affairs.

It was with some hesitation, therefore, that Sarah chaperoned Amabel to Almack's to take part in the first of the Season's august assemblies, but she was amazed to find just how different it could seem, merely because one no longer felt oneself to be the most drab female present. She had chosen that night to wear a most becoming round gown of the new Urling's net over a pink satin slip, its skirt heavily flounced and trimmed with tiny flowers and rouleaux of white zephyrine. One glance round the room told her that she need be afraid of being eclipsed by no-one, not even her divine sister-in-law, looking as charming as ever in a white gown of figured satin, trimmed with the palest of green ribbons.

Miles, always elegant, had chosen to accompany them on this all-important occasion, and had complimented them both enthusiastically on their appearances, adding with mock humility, "Why, my dear ladies, you are so fine that I feel positively shabby beside you. Can you possibly be content to go to Almack's with such a poor creature as myself? Don't spare my blushes, I beg, if you think I will not do."

"La, sir," replied his wife, mischievously, taking up his tone, "It is true that we are used to more dashing escorts, but, knowing your high regard for us, we cannot bear to disappoint you, for fear you might languish clean away."

"Your generosity overwhelms me, Ma'am, but if you feel that I put you too much to the blush, I beg that you will not hesitate to let me know and I shall immediately drown myself in Lady Jersey's nauseating bohea!"

"What an excellent idea, Miles," replied his sister, "for it could certainly do with some body!"

The first person Sarah recognized on entering the crowded assembly room was Freddy, who immediately made his way purposefully over to them and bowed low over Sarah's hand, blushing a little and murmuring rather incoherently, "I say, Lady Wil, by jove! Who'd have believed it? Do me the greatest credit Ma'am. Exceed all my expectation, 'deed you do! Complete to a shade!"

"Oh Freddy, are you really pleased with me? I am so glad for I was afraid I might not be just as you liked!"

Here Miles was moved to protest. "Well, if that doesn't beat all! Just as Freddy likes? What about me? A husband's rights you know? I have not yet forgotten that my wife prefers my cousin's advice to my own, you scoundrel."

"So she should, dear old boy, so she should," replied Freddy unruffled. "Well, stands to reason, don't it? Anyone would!" and without more ado he asked Sarah to honour him with her hand for the waltz just starting up, a dance which *now* had the complete approval of even the most strait-laced of the patronesses.

Sarah would have preferred to dance first with Miles, but since he made no move to ask her, she placed her hand in Freddy's. As they made their way onto the floor, Freddy murmured conspiratorially to her, "Thought I'd better get in quickly and ask you first, Lady Wil. Thing is, forgot to check! Can you dance? Stupidest thing to forget! Didn't enter m'head until I saw you just now. Shocking thing if you made a cake of yourself at Almack's you know."

Sarah squeezed his hand gratefully, thanking him for his kind consideration for her, but said that she rather thought her dancing would pass muster even in London, adding, with devastating honesty, "For when you get to my age,

Freddy, you have had plenty of time to master all the steps."

She was to prove her boast no idle one, for they were soon twirling around the dance floor in the greatest good style. Freddy was a smooth and immaculate dancer—it would have been less than good ton to be anything else—and he was highly gratified to find in Sarah an elegance and a grace missing from some even of the most polished of society beauties.

"Told you you'd be a credit to me, Lady Wil," he beamed, "and I wasn't mistaken. Right up to the knocker and everything fine about you m'dear. More than a match for anyone now, you mark my words!"

Since Elizabeth was not present that evening, Sarah had no way of putting Freddy's theory to the test, but she was more than grateful just to hear his kind words. She was certain that he only said them to put her at her ease, but that didn't lessen the real friendship which she knew prompted him.

By the end of the evening, however, she was less certain that Freddy had been only reassuring her, for, to her amazement, she found herself not the retiring wallflower she was used to be, but the centre of a great deal of attention. To say that she was inundated with partners would be to exaggerate, but she was never obliged to sit out and Miles was moved, on their way home, to protest at being unable to get near enough to claim even one dance with his own wife.

Secretly, he had been quite as dumfounded as had Sarah at how well his little wife had taken with the ton, and not a little proud. Really, it was astonishing how she had changed in the short time they had been in Town: she was certainly a credit to him. Although he had said little, he had not failed to notice her new elegance and he was gratified to find that she managed to combine a certain flair with complete propriety. He had even had the felicity of having Lady Castlereagh, the most stately of Almack's patronesses, make her way to his side during the evening to congratulate him on finding himself such a pretty-behaved and charming young countess. True she had had Freddy to guide her first steps, but it did not take Miles long to realise that once placed on the right track she could manage very well for herself.

As he lay thinking about her that night, he suddenly felt ashamed that his had not been the guiding hand for his wife's first faltering steps into the ton and he began to feel very low indeed. What had he been about not to have put himself out to help her, as Freddy most assuredly had? Well, perhaps it was not too late to make amends for it now, and he racked his brains to think of a way. What could he possibly do for her now that Freddy seemed to have done all that was necessary? Suddenly, he was struck by inspiration. She must have a carriage of her own!

****

The following morning saw a belatedly guilty Miles making his way to his wife's bedroom, where he discovered her in charming disarray sitting up in bed, leaning against her piled up pillows, a coffee tray across her lap while she sorted her mail. As he entered her room she instinctively put up her hands to straighten her pretty night cap and tuck in some stray curls, but he pulled her hands away, saying flirtatiously, "No, my dearest, I must protest. You look much prettier with your hair escaping so becomingly!"

She looked charmingly confused at this and to hide the breathlessness she always felt at his nearness, she laughed a little, saying lightly, "Yes indeed, for it must make you feel more than ever like King Cophetua with his beggar-maid!"

At this Miles frowned, "Is that how we appear to you, Sarah? I hope not, for I can assure you that that is not in any way how I think of us."

"Of course not, my lord," replied his wife, setting her face into serious lines, "I was only funning. Why, I will admit to being not one whit lower than first housemaid!"

"Sarah, you must not say so!"

"How you do jump, Miles! You should know my wayward humour by now."

"Little wretch! I swear you are the most provoking woman ever. I've a good mind not to tell you what I came for. I'm not sure you deserve it now and it would serve you well to do without."

"Now who is being provoking, odious man. You must know that women have no patience. Men I will allow to have the patience of Job: it is all to do with being the superior sex! But women alas are such simple childish creatures that they cannot wait five seconds."

"Continue to tease me at your peril, Ma'am," he warned her laughingly, "You are truly absurd!"

"There now," replied his wife, settling her face into prim lines and clasping her hands before her breast like a Puritan, "See how virtuous I am become. Dear Miles, please tell me your news."

"Hm. Very like a beggar-maid. But I shall not allow you to deflect me from my purpose, however much you deserve that I should."

When he told her that he had in mind for her to set up her own carriage, Sarah was overwhelmed. "What do you think I should have, Miles? Which is most suitable for a lady?"

"I rather think that a landaulet is proper and I recently saw one which might be just the thing. Will you trust *me* to choose something for you, or do you prefer Freddy's choice in this too?"

"I can see you are set on provoking me still further," replied his wife at her most dignified, "and refuse to be drawn in."

"Of course," went on her husband, warming to his theme, "Freddy would probably not do it as well as I, for he could not be expected to know that we must be sure not to buy anything too grand as it will contrast rather too strongly with your rags. And—yes, it may be that perhaps a farm-cart might be more in keeping with your station!"

At this, Sarah picked up one of her pillows and threw it hard at him, catching him squarely in his chest and he beat a hasty retreat down to the breakfast room, laughing softly to himself.

****

The Earl's plan found opposition in an unexpected quarter, for, on being told by a delighted Sarah that she was to have her own landaulet, Amabel turned to Miles, saying, "Why you would not be so mean as to give poor Sarah a landaulet, surely Miles?"

"Whatever can you mean, Ami?" he replied surprised, "I was not aware that it was quite the *height* of meanness to buy one's wife a new carriage.

"No Miles, do but consider—a landaulet! You cannot have thought. No-one, except old ladies like Aunt Stanham, goes round in a landaulet any more! I assure you that Sarah is not so old cattish! She has become truly fashionable now and only a barouche will do if she wants to be all the crack!"

Adding her entreaties to her sister-in-law's, Sarah was moved to say in a small voice, trembling with laughter, "I must admit, my lord, that I would truly *like* to be all the crack!" and, as a result, a very few days saw her the proud possessor of a very stylish vehicle indeed. Painted in the dark blue of their servants' livery, a darker blue for the wonderfully luxurious interior, with its gleaming silver metalwork, and wheels fashionably picked out in yellow, Sarah was sure that nowhere was there another carriage as fine. Just as admirable were the perfectly matched grays which Miles had managed to find for her at Tattersall's.

Now Sarah was really the last word, confided Amabel, for to be seen in the Park, during the Season, between the hours of five and six was considered absolutely necessary for members of the ton if the weather permitted and, though it was perfectly proper to be seen riding or walking, it was far more dashing—not to say more comfortable—to be driving, especially in an equippage so bang up to the nines as Sarah's!

It soon became a familiar sight to members of the ton for Sarah's modish carriage to be noticed bowling along through Hyde Park at a spanking pace, its fair owner and her sister-in-law sitting comfortably where all could see them, both dressed in the height of fashion and attended by a liveried groom. Even when they came upon Cousin Lizzie, as they did more often than Sarah liked, she did not feel outshone, for though Lizzie might be the more beautiful, Amabel declared that her cousin could not hold a candle to Sarah in matters of ton. Sarah often ruefully remembered how she had despised the high steppers when she had first come to London as a young girl, knowing instinctively that it was trivial to use fashion as a yardstick by which to measure people's worth, but having the honesty to admit to herself that it was also very agreeable, after so many years of inferiority, to be a member of the select band which drew all eyes upon them.

That all eyes were drawn to them was unmistakable and may have owed much to Amabel's divine fairness and indeed to Sarah's own new elegance, but they had a further advantage which assured them of receiving more than their fair share of attention, for Sarah had decided that poor Bess was cooped up too much in London and she now felt that it would be just the thing for her dog to accompany them on their almost daily rides.

Now many society ladies had dogs—almost always lap dogs of the pug variety—but it was quite unknown for a member of the ton to try to foist on them an animal of a lesser pedigree. At first Amabel was inclined to look upon her sister-in-law's whim with scepticism, but Sarah was adamant. Surely Amabel could not be so poor spirited? And anyway (amused) should they not be trying to lead fashion rather than meekly follow behind? Amabel was not optimistic, but as soon as she saw that their friends were inclined to consider it not an affront, but rather an endearing eccentricity, wholly amusing in the dashing new young countess, she breathed a sigh of relief and settled down to enjoy their innocent notoriety.

CHAPTER 17

It was one of their rides in Hyde Park which led Sarah into a new friendship. On a cold Saturday in early April, not too long after her triumph at Almack's, she and Amabel had taken themselves, a little earlier than was fashionable, into the park, just happening to be driving close to the Serpentine. Bess, alas unaware just how close she was to being disapproved, and being inordinately fond of water, took one glance at the smooth inviting surface of the pool and threw herself bodily from Sarah's barouche, heading for it singlemindedly in a straight line, tail flapping madly and one ear flying disgracefully as she went.

Sarah's groom, Sam, a willing lad, did all he could to catch her before she reached her watery goal, but a young man, however fit, is no match for a vigorous and extremely determined animal of Bess's ilk and she was soon splashing about wildly, just out of reach, clearly enjoying every moment of her unseasonable bathe, while Sam looked helplessly on.

What to do now, that was the question? Sarah was sure that if she called to Bess she would in all probability be recalled to a sense of duty, but she was equally sure that her doing so would entail much shaking and inevitable mud-splatterings for all foolish enough to be close at hand. Looking down at her smart pelisse of a particularly pretty peach-coloured kerseymere and at Amabel's attractive deep cream gown, she was reluctant to risk it.

She thought of leaving Sam to the unenviable task of catching Bess and bringing her home when she had had her fill of water sports, for she remembered that Amabel could drive a little, but she knew that certain high-sticklers among the ton would think she and Amabel very fast if they were seen driving without even a groom to accompany them and, though she would happily have chanced her own reputation, she was loth to risk Amabel. It certainly seemed that they must have all the discomfort of sharing their carriage with an extremely soggy dog.

It was at this point that help came from an unexpected quarter. Sarah had noticed, but had not really registered that the incident had attracted the amused attention of a man exercising a fine black stallion on the gravel path. While she was still trying to decide what best to do, the same man rode up to them and stopped by their carriage. Sarah was quite certain that she had never been introduced to him and was about to turn on him her frostiest glance when, to her surprise, Amabel cried out animatedly, "Why, Robert Cranesby, how marvellous! I had not thought to see you in Town so early. What brings you thundering back so soon?"

"How can you ask, enchantress? Could I allow my desolate heart to languish in Kent away from the reviving draught of your limpid glances?"

Amabel dimpled, "Limpid glances! I'll say this for you, Robert, you certainly know how to turn a pretty compliment, wretch that you are."

"I do, don't I? But you know it is so much easier when one has such inspiration. I swear that Byron himself could not have had better! I had the devil's own job trying to think of something charming to say to my late hostess down in Kent. Managed it, of course, but had a few sticky moments I can tell you.!"

"Stop being foolish and allow me to present my new sister-in-law to you," she giggled. "You know that Miles gets cross if I allow you to flirt with me too much. Sarah dearest, may I present to you one of my very oldest friends, Lord Cranesby. We have known each other all of our lives, for he used to be Miles's very best friend many years ago and his lands lie close to Beaumere. Robert, my sister Lady Wilberton—you must have heard that Miles had married again, I am sure. Now you two must promise me faithfully to like each other for my sake!"

"I think," Cranesby replied, lifting Sarah's hand to his lips, "that I shall have absolutely no difficulty in obeying you implicitly, my child, though I cannot promise that I shall only like her for *your* sake!"

Sarah found herself looking up into the face of the most

dazzlingly handsome man she had ever seen. She had heard of piercing blue eyes: now she knew what that phrase meant. But not only had he eyes of the deepest cornflower blue, surrounded by spiky, long, dark lashes, he also had hair which rivalled Amabel's for fairness, and sparkling, even white teeth, which would awaken envy in many a maiden's breast, could be seen glinting as he smiled. These handsome features were arranged delightfully about a face with very high cheekbones, over which the skin was tightly drawn and which, as if Nature was determined to spare him no advantage, led to a rather square chin, divided by a handsome cleft. And if this wasn't devastating enough, on the left side of his face, running between cheek bone and chin, was a thin straight scar, which lent his face such a romantic and rakish air that Sarah felt certain that those who had described Byron as the most handsome of men must not have been fortunate enough to have crossed Lord Cranesby's path.

He held Sarah's hand for several moments longer than was necessary, gazing deeply with those wonderful eyes into her own, and she coloured at the frank admiration she saw there. For one such as Sarah, so long left to blush unseen, this was a new and altogether exhilarating experience and few would have blamed her for allowing it to go to her head.

"Now Robert," remonstrated Amabel, "You are not to start one of your flirtations with Sarah. You know that Miles would not like it and I shall get the blame for introducing you. Why, I believe you only came across to us to get me to do just that!"

"Princess! How can you be so suspicious when I have come expressly to be a knight in shining armour to you? I saw your sad predicament with your . . . er . . . dog.— Obviously some exclusive new breed I've never seen before, I collect? . . . And I thought I owed it to you, in view of our long-standing friendship to help. It would never do to see such pretty dresses with muddy footprints all over them after ·all."

"I am glad that you are clever enough to have seen Bess's finer points, sir," said a laughing Sarah, recovering some of her usual composure. "Not many do, you know? I have even been asked on occasion if she is not a mongrel, if you can believe it?"

"Oh surely not! Why one can see at a glance that she is a very superior animal indeed. Even the duck-weed stuck behind her ear fails to obscure that! You really must allow a dog-lover like myself to assist you."

"How can *you* help, silly?" Amabel scornfully, "You can hardly throw Bess over your horse, can you? Admit it. You came over only to meet Sarah."

"I confess to being charmed to have done so, little suspicious one, but I really do wish to help. I must admit, however, that the drastic action you suggest had not occurred to me, though if that is what it takes to clear your mind of my perfidy then I will certainly attempt it! I have a feeling, however,—and I do feel that I must just mention it, however poor-spirited you may think me—that she may be too many for me!"

"Idiotic creature! How then did you think to help us?"

"My plan was, I regret to have to admit it, rather less energetic. I simply thought that we might leave your unfortunate groom here to await the animal's emergence from the murky depths, while I tied my horse to the back of your carriage and drove you home."

"Do you think you should, Robert? You know how Miles hates you to escort me anywhere—or indeed, even to speak to me."

"Oh I think that I am not yet *so* afraid of your brother. We are not *quite* at open warfare you know, though if Lady Wilberton has any objection, of course, I will withdraw immediately."

Lady Wilberton could conceive of no greater pleasure than having this paragon, who looked at her with undisguised appreciation, take her anywhere and said shyly that, far from objecting, she was quite sure that Miles could have nothing but gratitude for anyone offering his wife and sister such generous assistance. Having given her orders to her groom, therefore, Sarah and Amabel were then driven back to Berkeley Square in spanking style.

Arrived at Wilberton House, Lord Cranesby gave the reins of his horse to one of Sarah's manservants to hold, sent another for a groom to take Sarah's carriage round to the mews, and went inside with the ladies, to Mitford's obvious disapproval. Miles was nowhere to be seen and Amabel breathed an audible sigh of relief, throwing a wry little grin at her brother's butler, as he closed the drawing room door on them with what appeared to be very bad grace.

Lord Cranesby seemed to dwarf the drawing room, large as it was, for he was taller even than Miles and very broad. His air and bearing proclaimed his allegiance to the Corinthian set, those neck or nothing men, not to be beaten in any sporting venture, and he dressed with a careless elegance which showed that other things beside fashion were his preoccupation. Wherever men met for any sporting pursuit, there, almost certainly could be found Lord Cranesby. Most mornings during the Season would find him sparring at Gentleman Jackson's rooms in Bond Street, where he was seen to strip to advantage and was said by many to be a proper man with his fists; should boxing pall, friends might find him at White's, playing for high stakes, hour after hour, showing no sign of fatigue when the game continued far into the early hours; or he could be seen engaging in some coaching contest, demonstrating to interested parties why there had been no suggestion that he should be blackballed when he had applied to join the Four-in-Hand club. During the winter he hunted his own pack in Shropshire, for he was a bruising rider to hounds and an indefatigable huntsman, and he was often to be seen among the crowd watching a fierce pugilistic match or cock fight, laying his bets in careless abandon. The set to which he belonged were rather wild and had it not been for the size of his fortune, which exceeded even that of Lord Wilberton, there is little doubt that mothers of promising young daughters would have kept them strictly guarded from him. As it was, he was sure of a welcome wherever he went. Many were the lures which had been cast for him and many the girl who had thought to have captured his fancy. In spite of the fact that he was still single, though well into his thirties, it was too much to hope that any girl worth her salt would not try to land such a prize, though what kind of husband he would make to the girl fortunate enough to do so was anybody's guess.

Luckily, Amabel was not susceptible to his charms. She rather thought she knew the kind of life any wife of his would lead and had too much a sense of self-preservation to risk her person in such a contest. Flirtation was a different matter, however, and no-one was quite as satisfactory as Robert with whom to while away an odd half-hour, however cross it made her brother. It was with rather a sense of pique, therefore, that she noticed that today his quarry lay in an altogether different direction, for his eyes scarcely left Sarah's face and almost all of his remarks were addressed to the little countess. Really, it was the outside of enough! She began to wish that Freddy had not been quite so free with his advice! And the way Sarah was behaving was positively shameless!

Someone less grieved than Amabel might not have been as rigidly disapproving, but it was certainly true that Sarah was finding her conversation with Cranesby highly invigorating. She had for so long been used to thinking herself plain that even her late improvement had not been enough to overcome her customary diffidence. She knew that her recently acquired status and her new clothes assured her acceptance among the ton, but she was as much convinced as to her inferiority of feature as ever. How could it be otherwise when her own husband preferred to spend his time ogling his cousin to paying her compliments? Now, here was this god-like creature, not only prepared to spend half an hour with her, but apparently totally absorbed in so doing. It was enough to turn the head of a girl used to compliments: to Sarah it was simply heaven and she was not about to allow her sister-in-law's patent disapproval to spoil it for her.

Now she heard him saying, "I have been used to thinking myself a pretty downey fellow, Lady Wilberton—for I will pretend to no false modesty you know to one I consider so nearly connected as you—yet it passes my comprehension how it is that you have been tripping about in society without my having so much as a glimmering of your existence. It is the greatest puzzle on earth to me, I can assure you! I must only hope that my reputation does not suffer as a result, for you must know that it is said of me that I cannot be within a hundred miles of a pretty young girl without becoming better acquainted."

'I see no need to disturb yourself concerning your powers then, sir," laughed Sarah, "since I am neither pretty nor indeed young. Why, I have been out these five years and more!"

"Worse and worse! Can it really be that I have missed such an opportunity for five years? I begin to lose all confidence. Tell me," (leaning his chin on his hand and gazing familiarly into Sarah's sparkling eyes) "is it the custom in your family to bring out young girls from the nursery?"

"Lord Cranesby, you are a gross flatterer—no more and no less!"

"Oh surely not gross! I will allow 'flatterer' if I must—though in your case I must protest that flattery cannot be held necessary—but surely not 'gross'?"

"I see how it is with you, sir! You have such a reputation for flattery that you are to be considered a Master, but even a Master needs his practise and you must, of necessity, use the odd half hour here and there to round off the finer points of your art!"

"Lady Wilberton! Once more I must protest! That you should suspect me of such a purpose wounds me to the heart! No-one seeing you as I did today in that enchanting little bonnet, looking so bewitchingly helpless, could suspect me of subterfuge!"

Amabel could find no way to interrupt this interesting little tête-à-tête and Lord Cranesby seemed prepared to continue in this vein indefinitely, to Sarah's apparent delight, when the door to the drawing room was suddenly flung open and in stormed Miles, such a wild expression on his face that it caused his wife involuntarily to start up in confusion.

"Why Miles, what a shock you gave me! Whatever is the matter?"

To her surprise, he ignored her completely, turning straightway to Lord Cranesby. "So! You here! I knew I could not be mistaken when I saw the stallion!"

"It must be a great comfort to you to know that you have not lost your eye for horse-flesh, Wil!" replied Lord Cranesby amused.

"May I ask what you are doing in my house? I believe we neither of us need reminding that it has been forbidden you!"

"Why Miles," broke in Sarah, confused. "What are you

saying? I believe rather that you owe this gentleman a debt of gratitude than that you should berate him in this manner!"

"I think, Sarah that I am the best judge of what I owe to Lord Cranesby and I shall trust you not to interfere!"

"But I *will* interfere, my lord," replied Sarah stiffly, drawing herself up as tall as she could, "when you break the rules of hospitality in *my* name. Lord Cranesby is here at my invitation and, as Ami, I am sure, will tell you, he has this morning been gracious enough to offer his assistance to me in the kindest way. I think it unforgivable of you to insult him in this way for his goodness."

She looked to her sister-in-law for confirmation, but Ami seemed too shocked at the scene to add her voice to Sarah's and Sarah was forced to continue her defence alone. "Had it not been for Lord Cranesby both your sister and myself would have been made extremely uncomfortable indeed, for Bess you know was in one of her fractious moods and . . ."

"Do not trouble me with your explanations, Sarah! When you have said goodbye to your *guest* I shall expect to see you in the library!" With that Miles turned abruptly on his heel and walked swiftly from the room, the set of his shoulders indicating the enormity of his rage.

For several seconds no-one spoke. Then Ami said, in a soft, frightened voice, "I thought you should not have come, Robert. You knew how it would be if he came home!"

Unruffled as ever and even amused, Lord Cranesby replied, "Yes, one may always be assured of knowing in advance what Miles's reactions on seeing me will be! It becomes quite boringly predictable at times! I wish I could say that it worried me on my own behalf, but I cannot forgive myself for getting into trouble my new little friend." And taking Sarah by the hand, he asked solemnly, "Dearest Ma'am, can you possibly acquit me, for I fear you are in for the most tremendous scold?"

"I am not such a poor-spirited creature as to be afraid my lord, and anyway, you may believe me when I say that I know you have nothing to reproach yourself for! *You* have been most completely the gentleman. It is I who must ask for your forgiveness, though I know not how you can begin to give it after that disgraceful display you have been forced to witness."

"My dear Lady Wilberton, do not give it another thought. My fellowship with your husband is too long-standing for me not perfectly to comprehend his behaviour and too certain for it to disturb me. Yet I think I must leave now, for if I stay longer he will fret and fume at *you*, I think." At that, he picked up his hat and cane, which he had placed on a small table near to his chair and made to move towards the door saying, "I imagine, Ma'am that it is unlikely that we shall be allowed to pursue this friendship now that your husband is concerned in it. Allow me to say that I wish, with all my heart, that it might have been otherwise."

By now, Sarah was blazingly angry at her husband's behaviour and she spiritedly replied to Cranesby, "Why sir, how do you mean? I can assure you that my husband does not *concern* himself in my friendships, as you put it. If it is only Miles's interference which prevents you from pursuing our acquaintance, I beg that you will not allow it to stand between us. For my part, I could not bear to discontinue a budding comradeship with one who shows such a nice discernment in his knowledge of dogs—not to mention bonnets!"

"Ma'am, I offer Miles my felicitations! He has indeed found himself a gem in you. If you have spirit enough to proceed with our association I am your man! Why should Miles have all the luck? I feel, however, that prudence might best be served if I were to remove myself from this vicinity today to allow your lord and master to, may I say, cool down just a little?"

"An excellent suggestion, sir, and one with which I heartily concur. I trust that I can rely on you not to cut me, however, when next we meet?"

"You may be sure of that, I promise you," he replied, raising the hand he was still holding to his lips. Pausing only to say a terse goodbye to Amabel, sitting in a chair in one corner of the room, her head lowered, and still too shocked to speak, he left the house.

When he had gone, Sarah began to stalk angrily around the room in the most agitated manner imaginable. As Amabel raised her head to look at her, she was amazed at the expression she saw on her normally composed face, for her cheeks were blazing and her beautiful eyes had attained an extra brilliancy from the internal fury mirrored there.

"How dare he! How dare he!" was all Sarah could at first find to say, as she walked up and down on the rug in front of the fireplace, her fists clenched tightly and held at her sides, while her teeth ground audibly. Those back home in Staffordshire had, on occasion, been privileged to see Sarah in one of her tempers, but to Ami it was the greatest of shocks. Never had she seen her mild-tempered sister-in-law so much as utter an impatient word and she was afraid at the passion she now displayed.

"Darling Sarah, you must control yourself, I beg of you!"

"Control myself?" (voice rising by at least an octave), "Control myself? To be called to the library like a schoolgirl in front of a guest! And *I* must control myself? No Amabel, it is not I who need self-control, it is your brother. I do not know how you were brought up in *your* family. Perhaps in high and mighty families such as yours it is permissible to insult guests. I alas have not the advantage of such a grand education, so was merely taught that it *was not so*! Well, if he wishes to see me, he will come to see me here, for I am not moving one inch from this chair!" And at that, she sat down forbiddingly in a little gilded armchair next to the fireplace, to await events.

CHAPTER 18

She did not have long to wait, since Miles remained in the library only a very few minutes after hearing the front door close before making his way stormily back into the drawing room. As soon as she saw his face, Amabel hurriedly made her excuses and left the room, seeking the safety of her own apartments before it should occur to Miles to question just who had been responsible for introducing Sarah to Robert.

As the door closed behind her, Miles strode angrily over towards the fireplace and stood before his wife, still sitting in her chair, now studiedly reading the latest copy of *La Belle Assemblée*, which she had quickly picked up from a side-table on hearing his footsteps in the hall.

"I asked you to come to the library, Sarah!"

Sarah put down her journal very deliberately and turned to him purposefully. "No Miles, you did not *ask* me at all. Rather you *told* me, and I am not used to being ordered about like a servant!"

Miles flushed deeply and replied, "If that was how it sounded then I am sorry, but I lost my temper at seeing *that man* sitting there, calm as you please in *my* house."

"I was under the impression, my lord, that our marriage ceremony made this *my* house as well as yours and I was regrettably not aware that I was required to apply for your permission before entertaining friends in it. Certainly I feel that if that was to be one of the conditions of our marriage I ought to have been warned beforehand in order that I could decide whether it would be acceptable to me or not!"

"To entertain *friends* Sarah, indeed you do not need my permission, but that man can never be a friend to you and so you must understand here and now!"

"*Can* never be? And what makes you decide if he is fit to

be a friend to me or not?" she replied furiously.

"I am your husband, Sarah and that must suffice. Trust me and accept without question that I must know what is best for you."

"Must you indeed? Then if you *know* why he is not considered fit to be my friend, perhaps you will acquaint me with your reasons. Of course, being only a simple-minded *woman* I cannot claim to have your powerful intellect, but if you explain it to me *very simply*, in words of *one syllable*, perhaps I may be able to comprehend!"

"It is nothing to do with intellect, Sarah! And I have never imputed that you are any less capable of understanding than I am!"

"Tell me then your reasons for denying me the right to choose my own friends!"

"I do *not* deny you the right to choose your friends, I simply request that you keep Lord Cranesby at bay."

"Request? Ha! I like your way of requesting! You tell me in the most crushing manner that I *may* not see him again, and when I ask why not, you tell me that it is because *you* know what is best for me. You further refuse to give me any reason for your demands. A strange kind of requesting is it not?"

"And yet I do make such a request," said Miles quietly.

"Then I repeat that you must tell me why," replied his wife in a voice just as quiet.

"That I *can* not do. It does not only concern me you see. Were it just my secret I might tell you, but it is not!"

"You *might*? Very generous, I am sure. You seem to forget that I am your wife. Surely I should have a share in your secrets or is that privilege reserved only for others? Ours may not have been a love-match, but indeed until now I had always felt myself to be truly your wife. Now I begin to wonder if I have any rights at all in your eyes!"

"That is not fair Sarah! Of course you have rights and you are most certainly my wife in every way!"

"Chattel rather! If you felt me to be your wife in truth, you would tell me the reason for your demand!"

"Yet I cannot!"

"Precisely!" cried Sarah, turning away from him so that

he should not see the tears stinging her eyes.

"Do you not see that I cannot?" urged her husband, taking her by the arm to turn her towards him, "I cannot!"

"Then I am sorry, but I cannot obey. As you have said, I may choose my own friends, and I choose to befriend Lord Cranesby. He seems to be quite as unexceptionable as anyone to whom I have yet been introduced and until you can persuade me otherwise then I *will* know him. Why even your own sister says that you have known him for ever! I do not see why you are so determined to prohibit our association."

"And I do not see why you are so determined to continue with it! I wonder if you would be so set on seeing him were he less presentable. It is surprising how determined even the most sensible of women becomes at the sight of a pair of broad shoulders!"

"And how foolish even the most sensible of gentlemen becomes at the sight of a white bosom!" replied Sarah hotly, uncomfortably aware that his words held a modicum of truth, but also having in her mind at that moment a clear picture of Elizabeth in her cream dress.

"We were speaking of Cranesby, Sarah, so why bring up generalities?"

"Aye, far better for you to keep to our original subject, I can see why *you* should not wish to see its scenario enlarged!"

"Since I have not the slightest idea what you are talking about, I shall simply repeat my warning!"

"And I shall again insist that I refuse to accept it!"

"I have my own way of knowing what is going on in my household and my own way of dealing with things which annoy me, Sarah, and so you had better beware. Anything of a clandestine nature I simply would not stand for and so you had better be advised. I shall not hesitate to exercise whatever constraints may become necessary if you flout my wishes."

"You mean, of course, any constraints which *you* consider necessary, I am certain my lord. For only your opinion is of any matter! Yet I think I have not deserved censure from you, since, to my knowledge, I have never behaved in a way which might lead you to feel that such constraints would be necessary! My family, you know, has never been as well versed in the art of dalliance as some others, though, if you do not mind me just mentioning it, there are those in our immediate circle who could not say the same! Now, if you will give me leave, sir, I have to change for dinner. You may remember that Mr. Middleton and Viscount Anstey are taking Amabel and myself to the Haymarket this evening and it is necessary, therefore, that dinner be early. The gentlemen will, of course, be joining us—only with your *permission* of course!" and with that she walked in as dignified a manner as she could from the drawing-room, to seek what comfort she might in her own apartments.

When she had gone, Miles walked over to a little cabinet on which stood several decanters and he poured himself a large measure from one of them. By heaven, who would have thought she would have such a temper! She had always seemed such a biddable little thing! But he had to admit that she had a point, for even with all the admiration she had excited lately he had never seen her step one jot over the line. And she was certainly right. The same couldn't be said about some of the ladies in their circle. Why, only a week or two since there had been that embarrassing little incident with Lizzie in the library at his Aunt Stanham's. But then, Lizzie never did know where to draw the line. As he remembered that evening, he felt the moisture beginning to spring out on his brow. God, but the girl was a handful—in more ways than one. He wouldn't like the ordering of her, that was for certain. Remembering how she had tricked him into going into the library with her by pretending that Blissworth wanted to see him there and had then thrown herself at him, he felt himself going first hot and then cold. How awkward it had been to extricate himself without hurting her feelings! Not only that, but he had the uncomfortable feeling that somebody had walked into the room and seen them before he had had a chance to get Lizzie's arms from around his neck and before he had an opportunity to explain to her kindly that since both of them were married such improper behaviour would not do. Heaven knew what would happen if news of that little *débâcle* should ever reach Sarah's ears! And yet here he had been berating her in the harshest way just for speaking to Cranesby. One thing was for sure: his little

Sarah would never show him up the way Liz did poor old Bliss. She never did anything but make him feel proud of her. He began to feel that he had been very unfair to her indeed, and for a fleeting moment he considered whether he should not explain things to her and let her judge for herself whether he was not right to be angry. Indeed, he was about to start upstairs to make his apologies, when suddenly a vivid memory rose up before him which wiped from his face any trace of tenderness. Devil take Robert Cranesby! No, he *could* not explain it to Sarah, could not show poor Caro in that light! He *would* not apologize, for he had nothing to apologize for. Sarah might be quite innocent, in fact he knew quite well that he could stake his life on that, but he knew just as well that Cranesby was the worst fiend imaginable and if she persisted in this friendship, who knew where it might lead? He would be damned before he would allow Sarah to fall into the same trap as Caro. He just could not bear to go through it all again.

****

When Sarah reached the sanctity of her apartments, she found herself feeling so faint that she had to sit down. She despised herself for her weakness and for the tears she could not stop. How dare he criticize *her* behaviour when she had been made to look foolish any number of times by his behaviour with Lizzie? Why shouldn't *she* have someone around her who seemed to be attracted to her? All the married women she knew seemed to have cicisbeos, admirers who made up their court, and no-one appeared to think anything of it. Certainly Miles could not be jealous—he would not spend so much time running after Lady Blissworth if he really cared enough for herself to mind her being admired. No, he was simply being possessive. She just happened to belong to him, in the same way that Wilberton House belonged to him. Well, he would have to be made to realise that what was sauce for the goose might do just as well for the gander. She would show him that a Dagley was more than a match for a Greville!—Somehow, though, the thought could not comfort her at all, and she continued to sob.

When Jenny and Langley saw their mistress in tears,

they were resentful indeed. No-one in the house could have failed to hear that the Master and his good lady had had an altercation and few were in any doubt as to the cause. Both Jenny and Langley were, of course, at one with Sarah in thinking the Earl's attitude utterly unforgiveable.

When Sarah had taken on Miss Langley, there had been those in the Wilberton household who had predicted that no good would come of it. Never, said they, could two ladies' maids share one mistress in amity. Yet their fears had proved ill-founded, for Jenny and Langley worked side by side in total harmony and for this, it must be said, Jenny mostly deserved the credit. When Langley was taken on she, herself, fully expected to have to run the gauntlet of Jenny's hostility. What she found instead was a young woman quite as appreciative of her skills as would be enough to gratify anyone's vanity. The two had quickly become firm friends, united in their affection for Sarah, and now, when they saw how their master had treated her, their maidenly bosoms heaved in silent indignation! Men! They were all the same! Not worth a candle any of them!

When Sarah had sufficient command of herself to notice that Jenny and Langley were in her dressing room, she did her best to stop her tears, but their anxious faces only succeeded in causing her to sob even more vigorously. Jenny immediately put her arms round her mistress in sympathy, "There, there, my lady, don't you fret now! Come come, my little honey. There's nerry a one that's worth one of your tears, you mark my words! He don't mean nothin' by it m'dear. Why, men are like the bull old Farmer Hickley keeps in the long pasture at home. He puffs out his cheeks and bellows about a bit when the mood takes him, but when it is past, he can be led as easy as easy by the ring through his nose! It just needs patience 'til the mood is gone. And just look at you! Why, you'll make your eyes all red and swollen with weeping and then what will poor Miss Langley be able to do with you?"

Langley, less vociferous and not quite able to approve such familiarity, contented herself with making Sarah lie down quietly on the bed with soothing pads of witchhazel on her eyes to repair the damage and a cushion under her feet for comfort, while suggesting quietly, in her soothing voice, what she thought the countess might wear for the opera that evening. For Sarah, after the misery of the last half-hour, it was a haven of peace in a troubled world.

By the time Sarah was ready to go downstairs, no-one would have guessed that anything had occurred to upset her tranquility. Langley had spared herself no pains that evening to ensure that her mistress would charm her companions, believing that a woman looking pretty could more easily soothe ruffled feathers than a plain one, and she did indeed look truly beautiful in a new gown of crêpe, in a shade of lemon called couleur d'oreille d'ours, its low bodice deeply trimmed with blond lace. Her hair was dressed in light ringlets at the brow, the rest plaited and threaded so prettily with deep yellow ribands and strings of pearls, that even Langley professed herself satisfied with the result.

Sarah deliberately waited until she knew that Freddy and the Viscount had arrived before making her way downstairs: she had no intention of being alone with Miles and risking Langley's work by having another argument with him before their guests arrived. As it was, she was the last to enter the drawing room and the obvious admiration she saw in the eyes of all three gentlemen went some little way towards repairing the damage of the day.

Amabel, looking as pretty as ever, was down before her and seemed a little put out at the attention Sarah received, especially that reverence she could now command from Freddy. She was, however, more concerned to get Miles into a good humour than to cross swords with his wife in matters of fashion, since she was still by no means certain that Miles would not later call her to account for introducing his wife to Robert. As a result she spent much of dinner using her not inconsiderable wit to jolly him into a happier frame of mind, while Sarah confined her attentions to the others. She had succeeded so well that when Sarah's party left to go to the opera, Miles said that he might well choose to leave his card party early and call in on them all later at the Haymarket. He was not much addicted to cards, going to White's or to Watier's only because all of the men in his set expected it of him, and he was quite sure that the opera would prove more entertaining. Sarah had still not forgotten their quarrel and was very luke-warm in her reply to his suggestion, but as he helped her into her evening wrap, he touched her lightly on the cheek and said she was a "little pea-goose", which made her smile and say that if he did indeed wish to come on later, they would be sure and save a place for him in their box.

CHAPTER 19

The King's Theatre Opera House was a splended sight, with its tiers of boxes all hung with crimson draperies, fronts painted in white and gold, above which, by the flickering light of a multitude of candles in crystal chandeliers, could be glimpsed lavishly painted ceilings.

Sarah's party arrived unfashionably early, before the first act began. A lover of music, she liked to see the opera through and the others were happy to humour her in this, though she was well aware that this set her rather apart from her friends. For most of the ton the real business of the evening was not music; some went rather to enjoy displaying an expensive costume, others to begin a new flirtation or to finish with an old one, while many attended merely because it was the fashionable thing to be seen there. Members of the ton who could afford it hired a box for the Season, an extravagance of the highest order, just for the doubtful felicity of being able to spend each Tuesday and Saturday evening waving and signalling to friends in other parts of the theatre, but wherever one sat an evening at the opera was a costly business.

In the pit below were usually gathered young men of fashion, some from the dandy set, those to whom costume and manner was a matter for total absorption, while others adhered to the set which claimed Lord Cranesby, sporting men to whom a visit to the opera only gave an opportunity to ogle any lady who chanced to take their fancy, and who spent their time rattling their canes or taking snuff together, chattering loudly above the music.

Sarah had already visited the Opera once or twice since coming to Town, but tonight was special, for Mozart's *Don Giovanni* was playing for the first time in England, the famous Signor Ambrogetti taking the title role. Sarah was wildly excited and, the unhappy events of the day pushed to the back of her mind, she settled herself in her chair, her eyes agleam as she awaited the start of the performance.

She was soon totally absorbed in the music, hardly being aware of the noises of her companions' chatter, for one quickly had to become immune to such irritations at the Opera House. At the end of the first act, her mind dazed by the beauty of the music, she heard Freddy and the Viscount agree to walk out to see which of their friends had arrived early. Amabel declared it to be insufferably hot in their box and went too. Sarah too was hot and would have liked some air, but she knew her companions well and knew that she could place little reliance on their assurances that they would all return in time for the second act. It was not worth missing any of the music only to find herself in the company of Mrs. McBride and her like, so she remained where she was. She had not been sitting alone long, fanning herself to try to cool down a little and looking interestedly down at the seething mass below, when a knock sounded on the door of her box, and without more ado, in strolled Lord Cranesby.

"I thought I could not be mistaken, Ma'am! I saw you from my box opposite. What a delightful surprise to meet you here, and all alone too! May I join you, or would it be an imposition?"

"My lord, how d'you do! Yes of course join me. You cannot think how happy I am to see you again, if only to apologise once more for this afternoon, though I confess that I'd no idea you were a music lover."

"A music lover?" (quizzically), "As to that, I had no idea either that I was! Say rather that I am a lover of seeing people profess to love music!"

Sarah laughed delightedly, patting the seat beside her invitingly and saying, as he sat down, "At least you are honest, sir, which I believe does you great credit, for I never 'til lately met with more people who have told me how much they dote on the opera and then have talked the whole of the evening through, while I strain to hear the singers."

"Then I take it that you really are one to whom the opera gives pleasure?" he said, lounging uneasily on the velvet opera seat which looked much too small for him.

Sarah dimpled, "Now how shall I answer you, sir? I

should like very much to say I am, but how can I make you believe that I am not rather one of those who simply claim that pleasure?"

Cranesby took her hand and raised it gallantly to his lips, declaring earnestly, "It is enough that you say so, Ma'am, for prevarication is not, I think, in your nature," allowing Sarah's hand to remain clasped between both his own.

Sarah was by no means willing to accept such familiarity and gently removed her hand, saying, "How can you possibly know that, my lord, on such a short acquaintance?"

Without rancour, he replied, "If I say, Ma'am that I feel your character to be as open to me now as ever it might be were we to meet each day for a twelve-month, you will say that I am being familiar, yet so it is. I have never before met one whose character I am so certain will lose nothing by a more thorough knowledge, and as such it is a great source of happiness to me that you have chosen to disregard your husband's displeasure and honour me with your friendship."

"I hope I will never ignore any *reasonable* wishes of my husband, but this seems so unreasoning a taboo that I cannot feel held by it."

"I am only happy that you have the courage, Ma'am, but tell me, do you intend that our friendship should be secret or is the world to be allowed to look on?"

Sarah blushed. "I am not afraid of the world, my lord!" she said. "Certainly if it is interested it may look on as hard as it pleases since I am sure that it will see nothing which need disgrace either myself or you. I am indifferent to its suspicions."

"But you are not so indifferent, I think, to your husband's feelings. Tell me, was he not very angry with you this afternoon?"

"Forgive me, sir, but what he said to me was a matter only for my ears," replied Sarah gently.

He flushed rather but only said, "I honour you for your circumspection, my lady, and promise not to probe further. I must be only too glad that your conversation has not ended with my banishment!" Then, with an air of one turning to more pleasant things, "Tell me instead when I may see you again, for I am sure that your party will return any moment and we shall have no further time to talk."

"I do not perfectly know what will be my movements for the next few days. I am not able only to think of my own wishes, you know, for I am Miss Greville's chaperone."

"Ah, I see how it is, Ma'am. Now that you come to it you find yourself a little more afraid of your husband than you would have me believe. And, in truth, I do not blame you for he is certainly formidable."

Sarah's chin went up defiantly, "Indeed sir, you are mistaken. I am not at all afraid, it is simply that my activities are unsure. Of course, we shall be at Almack's on Wednesday."

"But you would not be so cruel as to ask me to wait four days to see you? Shall you not be at the worthy McBrides' on Tuesday for their party? I felt certain that you must, for they are in your set aren't they?

"Oh yes, I had forgot. And shall you be there also?"

"I had not quite made up my mind, but if you go, there can be no question. Of course I shall be there."

Sarah blushed delightfully. She was not yet used enough to flirtation to be able to affect the fashionable *ennui* of her friends and Lord Cranesby found in her open confusion an unaccustomed source of delight. He had decided to pursue Miles's wife simply because he knew how much it would annoy him. Certainly he had not expected that it would provide himself with much amusement. Now he found himself drawn to Sarah as he had not felt drawn to any woman for years. She really was a sweet little thing. Obviously he was in for more entertainment than he had envisaged. "And may I hope that you will spare me a dance on Tuesday, my dear friend?" he said. "I think I shall be able to get more easily through the next few days if I may be assured that privilege."

"I shall certainly dance with you, my lord, if I can, but my husband will be there and he may object."

"I was quite sure that he would be, but I cannot think that he would forget his manners so far as to upset a party, even at the sight of you in my arms, a state of affairs for which I assure you I can scarcely wait!" he replied audaciously.

Sarah laughed at this. "I believe, sir, that you are the most flirtatious gentleman of my acquaintance and I shall certainly not regard in a serious light any words of yours." Then, more solemnly she added, "But I would ask you not to antagonise my husband more than is needful. I do not know what is between you, but I am not beyond hoping that you may become friends at last. He is not often unreasonable, you know, in fact he is normally remarkably sweet-tempered. It shall be my intention to see you content in each other's company, and so I warn you!"

"I wonder if even you can achieve the impossible, my lady? I rather think you will find that we defeat you. And when I see how he behaves towards you I am more than ever certain that he and I can never be friends more."

Sarah sprang quickly to her husband's defence. "If you think that this afternoon's tirade was usual then you are sadly out. Why, as a rule he is all that is kind and generous. This is the first time we have been at odds, you know, since we were married."

"My sweet girl, I beg you won't jump down my throat!" he replied, laughing a little at her spirited words, while Sarah blushed at being thus addressed. "You must forgive my interference in matters which do not concern me, it is just that I do not know how you can affect to be so calm when you are forced to sit here watching him make love to another woman."

"What do you mean? How dare you say so!"

"Forgive me," he replied stiffly, "it is only that your husband seems mighty cosy with his cousin in her box— but perhaps you do not object?"

"Well, there you are quite out," she cried triumphantly, happy to be able to dispel the ominous fears assailing her, "for he is not here tonight. He is at his club with some friends, though he has promised to be here later for supper."

"Ah, my wretched eyesight! But I was certain that that was Miles sitting over there with his cousin—do not you see the man? Third box from the stage," and he raised his quizzing glass and held it before Sarah so that she could more easily perceive. She needed no more than a glance to confirm that it was indeed her husband, lounging comfortably against the side wall of the box while his beautiful companion glanced voluptuously up at him. Even as she watched she could see Miles speaking, a grin on his face, and saw Lizzie playfully tap his knuckles with her fan. She waited to see no more, but pushed away the quizzing glass, saying in a colourless voice, "Yes I see him now. You are quite right, it is my husband."

At her stricken expression Lord Cranesby moved his head close to hers and said quietly, "Ah forgive me, Ma'am. 'Fore God I did not wish to distress you. But I know Miles's ways and you are too sweet for me to wish to stand by while he deceives you. On my life I cannot understand why he should waste his time on his cousin when he might be with you."

"Oh really, my lord," said Sarah miserably, "there is no comparison as well you know! Why, she could command the admiration of almost any man."

"As you say, Ma'am, there is no comparison! She— forgive my blunt speaking—is the nearest thing to a harlot that we have in society. And I have yet to hear that there are no men of discrimination among the ton! It galls me that *you* are being passed over for the like of her. And what is so surprising is that you are willing to accept it!"

"What can I possibly do about it, Lord Cranesby? It is certainly no crime for Miles to appear in his cousin's box."

"And yet, he would deny you the right to be in my company."

"Indeed he will *not* do so, my lord," said Sarah with new vigour, her determination revitalized by what she had just witnessed. "I have already told you that I have defied him in this."

"Ah, would that I could believe that you really meant it. Yet I fear that Miles has only to lift a finger for you to obey."

"You are mistaken, I assure you."

"Of course," he replied smoothly.

"Why will not you take my word, sir?" she cried, exasperated. "What will it take to make you believe me?"

"I think that nothing could make me believe you lack

courage, my dear, but Miles would be too formidable an opponent for anyone."

"Not for me, I tell you plainly. Oh, I wish I could think of a way to convince you!"

He seemed much struck by her words and, looking down at the floor of the box, said slyly, "Perhaps there is a way."

"Anything, just tell me," said Sarah, heedless in her overwhelming desire to prove to this man that she was not her husband's dupe.

"Then allow me to escort you to Vauxhall on Monday," replied her tempter. "There's an indoor Masquerade in the Rotunda—the first of the Season. If you are not afraid of Miles what better way to show it?

"But surely it is improper to go to Vauxhall?"

"Oh, you have to be most old fashioned to think so, my lady. And besides, we should go masked. If we are careful and leave before the unmasking at twelve who will know we were there?"

"I had not thought the Gardens open yet," she said, faintly.

"Oh the gardens are still closed, but this is an indoor Masquerade. You need not fear, it is quite warm within the Rotunda!"

She continued to hesitate. "I could not come alone, my lord, for how could I leave the house? You have forgot that I am supposed to be Amabel's chaperone—though how I should be considered suitable when I am thinking of such a scheme as this . . . And if I tell Miles I am going with you he will certainly forbid it as well you know."

"That is certain," he replied at once. "Miles must know nothing of it. But if I know anything of our little Amabel this would be just the kind of lark she would appreciate. Why not enlist her to join the party? It will not be quite the same, I admit, but much better than nothing."

"Well, I suppose I could try," she murmured doubtfully. "I think you are quite right to suppose she would like it of all things, for she has a regrettable tendency to high jinks."

"Well then?"

It seemed to Lord Cranesby that she was weakening,

when she remembered that she and Amabel would never be allowed to go out at night without an escort and obviously Lord Cranesby could not collect them from that house, "I would ask Freddy for his escort—Mr. Middleton, you know?" she explained hastily, "for he is probably my best friend, but he is so strait-laced at times I fear he would not only refuse but he might even tell Miles of our plans, and then all would be up with us."

"Certainly, then, not Mr. Middleton," he agreed, a little smile of amusement playing around his mouth as he watched her puzzling for a solution.

They seemed to be at a standstill, when Sarah, who was beginning to develop something of a liking for the scheme, cried out, "I know just the person! Why, Viscount Anstey has been dangling after Ami for ever. He would be grateful for such an opportunity, I'll warrant."

This main difficulty being overcome, they had time only to settle that Lord Cranesby would acquire dominoes and masks for them at Rickman's and that they would meet on the corner of Clarges Street and Piccadilly at eight-thirty, before the door opened to reveal the rest of her party, bringing with them Mr. and Mrs. McBride. On seeing them, Lord Cranesby rose at once from his seat and bowed, receiving a very gracious greeting from the McBrides. Sarah was surprised to see that Freddy, usually so punctilious in all forms of social address, gave Lord Cranesby only the slightest of bows in return and this accompanied by a most serious and searching look. His welcome from Ami was little better, for after the events of the afternoon she had decided on prudence. Unruffled as ever, Lord Cranesby bowed deeply over Sarah's hand, which he pressed briefly and, reminding her in a whisper of her promise for Monday, was gone, very satisfied with his night's work.

While the others were settling into their seats, Freddy took Sarah to one side and whispered, "Who asked *him* to come in here, Lady Wil?"

"I asked him myself, Freddy. He was so kind as to keep me company in your absence."

"If you did not wish to be alone, better that you had asked me to stay with you. Only too happy, assure you! Shouldn't be alone with Cranesby. He's a bad man. Miles wouldn't like it. Can't say I'd like any wife of mine to be seen alone with him, but especially important that you ain't."

"Why me?"

"Bad blood between him and Miles. Can't bandy all the details round town, but Miles can't stand the man."

"Freddy, you are as bad as Miles! You say I musn't know him, but won't tell me why. It is absurd. Everyone else seems to be happy enough in his acquaintance. He told me himself that he will be at the McBrides' on Tuesday."

"Didn't say he wasn't accepted—perfectly good ton up to a point, so no reason to refuse him anywhere. Just that he don't get on with Miles, so better you don't get too pally."

"What are you two whispering about," demanded Amabel sulkily when she saw their two heads close together. "I thought you were a lover of music, Sarah, and yet here is the second act begun and you not even listening. Nor have you yet spoken to Mr. and Mrs. McBride."

Sarah was mortified to have to agree that she had not noticed that the proceedings had recommenced and, with a late, rather perfunctory handshake with the new arrivals, she settled down, still feeling troubled by Freddy's remarks, and with her mind a seething mass of hopes and fears, to listen.

CHAPTER 20

When Sarah and her sister-in-law arrived back in Berkeley Square late that night they were surprised to be informed by Mitford that the Master was before them, and further, that he had been home for some time. At the opera, Sarah had steadfastly refused to allow her gaze to wander again to Lizzie's box until the second interval, when she could resist the temptation no more. By that time, her husband was no longer in situ, but since Lizzie too had disappeared, she was not unduly surprised when Miles failed to put in an appearance in her own box. His absence served only to stiffen her resolve wth regard to the Masquerade party and she had made an opportunity, while Freddy was away securing supper, to enlist the willing co-operation of Amabel and the Viscount without his suspecting anything. Now she wanted nothing more than to avoid her husband's company, so, taking time only to whisper to Amabel that she must be sure to keep her own counsel, she made her way quickly to her apartments, her nerves much overset.

However often Sarah had begged them not to wait up for her, both her maids knew their duty too well to heed her words, so that a few minutes found her divested of her evening apparel and in a pretty nightgown and wrapper, her hair having been brushed by Jenny, while Miss Langley shook out the creases an evening sitting at the Opera had made in her evening gown. One look at their mistress's face had been enough to silence the two faithful women who served her and instead of their usual chatter, after exchanging speaking looks behind her back, Miss Langley contented herself with rubbing Sarah's temples with cologne to ward off the headache she was persuaded troubled her, while Jenny made some tea, her cure for all ills.

Sarah's husband found her sitting by the fire in an

armchair, sipping fitfully at a dish of tea, which she held between both her hands as if to warm them, while her feet rested upon a beaded footstool. If Sarah was just beginning to feel more the thing, one look at her husband was enough to ensure that all comfort was now at an end, for in spite of the inevitable courtesy he showed her ladies when he asked them to leave the room, a murderous rage showed in his face and a pulse beat ominously at his temple. So patent was his fury that Jenny and Miss Langley both courageously looked first to Sarah for her consent before, with obvious reluctance, they left her alone with him. Only a fool could be unaware that Miles was in high dudgeon over something, but his wife refused to be intimidated. Instead, she said mildly, "Well, sir, a pretty way to behave indeed, is it not? I believe you have scared Jenny half to death!"

"But not you, my lady, eh? No!—certainly not you! You, I believe would remain unafraid were I to wring that pretty little neck of yours," replied her lord in a thunderous tone. "Are not you afraid of anything?"

"I trust that I may have no reason to be afraid of you, my lord," replied his wife, unconfortably aware that she was beginning to sound a little like Desdemona to her husband's Othello.

"You trust? You trust?" said Miles, spitting out the words in his anger, "Aye, you do trust Madam, I think. You trust to my good nature indeed, but perhaps you trust too far!"

Sarah laughed briefly, a piteous choked laugh which had nothing of humour in it, "I think that I can have had little reason to congratulate myself on your good nature today, my lord, however I may have done so before."

"Then perhaps you should look to your own behaviour to explain such a *volte face*. Did I not, this afternoon, explicitly forbid you to see Cranesby? And can you deny that this evening you disobeyed my wishes?"

Finding her own fury swelling to match his, Sarah put down her dish on the hearth and rose to her feet. "Your wishes and my behaviour seem to you to be one and the same, my lord, but can you have forgot that I did not agree to obey you in this? I seem to remember telling you, forgive me if I'm wrong, that your desires in this matter seem to me to be high-handed and totally unreasonable!"

"You dare to call me high-handed? What do you call your behaviour madam, when you deliberately allow Cranesby to visit you alone in your box—And don't say that you did not, because I saw you with my own eyes!"

"Aye indeed, so you did! And you remind me to ask what you were doing at the Opera so early when you had told me that you would be at one of your clubs until supper?"

Miles started, thrown completely off balance by her unexpected counter-attack, but managed speedily to collect himself, replying more fiercely, "If you think to wriggle out of this, my girl, by decrying my behaviour, you have mistaken your man, for I went early only to see you. I thought that you might like me to show a flag of truce."

"Oh stuff!" declared Sarah inelegantly, "That really is doing it rather too brown, do not you think?"

"What charming sayings you seem to have picked up during your sojourn in town. And do we have Cranesby to thank for teaching you phrases suitable only for the stable?"

"Perhaps I am forced to apply to Lord Cranesby for tuition, my own husband apparently preferring to spend his time teaching his cousin, heaven only knows what?"

"Am I supposed to infer something from your words, for if so you must be heartily disappointed since I have not the remotest guess what you are talking about!"

"Do you seriously think me caper-witted, sir? Depend on it, I am no such thing and that being the case, I can see little difference between my entertaining a friend along in my box and Lizzie doing so."

"What has Lizzie's behaviour to say to anything? What makes you keep bringing her into this?"

"Why, only that just as you were so fortunate to see me, my dear sir, so was I happy enough to see you—in Lizzie's box and looking as comfortable as may be. I trust I am not one to refine too much upon trifles, but it would afford me some satisfaction if you could explain to me why, when you wished to present a flag of truce to your wife, you ended up with her!"

"I had not realised that you had seen me in Lizzie's box,"

replied her husband uncomfortably.

"Had not you indeed? Why, I never would have guessed," returned Sarah, the deepest irony colouring her voice.

Quickly picking up the inflection in her tone, Miles said irritably, "What nonsensical notions have you in your head now, woman? You cannot seriously think it improper that I was with Lizzie. Why, she is my cousin."

"My felicitations, I am sure. And does that explain why you went to see *her* before you came to me?"

"Why, as to that, there is nothing in it. It is simply that I bumped into her in the foyer and it would have been churlish to refuse to escort her."

"And was she alone when you met?"

"No, with a party—but they chose not to return to their box," replied her husband, uncomfortably aware that he was being forced into a corner.

"How very convenient for you. It must be agreeable to have such friends."

"If you think to lead me away from my path, Sarah, you are sadly out. I am here to discuss your behaviour with Cranesby, not some freakish suspicions you may have."

"Oh of course, mine are *freakish* suspicions. Only your suspicions are God-given!" shouted Sarah furiously.

"There can be no comparison in the circumstances, Sarah!" exclaimed Miles, just as angrily, "Lizzie is related to me—almost like a sister! Cranesby is my enemy and I have forbidden you to see him!"

"You mean, I think, that you have allowed me to know that you would *prefer* me not to see him again," Sarah replied, with awful calm, "but regretfully, as I have said, I *will* see him."

At this Miles began walking rapidly about the room in an effort at self-control rather than trust himself to remain too near to his wife.

"But I say that you will *not* see him! I will *not* have you defy me Sarah!"

"Oh really, Miles," retorted Sarah, laughing in spite of herself, "You make it sound as if I am a little girl defying her governess."

At the sound of her laughter Miles lost his temper completely and, taking her by the shoulders, he began to shake her. "How dare you laugh at me! Are you lost to all sense of propriety? What kind of woman is it that refuses to obey her husband?"

"As to that, my lord, I think I am every bit as much a woman as you are a man, it is just perhaps that you find your cousin more to your taste," replied Sarah savagely, unsuccessfully ripping at his fingers in an effort to make him relinquish his hold on her.

"And perhaps you think Cranesby is more of a man than me?"

"Perhaps he is!"

Miles caught his breath at her words. As his figures continued to bite into Sarah's shoulders, he shouted, "You little drab! We shall see how much of a man I am," and he began to force her backwards towards the bed. Before she could stop him, he had pressed her against the heavy silk coverlet, the edge of the bed hard against the back of her calves.

"Don't Miles, I beg of you," cried Sarah aghast, as his mouth came towards hers, but he was too incensed to heed her and his lips found hers in a brutal kiss, deliberately stripped of any trace of tenderness. She tried to push him from her, but he held her close to him while she struggled, not caring how his nails bit into her flesh, until eventually defeated, she lay still in his arms.

The moment of her defeat saw his passion change. His kiss was no longer harsh: instead it was gentle and lingering, bringing a response from her she had never dreamed of. She felt her body quiver traitorously as his hands began to caress her. Then her own arms were around him, her longing exploding spectacularly into life and she began to exchange with him kiss for kiss, kisses which became ever more urgent as her need for him increased. Before she closed her own, she saw his eyes gleaming recklessly as he tore frenziedly at the thin material of her wrapper and she heard his breath coming fast as his desire began to engulf him.

Suddenly, as if wrenched away by some gigantic hand, she felt him tear himself from her. She guessed, rather than saw the super-human effort he had made, and could only marvel that his wish to hurt her could be stronger even than the passion they shared.

"Well, my dear," he said derisively, gathering the threads of his dignity around himself, "now you have something with which to compare Cranesby's kisses," and with a last scornful glare, he turned on his heel and left his wife's bedroom.

After he had gone Sarah continued to lie where he had left her, pulling her torn wrapper tightly to her as if for protection, though she knew full well that she wanted nothing more than for Miles to return and take her into his arms, however harshly, once more. For the first time since her marriage she allowed herself to see the truth and she wondered how on earth she had been so blind to it before. She had for so long schooled herself to think of hers as a marriage of convenience that she had never questioned whether it could ever be anything more. Yet for her, of course, it was much, much more, had probably been so indeed from the first.

The realisation that she loved Miles, blinding though it was, gave her no comfort at all for she could not flatter herself that marriage had brought them closer: indeed, she was quite certain that Miles despised her—how could he so openly conduct his liaison with Lizzie else? Yet had he not seemed jealous tonight? Aye, as jealous as he might be if someone were to steal his favourite horse! Well, she must be more on her guard than ever now. She had always had to hide from him the depth of her passion: it should not be impossible to keep from him the fact of her love.

* * * * * * * * *

On leaving his wife, Miles strode angrily along the passageway to enter his own apartments, closing the door behind him with a crash and then suddenly leaning weakly against it as he felt the enormity of what had just taken place. He was furious with himself: it was unforgivable to allow his anger to goad him into behaviour more fitting for the brothel than his bedchamber, however much he felt himself to be in the right of it.

As he allowed his thoughts to dwell on his wife, he was aware of an overriding wish to return to her. He had been shocked at the strength of his desires and more so at her uncontrolled response to them. What a strange thing indeed? It was hard to believe that he had ever doubted that he would enjoy making love to her, for surely even the most potent love match could not produce such fire. He grinned a little to himself. It would be worth swallowing a little pride to be allowed the privilege of such delights as the night seemed to promise. He had almost persuaded himself that he should go back to see what welcome awaited him when along with Sarah, the image of Cranesby once more took possession of his mind. A tremor of fury ran through him and he knew that he would not return to her that night.

To remain in his apartments was impossible—the torment of her presence on the other side of his dressing room door would be too much for him. Cards were a bore but anything was better than staying here. Perhaps Watier's, to lose a few pounds on the cards or dice? "Better had I gone there earlier as I was supposed to," he thought, ruefully.

Although it was after two when he arrived at the corner of Bolton Street and Piccadilly, Watier's, known by all and sundry as the 'Great-Go' showed no signs of emptying out. Here play did not start until nine, and then it continued all night, its members, only the pink of the ton being allowed to claim that privilege, playing deep, at hazard and macao. Miles was fortunate enough to meet up with a crowd of acquaintances, which included not only Viscount Anstey and Freddy, who had decided to round off their evening there, but also his friend Mountjoy and some other lesser men of his set, and Miles was soon engaged in a game of hazard. Even to the least perspicacious among those at his table, it was clear that the Earl was not himself, for he drank heavily and showed himself to be reckless in his bids, playing with a carelessness which was totally uncharacteristic. No-one seeing the scowl on his face felt inclined to chance their luck in asking him to account for it, however, for despite his habitual good temper, it was well known that, on the odd occasion, he could come the nasty as well as any man, and more thoroughly than most! As a result, even the most foolhardy among them declined to enquire and he was left to dwell on Sarah's iniquities in peace, while the game went on around him, almost without his being aware of it.

His scowl deepened as his mind dwelt on the words which anger had torn from Sarah, while Freddy watched him shrewdly from the corner of his eye. So, she thought Cranesby more a man than he was! Well she would certainly think so now, when he had left her in that stupid way. At the thought of her lying in the torn nightgown, desire mingled with his shame. He felt his blood heat, but knew that to be stupid! They'd been married an age, and he was no schoolboy to be so moved by such a scene . . . He continued restless, making no conversation, but gazing deep into the dregs at the bottom of his glass.

What a fool he'd been to marry again, he reflected bitterly. He'd been at such pains to marry someone totally unlike Caro and here he was in trouble again! Women were the very devil! With a man you knew where you were. Women were impossible to fathom. He settled down contentedly to a thorough diatribe against females, grateful to have escaped the ignominy of being one of the despised gender.

Such comfortable thoughts could not long continue. Vicious tweaks of conscience nipped through his self-indulgence to present him with an unwelcome alternative. Could any of this be his fault? It seemed unlikely, but perhaps if he had tried harder to engage her affections, they might by now be on perfectly amicable terms? As things stood the thought was not a pleasant one, for no two people could be more estranged than he and Sarah had become during the last twelve hours, and his behaviour this evening must certainly have given her a disgust of him not to be easily overcome. More to the point, how could they live together now that she fancied herself in love with Cranesby? The muddle was more than he was capable of sorting. He should have tried harder to include her more in his life . . . And Sarah was such an affectionate little thing . . . The roseate picture forming in his mind of his wife as she had been when he proposed to her was shattered abruptly and replaced by one in which she was joined by Cranesby. Incensed, he clenched his fist and, to the consternation of his friends, brought it down hard on the table, knocking over piles of coin and vowels which had mounted up in play, and producing a desperate muddle.

Theirs was no love-match, but Sarah would soon discover how short he fell of being a complaisant husband!

CHAPTER 21

It was just as well that only one day had to be passed
before the Vauxhall masquerade since to Sarah never did a
day pass more slowly or more miserably. Certainly when
she was at last being put to bed by Jenny on Sunday
evening, she reflected that, had there been a conspiracy to
make her day as unpleasant as possible it would have been
difficult to imagine even the worst of her enemies being
able to discomfort her more than those she had been wont
to imagine her friends.

The day had begun with her decision not to attend
Morning Service at the Chapel Royal, for so fitfully had she
passed the night after Miles had left her room, that she felt
entirely unequal to meeting with those tonnish
acquaintances she was sure to encounter there and so
pleaded a headache, not entirely a fiction, since her head
really did throb quite abominably. Amabel was all
solicitude, proferring laudanum in water, cologne for her
temples, Dr. James's powders and any number of other
cures which came into her head, even offering to stay at
home with her if she really felt unable to leave the house.
Sarah refused all of Amabel's cures, assuring her that if she
lay quietly in bed for a while she was quite certain that her
headache would go away. Nor would she hear of her sister
remaining behind with her, for she knew that Amabel
enjoyed nothing more than being seen at the Chapel Royal
wearing yet another new creation designed to add to the
number of her admirers.

It was not until Amabel had left for Church, looking
delicious in a froth of white muslin, that Sarah realised that
she must be alone with Miles in the house, with only the
servants for company. Supposing he came to her room!
Supposing he was not yet rid of his fury! The thought was
enough to make Sarah quickly summon Jenny and Miss

Langley to her. Better that she should be dressed if he did indeed come to find her, for she had not relished playing the role of victim and was determined not to do so again.

She was quickly helped into a round dress of oyster-coloured cambric muslin, which just happened to be one of her most becoming, and was soon making her way downstairs, with a fair assumption of nonchalance, towards the breakfasting room, wondering how she should act when she came face to face with her husband across the breakfast table. She need not have concerned herself, for he was not to be seen, and casual enquiries of Mitford as to the Master's whereabouts elicited the information that he had gone out on horseback very early and did not expect to be back until late that evening—probably after Lady Wilberton had retired. And no, there had been no message left as to his direction!

"There you little fool," said that lady now to herself, angrily biting through a piece of bread and butter, "He means you to know by this how little he cares for you. Why, he does not even think it worthwhile to try to patch up our quarrel. What a great booby you are to care a fig for him. I think that there can be no-one for whom he holds such indifference."

It was a very serious Sarah to whom Mitford presented a gentleman's calling card some half an hour later. She had been sitting with Bess on the rug before the blazing fire in the drawing room, heedless of her complexion, telling Bess all her troubles as Bess, trying to look sympathetic, obligingly moved herself into precisely the correct position to ensure that Sarah's stroking should not miss any of those parts around the ears specifically designed to allow a dog to lapse into a state of ecstatic imbecility. Seeing the name on the card, Sarah sprang up from her place, dislodging Bess as she did so, and bade Mitford show the gentleman in, first ensuring that he took her dog away, since her visitor, she remembered, had an inordinate dislike of having paw-marks on his creaseless pantaloons. A few moments later and Sarah was shaking hands with him, saying, "Freddy, you cannot imagine how pleased I am to see you."

"Pleasure's all mine, Lady Wil," replied her cousin suavely, "Miles not in?"

"No, he has gone out riding. But why are you not at

Church, Freddy? I am sure that Amabel expected to see you there."

"As to that, wouldn't do to be seen there every week! Bad ton. Don't want to have 'em saying I'm in line for a curacy, don't you know. Moderation, that's the key word m'dear. I've found that everything stays all right and tight as long as you don't over-indulge."

At the thought of Freddy over-indulging in church-going Sarah was forced into a gurgling laugh in spite of herself. "I swear you are as good as a tonic, Freddy, really you are."

"That's more like it, Sarah, don't like to see that pretty little mouth drooping." He paused significantly. "Mind, can't say I'm altogether surprised to see you out of salts today."

Sarah had not been intimate with Freddy all these weeks without having a pretty shrewd notion that his commonplace exterior hid a great deal of wisdom, so she said only, "Oh Freddy, do you indeed *know* about our quarrel?"

"Hang it, Lady Wil, not so fast! Don't know anything at all, so no need to rush to confide in me. Only that, well, ran into Miles at the Great-Go last night. Looked as if the devil was in him. Tell you, it gave me quite a shock! Not at all like himself—play all to pieces, betting wild, bosky-looking, that style of thing. Remembered that I'd seen you earlier with Cranesby. Thought perhaps some gabster had made himself busy? Somebody blab, eh?"

"Worse, Freddy! Much worse! He *saw* us together and was out-of-reason furious."

"I should think he was! Told you it wouldn't do for Miles to get wind of it. Knew he'd be as mad as fire. Lord, Sarah, I never thought you was so shatter-brained."

Sarah lifted her chin defiantly at this. "Well you don't know it all Freddy, so there. We did not only argue about Lord Cranesby, for I saw Miles at the Opera too, and he too was alone with somebody in *her* box. And I think that I will not need to give you three guesses who it was."

"Are you telling me you took him to task for being with Lizzie? You little nodcock! Are you determined to put his back up? No wonder he was as mad as old Nero when I ran into him."

"Why is it that men can only see a man's point of view, Freddy? I had thought you my friend, and now you make it seem as if you believe all to be my fault," she replied, angry tears stinging her eyes, "Can you have forgot that scene at Lady Stanham's? My memory is not so short!"

Freddy, immediately contrite, handed her a spotless handkerchief taken from his pocket. "Come now kitten, don't start blubbing. Never could stand it, you know. Be a good little thing."

Taking the handkerchief, Sarah obediently wiped her eyes and they were soon seated side-by-side on a sofa near to the fire, while Sarah gave Freddy all the details of her quarrel with Miles that propriety allowed.

To Sarah's annoyance, Freddy continued to hold by his opinion that she should not have shown her jealousy of Lady Blissworth, "For mark my words, it may well be that he has never thought of her as anything more than his little cousin—not saying that that's how it is, mark you, just that we can't discount the possibility—and now, you may have put goodness knows what into his mind! Always best to be on the safe side in these matters until you know the lie of the land. M'father always says—dashed knowing man, m'father. Military.—Always says, get over heavy ground as light as you can! That's just what you haven't done m'dear and so I tell you. Might never have found it necessary to come the heavy over Lizzie. Besides, nothing less attractive than a jealous woman. Ever occur to you that with all the attention you have been getting lately Lizzie might well be jealous of you? Might think Miles could become more attracted to his wife than to her? Never can tell with these affairs. Don't you see how much better it would have been if it had been Lizzie who had been enacting Cheltenham Tragedies for Miles rather than you? As it is now—played into Lizzie's hands I shouldn't wonder."

"Oh Freddy, you are quite right! How stupid of me not to realise! Is anybody more truly wise than you? But what can I do now?"

"Well, first," he replied, after considering the problem for a couple of seconds, "I suggest that you come out with me for a drive in the park. Curricle outside. Looking a trifle peaky, m'dear, if I might say so. None of your usual bloom. If Miles sees you looking so washed out shouldn't wonder if he rushes off hot-foot to Lizzie. Or, indeed, anyone else! Come out for a while and see if we can't put the roses back into your cheeks. We can put our heads together at the same time about this business. See if we can't come about. Don't like to say too much with servants around. Business will be all over town before we know it if we are not careful. Tell you what, Sarah, I'll let you tool the ribbons if you like. Been thinking lately, good thing for you. Add a new dash if you could learn to drive a carriage."

"Will you really, Freddy?" asked Sarah, beaming. "How handsome of you when I have behaved so foolishly. I must admit that I have the headache abominably and I am sure that an airing would be just the thing."

Twenty minutes later found Sarah driving with Freddy in his curricle through the Bath Gate and into the Green Park. It was much milder than when Bess had taken the plunge that day before, indeed, the sun was quite warm through her pelisse. As soon as they were through the gates Sarah took the reins and her headache was soon forgotten in this new pleasure. Freddy said that he could see that she had light hands and a natural aptitude, and handsomely declared that he would not be surprised to see her driving her own barouche in the park very soon.

However enjoyable was her drive, for once Freddy and Sarah were not in complete accord. While she was prepared to allow that he might be right when he told her to behave towards Miles as if nothing untoward had occurred, and while she admitted too that it was probably a mistake to show her envy of Lady Blissworth, she *could* not approve Freddy's advice with regard to Lord Cranesby. No matter how he tried to convince her that she must accept Miles's dictum concerning his old enemy, Sarah refused to believe it to be necessary. If Freddy would only tell her why, then maybe she might reconsider, but until he did so, she must regretfully be guided by her own instincts. Freddy, of course, could not do so, but had no hesitation in telling her roundly that for once her instincts were at fault. It was in less than his usual good humour, therefore, that he returned with Sarah to Berkeley Square for luncheon.

If Freddy thought that the most disagreeable part of his day was at an end, he was quite out, for when he was shown into the drawing room, it was to be brought face to face with Amabel: but it was an Amabel he had never seen before and one, moreover, whose face was pregnant with the full fury of womanhood wronged. Her first words, however, were directed not at Freddy, but at Sarah, for no sooner had her sister-in-law shown herself at the drawing room door than, without even waiting for Mitford to close the door behind her, she began coolly, "My dear Sarah, how absurd you are to *pretend* to the headache. Had you simply said that you had a rendezvous with my cousin I should most certainly not have tried to insist that you come to Church."

"Why Ami, I had no idea that Freddy was coming here this morning, had I Freddy?" replied Sarah, faintly disturbed at the colour in Amabel's cheeks.

"Couldn't have, Lady Wil. Well, stands to reason, don't it. Had no idea last night that I should call myself," said Freddy, directing a fierce stare towards Mitford, who had been interestedly listening to these promising beginnings of a quarrel, but was now forced to close the door on them and take himself off.

"I assure you that you have no need to hide your meetings from me. Surely it is rather Miles that you must needs be afraid of."

"I haven't the least idea what you are talking about, Ami," said Sarah a little shortly, for her headache has returned, "but I wish you might explain it to me, since I declare that I am too stupid for guessing games today."

Freddy was less inclined to allow Amabel the luxury of enlightening them as he thought that he was beginning to have a fair notion of what was in her mind. "If you are thinking what I am pretty sure you *are* thinking, my girl," he now said, "then you are more of a booby than ever I thought you could be. And what is more, you have far less delicacy of mind than I gave you credit for."

"Well, you are almost bound to say so, are you not Freddy? Even you could not pass off as good ton having an illicit liaison with your cousin's wife!"

"Is that what you think he has been having, Ami?" asked Sarah incredulously, suddenly understanding, "Why you little goose! Surely you know us better than that. If you must know, Miles and I had a quarrel last night and Freddy is teaching me to drive to make me feel better. It is the greatest piece of folly to suspect any blacker motive."

Amabel's face flamed redly. Freddy had always refused to teach *her* to drive. "How nice and pat you have your story, Sarah. You must think me a goose indeed to believe it. Just tell me, if you can, how he knew that you had had this precious quarrel! No, it is too obvious, for you are forever in each other's pockets: if it is not shopping alone, then it is waltzing at Almack's, or sitting together whispering at the Opera, and now driving. There is never a time when you are *not* together. Why, if you are not careful you will find that you have become one of the on-dits of the town and how will you like that?"

"By heaven," declared Freddy wrathfully, striding over towards her and leaning over her, resting his hand on the back of her chair, "now you go too far, my girl. It is time that someone told you what is what, and it seems that I am to be that someone! So be it. You appear to have a mind like a gutter urchin, so there is not a moment to be lost, and if you have no more discrimination than to think Sarah could be guilty of the crimes with which you insult her, then I should think that your wits must be going begging." He paused, as if struck by a further thought, then continued damningly, "Moreover, I must say that it depresses me to find that a young lady (and I use the term loosely) given the benefit of every aid to education, should end up so sour-tongued as you! Very pretty behaviour we have been met with today, Miss. It makes me ashamed that you should be related to me at all, so it does."

Sarah watched fascinated as he left hold of Amabel's chair and began to walk up and down the room unable to control his rage. Amabel took this opportunity to say sharply,

"And who do you think you are to dare to set yourself up as an arbiter of manners? You may think that you know all there is to know about the world, but let me tell you that not everybody thinks you are so perfect yourself."

Her outburst did nothing to cool Freddy's temper, and he once more turned on her, saying through clenched teeth, "I'll tell you what, Miss precious high and mighty Greville, if you don't watch that tongue of yours you will find that none of the suitors you have kept dangling on strings all this time to serve your own vanity will come up to scratch and you will find yourself ditched. It's been known before, don't you know, that a girl who seems to have it all, good looks, fortune, breeding, the lot, ends up on the shelf because her tongue is too sharp and makes her past bearing with. And incidentally, you might also wonder in what light you appear when it is seen that you had rather keep a whole load of ninnies wrangling over you than behave like a delicately-nurtured female ought and choose one of them. Heaven knows you have enough of the boobies to satisfy even a Cleopatra—and *that* you *aint*! I thank heaven that I am not one of your suitors, but if I were, your performance today would have cured me pretty quickly."

Throughout this tirade, Amabel preserved a rigid silence, refusing either to look at him or to give him the satisfaction of a reply. His last barb really went home, however, and she turned on him in fury. "You? A suitor of mine? Why I'd as lief have a tame monkey than have you dance about me. I cannot think of any one of the men who have asked me to marry them that I would not prefer to you."

She had the satisfaction of seeing Freddy flush a deep scarlet before he gave Sarah a brief bow and, without another word to Amabel, left first the drawing room and then, with a loud bang of the front door, the house.

For a few moments after he had gone, the ladies said nothing. Sarah was too appalled at what had occurred and Amabel could not trust herself not to allow the tears which had been gathering at the corners of her eyes to overflow. Then, pale-faced, Sarah comforted, "He did not mean it you know, any more than you did. He was merely angry."

In a very quiet voice which tremored slightly, Amabel replied, "Yes he did mean it! He meant every word of it! And it is true Sarah that I *was* sharp-tongued to *you* without reason. Of course you are innocent, just as he says. Please forgive me dearest. I cannot think what came over me."

"Oh love, say no more about it, I beg of you," said Sarah, beginning to have a fair idea, "And I know that Freddy will be back to apologize as soon as he has cooled down—for you know he will think it the height of bad ton," she giggled weakly, "to argue with a lady."

"Freddy?" questioned Amabel faintly, as if the name conveyed absolutely nothing to her, "Good gracious, as though I care what Freddy thinks of me. If he thinks me so abominable then he is quite free to do so. There are many others who feel quite differently about me as he shall find out before he is many days older."

"Of course there are, my dearest," assured Sarah, not liking the martial light in her eyes, "but I think you will find that Freddy will already have regretted saying such horrid things to you, for to be sure he admires you so."

"You do not have to flummery me, Sarah dear. No-one who admired me could say such beastly things. He was never one of my court, which is why, I suppose, I was a little peeved that he attached himself to you so obviously when you came to town. He was a challenge to me, nothing more I assure you."

"Oh, but there was nothing in his attaching himself to me, my love, for you know how dreadful I looked when I came up from the country. It was only that Freddy was kind enough to help me to know how to go on. That really was all that there was between us. It is true that I count him one of my best friends, but how could it be otherwise when he has been so very kind to me?"

"There is no reason to justify your friendship to me, Sarah dear, since Freddy is of no consequence with me at all. I admire Freddy no more than he admires me. Why, he is just a tailor's dummy. There is nothing to him at all. He is little more than a joke, so how could his opinion be thought to weigh with me in any way?"

Since she had accompanied this harsh little speech by walking distractedly around the room chafing her hands, Sarah gave it all the credulity it deserved, and she found the afternoon, during which Amabel returned every few minutes to Freddy's perfidy, to be one of unrelieved gloom. Added to her desire to reassure her sister-in-law that Freddy did not *really* hate her was her fear lest Miles should return in as ill a temper as his sister. By eight that evening the headache from which she had been suffering all day had reached monumental proportions and she wanted nothing more than to be allowed to reach the comfort of her bed. She was quite certain, however, that

Amabel would think her a monster of heartlessness to leave her alone with her misery and she endured an hour more of her rantings before Amabel too admitted to a headache and sought her own apartments. Having helped to put Amabel to bed and soothe away her tears, she was finally free to make her own weary way to her bedchamber, where she was helped by her faithful henchwomen to glide gratefully between her cool sheets.

CHAPTER 22

As Jenny opened her mistress's curtains punctually at ten the following morning the light streamed into Sarah's room. It was a beautiful cloudless morning and even so early the sun felt deliciously warm as it fell on Sarah's face and her outstretched arms. For a few moments her spirits lifted, for surely spring had, in truth, arrived at last and she was not yet so old that she did not feel its usual promise. Her optimism could not last long however, and her face clouded suddenly as she remembered in what mood she had left poor Amabel the night before. She must go to her at once. Spending less time than usual at her toilette, Sarah made her way to her sister-in-law's apartments, half expecting her to be still in the glooms, but she found, to her surprise, that Amabel was already up and about, no sign of yesterday's ill-humour on her face.

"Good morning, Sarah my love," she called, as Miss Bidmore let Sarah in. "Is your head better today? I must say that I feel wonderful!"

"Oh yes, certainly, my headache is completely gone and I am so glad to see you in such spirits, dearest."

"Spirits? Whyever should I not be in spirits on such a lovely day?" replied Amabel gaily. "Surely nobody could feel low with the sun shining so beautifully. And it puts me in mind, by the way, that I need some new parasols. Shall we go to the Pantheon Bazaar today to see what they have to offer? I want one to match the ribbons of my muslin and another for the silk. Oh, and I need to go back to Mr. Botibol's shop since the Ostrich feathers I bought last week to match my new evening gown are not quite the shade I wanted after all and I wish to see if he has some nearer it. No-one, you know, has such a fine selection as he."

If Sarah was rather taken aback to see Amabel

apparently in such a sprightly mood, she rather thought she could account for it, and anyway, she was not one to cavil at good fortune. The two were soon on their way down to the breakfast room, therefore, Amabel's arm affectionately around Sarah's waist, as they discussed the relative merits of matching or of constrasting parasols for the best effect.

Amabel's noticeable good humour was responsible for making Sarah's first meeting with Miles since their clash on Saturday less awkward than she had feared, for seeing him already at the table, reading his newspaper, his sister leaned down and kissed him on the cheek, saying as she did so, "Ah, here you are, Miles dear. Isn't it a perfectly heavenly day? Why, there is not a single cloud in the sky."

"Good heavens, Ami," replied her brother, taken off-guard for a moment and relinquishing the tight-lipped demeanour he had intended to sport for his wife. "I'm not sure that I am up to you being so affable first thing in the morning. In fact, I am almost certain I'd as lief face your usual morose breakfast face, even when accompanied by your habitual growls and grunts should anyone dare to speak to you."

Since it was well known that Amabel was the touchiest of creatures before she had breakfasted, they all three laughed and the ice was broken. If Sarah was quiet, brother and sister made enough noise for it to pass unnoticed by Amabel, and the meal went forward quite easily. As for Sarah, she could only be amazed at the difference between the urbane Miles who now confronted her and the man who had been in her bedroom two nights before. Looking at him now, immaculately dressed as ever, in a perfectly fitting black morning coat and a pair of the black trowsers so much despised by Lady Stanham, his spotlessly white waistcoat and shirt topped by a starched and intricately folded cravat, and his manners just as immaculate as his clothes, it was difficult to imagine that he could ever be discomposed in any way, certainly that he could become the desperate creature she had been privileged to see.

Had she been able to read his mind, she might have had less reason to be amazed, for his self-control had been pushed to the limit to enable him to appear nonchalant. Unlike Amabel, he had not failed to observe how quiet she was at breakfast and longed to know what she was thinking. Was she remembering his despicable behaviour on Saturday, or worse, was she angry with him for leaving when he did? He wished he knew what to think. If only he'd had more self-control, for then at least he could have continued to share her bed. Much easier then to keep her from another man's! Now it was impossible for him to go to her at all. Yesterday he had returned from Watier's in the early hours, intending to bring the whole matter out into the open. Daylight lessened his resolve and it seemed prudent not to risk further estrangement by hasty accusation. A day's riding and a boisterous bachelor gathering had not taken her from his mind and he had returned home late on Sunday determined to make his peace, only to be told that both his wife and sister had been in bed for several hours. A further night's reflection was enough to convince him that he was wasting his time anyway, since however attracted Sarah was to Cranesby she would naturally continue to deny it to her husband! And in the end—a decision that it was best to avoid her as much as he could. At least then he would be spared explanations which could only hurt his pride. Perhaps a few rounds sparring at Gentleman Jackson's might be just what he needed to take his mind off things.

About an hour later, he was seen striding through the door of the great man's rooms, ready for sport. Like most members of the ton, Miles saw nothing strange at all in hobnobbing with 'bruisers' like Tom Cribb and Belcher, Bill Neate or the Gas-man. He was a member of the Pugilistic Club, and it was not at all unusual to see him, or indeed any of his friends, walking arm in arm with one of his bruiser friends down Bond Street or St. James's, although they would heartily have despised the man who did so with anyone else of that class. Some noblemen, too, took boxing lessons at one of the fighting schools, like the Fives Court in St. Martin's Street or the Thatched House Tavern in St. James's.

That run by Gentleman Jackson, the ex-champion of England was, however, the most famous of them all. Here, even Lord Byron, who had nicknamed Jackson 'the Emperor of Pugilism', had taken lessons and here Jackson could still be found each day, in his famous scarlet jacket and lace cuffs, ready to give advice to favoured personages while the sporting gentry treated him with a deference only occasionally paid to princes.

He greeted Miles with something of the familiarity of a long-lost friend, scolding him on not making an appearance for so many months, declaring that he was sure he could see a little thickening around his waist and honouring him by promising to go a round or two with him himself to see just how 'flabby' his lordship had become. Already Miles felt his spirits lifting and he was just making his way over to a cubicle to begin to strip for action, when he found himself surveying Lord Cranesby across a distance of some yards, obviously on his way from the rooms. Unhurriedly making his way towards him, for he was unwilling to give Cranesby the satisfaction that he had in any way ruffled him, Miles was soon standing before him.

"Ah Wil," drawled Cranesby on seeing him, an insolent note in his voice, "you honour me with your attention, indeed you do old fellow."

"Dear me," replied Miles, "how very remiss of me to be sure. I am certain you know that nothing could be further from my wishes."

Cranesby instinctively raised his fists, only to immediately drop them again since here, of all places, spontaneous bouts of fisticuffs were frowned upon.

"Just so," said Miles, glad that his message had gone home, "but if you do indeed wish to chance your luck in a few rounds, I beg that you will see no further for a partner, for it is one of the few, the very few things I would be happy to oblige you in."

"Yes Miles, I am sure that nothing would give you greater pleasure than to plant me a facer, would it? Provided, of course, that you could do the trick, which I beg to suggest is by no means certain. I have not forgotten, you see, how evenly matched we were as boys, and I venture to think that I am in prime twig, whereas you are looking perfectly whey-faced, if you don't mind my saying so." He added, his tone calculatingly insulting, "Of course, I have not had the demands of that pretty little wife of yours to drain my strength, have I?"

"By Hell, Rob," the Earl blazed, unconsciously lapsing into his childhood name for his old friend, "do not push me too far. You have been the cause of one scandal in my house, but I warn you that should you attempt such a thing again, you will not come out of it unscathed!"

Lord Cranesby ran his finger lightly down the scar on his left cheek, a strange gleam in his eye, and said, "Surely you mean *comparatively* unscathed, my dear fellow, and this pretty mark on my cheek was not the only one I won in that little encounter, as you may remember."

"Perhaps it should be you who remembers, my friend, for it may give you pause to think before allowing your usual hot-headedness from plunging you into an adventure which cannot be to your good. For mark me, Cranesby, and mark me well. I swear that, should you attempt to damage my wife's reputation in any way, you will not live to reap any benefit."

"You interest me, Miles, indeed you do. I had not thought ever to see you again in the throws of, well, shall we say the tenderer passions? Though the little Dagley is certainly not in the common mould, I grant, and it is not difficult to understand why such a connoisseur as you should have beaten the herd in noticing it. Obviously reports of a marriage of convenience have been wide of the mark?"

"My reasons for marrying are my concern and the best way for you to preserve those good looks of yours Cranesby, is to ensure that they *stay* my concern. Involve yourself in my marriage at your peril! I have offered you the chance to go a few rounds with me: if you have not burned up your hatred of me long since, far better that you try to get back at me in that way than attempt anything more foolish."

"Almost, my dear Miles, I am tempted, but alas it cannot be. You see, I am fairly certain that my "good looks", as you are so kind as to call them, must be your target in such a contest and while I feel reasonably certain that I should emerge the eventual winner, it is probably too much to hope that you would not land one or two lucky shots. While I hope that I am not such a coxcomb as to mind a swollen lip or black eye, tonight, I must confess, I have an assignation of the greatest importance and should not like to insult the lady by appearing in less than pristine condition. Perhaps another time . . .?" and with an ironic bow, he passed on his way, stopping only to exchange a little banter with Jackson before walking out into Bond

Street sunshine.

* * * * * * * * *

In its own way, Sarah's day was quite as energetic as her husband's. Amabel was clearly in the mood to indulge herself and dragged Sarah round dozens of exclusive shops in and around Piccadilly, purchasing any expensive trifle which took her fancy. When even her extravagant mood was satisfied, Amabel begged an uncomplaining Sarah to accompany her to Hookham's Library in Bond Street, where she hoped to pick up a copy of Miss Austen's latest book, a must for any lady of fashion, dedicated as it was, to the Prince Regent. They were just about to go inside, when they bumped into Mr. Middleton on the step coming out, two books with marbled covers he was collecting for his sister, under one arm. Sarah was going to give him her usual greeting when, to her astonishment, he made only the slightest of bows to Amabel, and then, with a rather deeper bow and a smile to herself, passed on without a word. How shocking! Sarah's head swivelled immediately to Amabel to see how she bore up under such cavalier treatment, but that young lady, a slight flush mounted in her cheeks, only lifted her nose a little higher in the air, as if to indicate to the world at large that he was beneath her notice anyway.

Sarah was afraid that she was to be subjected to another bitter diatribe from Amabel concerning Freddy's numerous faults, but instead, Amabel seemed to find Freddy's distant demeanour a cause for congratulation, "for mark my words, Sarah, it would have been just like the odious creature to walk in on us this evening just as we were leaving for Vauxhall with Anstey, and then he would have thought it most odd in us had we not invited him to join our party. And you know that when he found out where we were going, he would have become tight-lipped about it and said it was not suitable for us to be seen there. No, we are far better off with him at a distance."

Sarah had been having second thoughts about Vauxhall almost from the moment she had been tricked by Cranesby into agreeing to go, for a few hours' reflection had been sufficient to make clear to her that she had indeed been tricked by her clever admirer. When Freddy had continued firm in his opinion that she should not know Cranesby, she had been given further food for thought and surely to go with him to Vauxhall would only compound the crime. Now, a trifle hesitantly, she confided to Amabel, "I confess, my love, that I am in a quake about tonight. I have been wondering any time since Saturday whether it should be attempted. Do not you think it would be felt very fast in us should any of our friends find us out?"

"Oh, never say that you are going to cry off, Sarah!" wailed Amabel, "Indeed, I did not think you so poor-spirited. Why, it will be the most famous lark and no-one will recognise us so long as we keep on our masks and hold our dominoes right round us. We shall leave before the unmasking you know?"

"But I am persuaded that Miles would dislike us to go of all things, even if we were not going with Cranesby. I am sure he must disapprove of Vauxhall."

"Oh stuff! Miles is not so high and mighty. Why, he's been to Vauxhall himself often enough, in fact, we have even been together," she said, with the air of one handing over a clincher, "and more than once too. I promise you it is the greatest of good fun."

"Have you really been with Miles? You would not joke me?" asked Sarah earnestly.

"Well, I like that! I'm no fibster, whatever I am," feeling it to be unnecessary to add that it had been to concerts and not Masquerades that Miles had taken her.

"No, of course not, my love. I wonder, then, why we need keep it secret from Miles. I understand, of course, that we cannot tell him that Cranesby is our escort, for that would make him cross as crabs, but why may not we tell him that we are going with the Viscount?"

"Oh no, Sarah!" cried Amabel hastily, "for then he would be sure to say something odious."

"There!" cried Sarah, with a touch of triumph. "I thought that it was not quite the thing and now your words have convinced me of it. Certainly we must cry off!"

'Oh don't talk such fustian, Sarah! I shall do no such thing! Why all the arrangements are made and we cannot possibly get in touch with Cranesby in time, even if we could warn Viscount Anstey. He will have the costumes.

Anyway, my love, you refine too much upon trivialities. All the ton go to Vauxhall: they just don't admit to it. So why should we be different?"

"But you know how cross Miles is with me already, Ami. I do not know why I let myself be talked into this silly venture, but I wish we might not go after all."

Amabel refused to be persuaded to give up the treat and it was with a mind full of misgivings that Sarah got ready that evening. Miles had left a message to say that he was dining out, for which Sarah was entirely thankful. At least she did not have to give him the lie direct as to her destination.

Viscount Anstey, in high spirits, dined with them in Berkeley Square. Although he was a passably well-looking young gentleman, though inclined to a little corpulence and possessing a rather higher colour than Sarah could find pleasing, she was surprised to see Amabel flirting with him in what she considered to be a most dangerous manner, since she had never thought that Amabel favoured him above any other of her escorts. True, he was extremely good-natured and said to be quite prodigiously wealthy, but she had never known Amabel moved by considerations only of wealth and Sarah would have sworn that she knew her sister-in-law well enough to discount her having formed a warmer regard for him. Tonight, however, it seemed that she was determined to turn his head with smiles and dimples and a quite surprising degree of familiarity, which caught the young man as much unawares as it did Sarah, though, since he had admired Amabel for more than a year, he could hardly be blamed for taking every advantage of her mood.

Sarah was quite relieved when the clock showed a quarter past eight and it was time to leave in the Viscount's town coach to meet Cranesby, for she began to wonder if things were not becoming out of hand.

Their carriage drew up close to the corner in Clarges Street under one of the gas lights which now lit London, and waited only for a few minutes before Lord Cranesby's curricle pulled up nearby. He jumped down, holding over his arm two black silk dominoes and two rose-coloured ones, while masks dangled from strings in his hand. With a cheery word to his groom to be off home, he was soon among them in Anstey's coach, handing out the costumes. Amabel, her eyes glinting with excitement as they put them on, said "Oh, how clever you are, Robert, for see, I have pink ribbons to my dress and Sarah's dress is pink as well. Why, we shall look splendidly."

"I hope you too are pleased, Ma'am," said Cranesby, bowing to Sarah, who was by now quite distracted with fear.

'Oh yes, they are very pretty to be sure. But should we not be going, for we are so near to home that there is no knowing who might see us."

"Sarah is all in a quake, Robert, in case Miles should get wind of this," explained Amabel, with the air of one making excuses for a very young child. "She is not yet used to such outings and feels herself to be very wicked."

"Then we must be off immediately, Anstey, for it would not do to make Lady Wilberton uneasy," he replied gallantly, staring at Sarah in a way which brought the blood rushing to her cheeks.

The Viscount was all complaisance and gave his coachman the word to "Spring 'em!"

CHAPTER 23

The evening was so mild as they made their way through the streets of London that Amabel could not help wishing that they had decided to go to Vauxhall by wherry across the Thames instead of by coach, for "to be rowed across by one of the watermen was of all things delightful!"

Cranesby, always willing to oblige a lady, promised to see if he could not arrange something for their journey back and Amabel professed him to be her "very favourite man" as a result, although in truth it did not seem as if he returned the compliment, for, to Sarah's great confusion, his eyes scarcely left her own face and he addressed almost all of his conversation to her in a way which, though it made her blush becomingly, made her wish heartily that the evening was safely over. Pleasant as it was to be the object of a gentleman's attention, she found that somehow she could not be quite comfortable at such very particular behaviour.

Although Vauxhall was not yet opened for the Season, its thousands of coloured lamps were lit for the pleasure of the assembled company as it wandered down long avenues of trees admiring fountains and statues, and Sarah was entranced to see them hung in festoons to light the walkways. Almost it seemed a pity to have to make their way inside the Rotunda to the masquerade, but Amabel, holding tightly to the Viscount's arm, assured Sarah that, not only would she enjoy the proceedings enormously, but that, if they did not hurry, she would miss seeing the Cascade, one of the sights of London. Still reluctant, but unwilling to disoblige her, Sarah wrapped her silk domino tightly around her and checked that the strings of her mask were firmly tied, as the sound of an orchestra playing guided them to their destination.

Sarah had never before been to a masquerade, and she

checked on the threshold of the large circular building, her eyes wide with amazement, as crowds flocked about her, spilling onto the walkways at the entrance. Surely she had entered some strange new world, for here, as far as the eye could see, showing up clearly in the flickering light blazing from masses of candles in huge chandeliers, were crowds and crowds of masked people, some in normal evening dress with only a domino for disguise as in their own party, but by far the majority in the most extravagant of fancy costumes. Here was to be seen every kind of disguise which ingenuity could devise: Harlequins made merry with their respective Columbines, vying for the title of chief mischief-maker with at least as many figures of Punch: here too Sarah could see Turkish princes escorting ladies of the harem, saucily and gaudily costumed, who contrasted strangely with a fair sprinkling of ladies dressed as the Goddess Diana, chaste and fair, a crescent or an arrow in their hair so that all might know which character they played. As Sarah made her way through the crowd on Cranesby's arm, feeling sadly crushed in the throng, she was suddenly startled by a nearby woman, shrieking at the top of her voice and tearing at her clothes and hair. She was about to try to offer the demented woman assistance, when Cranesby, amused at her ignorance, informed a shocked Sarah that the character of madwoman was one of the most popular disguises of all, for once it was assumed, it excused any impropriety of language or deportment. Just as shocking to Sarah—perhaps even more so—was to see, as she did all about her, women disguised as men, though no disguise, she thought, could be more inappropriate than those worn by several ladies pretending to be nuns. When she made her views known to Amabel, she was surprised to hear that delicately brought-up young female declare that she thought Sarah quite prosey, "For I can assure you, love, nothing is quite so provocative to the gentlemen as a nun unmasked!"

It all seemed most off to one so carefully nurtured as Sarah, and not a little wicked. Indeed, she began to feel quite uncomfortable, especially as, safe behind her mask, Amabel began to flirt audaciously not only with the Viscount, but even with one or two gentlemen not of their party who were persistently ogling her, being determined to take advantage of her state of incognito and enjoy her romp to the full.

Sarah did not see it in the same light. She suddenly became aware that here she was out of her depth and knew instinctively that Miles would be rightly furious could he see her in such company and would probably be even more so to think that she had given Amabel such licence. When she begged her sister-in-law to keep her behaviour within the bounds of propriety, Amabel laughed and called her a great gooby for not enjoying herself to the full, accepting most cordially Anstey's invitation to take to the crowded floor with him in one of the country dances now forming. Before she could stop her, Amabel had disappeared with him into the throng and the crowd had swallowed them up, closing in behind them until she could not even catch a sight of them.

All this time Lord Cranesby was watching Sarah in unalloyed amusement, her innocence a delight to him.

"Well, my lady, and how are you enjoying your first masquerade ball?" he now asked, when the others had gone.

"It is not at all as I imagined. Indeed, I wonder if it was not a mistake for me to come. Surely many of the people here have already imbibed rather too freely. I am certain that the ton could not be entertained by such untoward proceedings!"

Cranesby could not stop himself from laughing out loud at this. "My dear girl! Can you have been in town for so many weeks without realising that nowhere is hypocrisy more rife than among the ton? True, we are the first to cavil if someone is *seen* to behave improperly, but I would stake my life that half the people here—yes and many of them the very ones that have, as you so sweetly put it, imbibed rather too freely—are our very good friends, oh well-disguised, of course, but members of the ton for all that. We have only one rule to obey and that is not to be caught! As long as we are discreet, no doors are closed to us." He took Sarah's hands then, and pulling her gently very close to him, his face only a few inches from her's, murmured coaxingly, "Just think, my little one, what that might mean to us."

Sarah wrenched her hands away, her eyes glinting furiously through the slits in her mask, "Well you must forgive me then, my lord, for allowing myself to be drawn into such proceedings and I trust that you will put my 'hypocritical' behaviour down to the fact that I am not yet so sophisticated as you and your friends. In truth, I little suspected that it was your intention to draw me into such riotous company. And when I remember that I have brought Amabel too, I declare that I am ready to sink with vexation."

Seeing that she was indeed vexed, Cranesby realised that he had been too precipitate. Her anger suited him not at all, so he was forced to say, placatingly, "Come, Lady Wilberton, you are taking this much too seriously. You cannot really imagine that I would put *you* at risk, or do ought to displease you, such friends as we are?"

"If that is really so," she replied, ready to be reassured, "you can have no objection in agreeing to leave. And I can tell you that it would oblige me greatly could you find Miss Greville and the Viscount and bring them away at once. Believe me when I say that it is by no means amusing to me to be in this mêlée and for an unmarried girl like Amabel the result might be disastrous. Surely you must see that? It distresses me that you could call me friend and yet think this a suitable place to spend the evening."

"Ah, my dear," he simpered, taking her hand once again and pressing it, "I've made you cross—something I never wished to do. Perhaps you are right and it is not quite the thing for you, but I cannot let you go until you acquit me of ill-intent. Will you believe me when I say I only wished for your pleasure?"

Sarah, too embarrassed to take her hand from his again, was willing to believe anything he said if only they might get away from this appalling crush, and replied, "If we may only find Amabel and leave, I shall not give it another thought."

"Your ladyship is more generous than I deserve," he said smoothly, "though I fear it is not so easy to obey your wishes in this crowd. I confess that I have not caught sight of them since they left our side."

By now, Sarah was beginning to feel really depressed. The heat from the candles and the crush of bodies was making her wilt and she would have given all she owned for a sip of ratafia. She was also uncomfortably aware that to continue allowing her hand to rest in his gave their friendship an intimacy which went far beyond the limits she had set. "What do you suggest we do, sir?" she asked impatiently, straining to keep her temper.

"If you are agreeable, it might be best if you stayed here in this corner while I search the room. They are somewhere on the dance floor, that much we know, so it should not take me long to find them. You will be less crushed here than if you try to come through the crowd and I can see that you are badly heated already. See, here is a chair for you. Sit down and wait only a moment and I will bring them to you."

Sarah was more than thankful to be able to sit on the little hard chair in the corner, as, giving her hand a last squeeze, Lord Cranesby went on his quest, but her relief lasted only a few moments, since, to her consternation, a rotund man in a red costume, which she thought was supposed to represent Henry VIII, stumbled blindly over towards her, making her a grand, if somewhat unsteady bow, which almost caused him to topple over. In any other circumstances, Sarah would probably have been inclined to giggle, for his hat had fallen down over his forehead and his false beard was coming adrift, but the events of the evening had considerably dampened her sense of humour and she could not find him in the least amusing. His mask covered only his eyes, and Sarah could see how flushed he was from the effects of wine, and also that he was perspiring profusely, tiny droplets standing out on his upper lip. With a sigh of dismay, she resigned herself to the fact that he had chosen her as the object of his gallantry and tried to prevent him from meeting her eye by turning pointedly the other way. It was to no avail, for he continued to stand over her chair and beam at her, making so bold as to enquire of her, in a voice slurred, yet withal, very good-humoured, "Well, my little bird of paradise, and what is a pretty, sweet thing like you doing sitting here all alone? Why, Tom Bartlett would be a poor fellow indeed to allow such a dreadful thing."

Sarah, refusing to look up, made no reply, hoping against hope that he might be discouraged and leave her alone. She was not so fortunate, for he would not be abashed and, taking a chair next to her own, he continued to leer at her while she fanned herself briskly, trying to prevent his wine-soaked breath from reaching her and overwhelming her with nausea.

"Don't be so bashful, my pretty, for I'll be bound you came for fun just as I did," he persevered bravely, "and I'll wager that behind that mask of yours is the sweetest face a man could wish to kiss!" At this, he lurched towards her as if he would indeed try to kiss her and Sarah put up her hands to his chest in horror, as the wine fumes reached and threatened to engulf her. Never had she been more angry, pushing against him with all her might and catching him offguard, causing the unfortunate man to lunge wildly at her in a last attempt to grab hold of her arm and so keep his balance. He missed, and succeeded only in catching the edge of her mask with his hand, before falling from his chair in a heap at her feet. But to Sarah's horror, her mask was torn from her face, leaving it exposed for all to see! As luck would have it, most of the people around her were either too busy with their own concerns to notice the incident or were too amused at the sight of poor Mr. Bartlett on the floor to notice the face of the lady who pushed him there. Indeed, only one person, a fresh-faced gentleman, sitting with some friends nearby, recognised Sarah before she speedily retied her mask, but he gave a long, silent whistle, wondering as he did so if he should intervene on Sarah's behalf. While he was debating with himself, Cranesby returned to Sarah's side, which decided matters. He must certainly keep an eye on the Countess, for so he knew her to be, since if his suspicions were correct as to the identity of her partner, it might well be that she would find herself in some deep water later on.

"Thank heaven you are returned, my lord," said Sarah gratefully as she saw Lord Cranesby, at the same time showing Mr. Bartlett baleful eyes through her mask, "please let us get away from here!"

"As always, Ma'am, I am your servant," he replied smoothly, unaware that it had been with Sarah's aid that Henry VIII had reached his come-uppance, and the two walked off, Sarah carefully drawing her gown to her and preventing so much as the hem of her domino from touching that poor dethroned monarch.

"But where are the others?" she asked then, looking all around her, "Have you not brought them back?"

"I regret that they are nowhere to be seen. I have searched everywhere, but they must have taken themselves off for a walk outside to cool off, since it's so damnably hot in here. If you are agreeable, I think we would do well to go outside ourselves and seek them there."

So attracted was Sarah by the idea of escaping from the abominable heat in the Rotunda, that she did not immediately perceive the impropriety of going outside alone with him, and taking his arm gratefully, expressed her thankfulness to leave: nor, in the blessed coolness of the evening, was she straightway discontent. They could see no sign of Amabel and the Viscount among the crowd taking an airing immediately outside, and Cranesby, silently offering up his thanks for Amabel's waywardness, proposed that they make their way round some of the walks so as to find them. Foolishly, it did not occur to Sarah to mistrust him, but when some few minutes later, she found herself being led past the Chinese Pavilion and into one of the dark walks, her heart gave a momentary lurch of suspicion.

"I don't think Anstey would think it proper to bring Amabel here do you?" she asked, turning to look into his face. What she saw there only served to increase her disquiet, for instead of the amusing companion she had been wont to consider him, she found herself staring into eyes which suddenly seemed to have become much darker, and she noticed a pulse beating wildly at his throat, as if their situation excited him. Now he suggested, in a carressingly smooth voice she found disturbing, "Let us forget about the others for a little while, my dear, and not let them spoil for us these few precious moments."

"Forget, my lord, indeed I cannot, since I am responsible for Amabel."

"Devil take Amabel," he said irritably, and then, retrieving his slip, more tactfully, "I do not ask you to forget her, of course, but it is useless to go round in circles. If we sit here and rest for a while we can decide what is best to do," and he led Sarah firmly by the arm to a bench seat, cunningly set into a leafy embrasure to one side of the walk in such a way as to hide its occupants from prying eyes.

Now Sarah really was afraid. She remembered Freddy's

warning that he was a "bad man" and for some reason was suddenly quite certain that Freddy was right all along. Determined not to show her fear she answered him in a calm matter-of-fact voice, which she hoped would suit, "Now what do you think is best to do, sir? How shall we find them?"

He did not even bother to answer her. Instead, almost before she finished speaking, his arms had encircled her shoulders, his strength almost crushing the breath from her body as his lips searched for hers. She wrenched her head to one side, crying out wildly, "No! Do not, I beg of you, sir! You do not understand!"

In answer, he laughed exultantly and covered her mouth while she struggled furiously to break free from him. But he was too strong for her, holding her quite easily in one arm, while his other hand loosed her mask.

"Now I can see you, my lovely girl," he murmured thickly, as his lips kissed first her eyes and then, to Sarah's dismay, moved down to her throat.

Not one to give in without a struggle, she continued to fight him for all she was worth, though her struggles only seemed to heat his blood, "Egad, Sarah, I swear you are an exciting woman! Don't pretend that you don't want this as much as I do, for I'll swear you have been as hot for me as I am for you."

She was stung to reply, breathlessly, "You are mistaken, my lord, and if I have made you think so I can only apologize. I do not want you, I have never wanted you, nor will I ever do so."

"You lie," he rasped, "Why else would you defy Miles to meet me?"

Sarah, who had begun to wonder herself what on earth could have possessed her to be so foolish, could not answer, an omission which he took to be an acceptance of his attentions. His hand moved towards her bosom and she felt the thin stuff of her dress tear as he reached to find bare flesh. She was almost fainting now in horror, her strength deserting her rapidly, when suddenly a voice rang out from the shadows, to say in the most matter-of-fact way,

"I think, Cranesby, that the lady finds you not to her taste!"

So shocked was he at the unwarranted interruption that Lord Cranesby loosed his hold on Sarah, who immediately took advantage and sprang up from the bench, clasping her domino around her with shaking hands to hide the damage to her gown. Looking round to ascertain the identity of her rescuer, she saw a figure emerge from the blackness, untying the strings of his mask as he came. As the mask fell and she saw his face, Sarah cried out thankfully, "Lord Blissworth, thank heaven it is you!"

CHAPTER 24

"Well now, Lady Wil, won't you tell me all about it?" encouraged Lord Blissworth, as the waiter moved off and they began to tuck into the wafer-thin slices of ham for which Vauxhall was famous. Sarah was feeling much more the thing, for, with only a few words, Lizzie's husband had miraculously managed to get Lord Cranesby to decamp, only a slight shrug of his shoulders to show his discomfort at having been found in such an undignified situation. Her rescuer had then carried her off to one of the supper boxes littered about the gardens. Intrigued to see her with her husband's professed enemy, he hoped for an explanation when she had regained a measure of composure. Once there, she had found an opportunity to repair the tears to the neckline of her dress with some pins from her reticule, while he ordered supper.

She was as much aware that her rescuer deserved an explanation as he could ever be, but where could she begin? Now that she knew Lord Cranesby for a scoundrel, it seemed incomprehensible to her that she could have been so taken in by him—more, that she should have disobliged her husband to do so. Her resulting explanation was rather halting and, at times, so confused as to make it almost incomprehensible to all but the most astute of men. She was lucky, therefore, that Lord Blissworth was such a man and, although he felt that some of the finer points of the tale might have escaped him, he was pretty certain, by the time she had finished speaking, that he had the gist of it. He had, after all, one or two pieces of information in his keeping which would have been denied to other would-be followers of her narrative and which were undoubtedly of help in the untangling of Sarah's adventure: he was, for one thing, well acquainted with the cause of Cranesby's estrangement from Miles and knew that he would leave no stone unturned to serve Miles a facer: he was also fairly certain that Sarah suffered, as did he, from his wife's infatuation with Lord Wilberton and he rather thought that these two facts served to fill any gaps Sarah had left in her story, including why she was so determined not to obey her husband's wish that she should keep Cranesby at bay. When she ended her speech by saying, in a rather distracted way, "Oh dear, this must sound like so much nonsense to you, my lord," he felt quite able to reply that, on the contrary, the facts were now perfectly clear to him. "And I can only say that I am more relieved than you can know that I wasn't too fastidious to come here myself, with my friends, or all might have been up with you." He paused, looking at Sarah with kindly eyes, "You say, my dear, that you disobeyed Miles because he would not explain about his quarrel with Cranesby. You will forgive me, I know, when I say that I think that is not your only reason. My wife? . . ."

Sarah only nodded at him, a tight constriction in her throat making it impossible for her to answer him. There was an uncomfortable pause, and Lord Blissworth sat looking at her for some moments, much to her discomposure. Then, as if he had come to a difficult decision, he began briskly, "Well, Miles will be angry with me and Freddy Middleton may say that I have no business to tell you, but I am going to explain to you just why you should not make a friend of Cranesby, for I am sure that, had someone done so before, you would not be here now. And in any case, you have a right to know. I must warn you at the outset, however, that it is not a very pretty tale."

Sarah was suddenly not at all certain that she wanted to hear it, for Lord Blissworth's face told her that it must be bad. "Do you think you should tell me, sir, if Miles does not wish me to know?" she asked in an awed voice.

"Yes, my dear, I do, though I shall do so as briefly as possible, for I must explain to you at the start that Miles, Cranesby and I were once the best of friends together and it mislikes me to speak ill of either of them. Funny thing, friendship, you know? Cranesby could have knocked me down tonight, easy as blinking—but he didn't. Friendship, do you see? Difficult to knock down a fellow with whom you went fishing as a lad. Well, as I say, we were all friends—our lands march close by each others' and we were brought up more or less together. Always I was less of a blade than they, which once gave me cause for envy, but which has since often made me thank the heavens!"

"You may say so, sir, but after tonight I find it difficult to believe that any woman would think you wanting in dash," broke in Sarah earnestly.

"It is enchanting of you to say so, my dear, but compared with the other two, I was a very poor specimen indeed. You cannot know just how magnificent they were. Big, strapping, handsome fellows, both of them and always in mischief—well, we were all *that*, I suppose. They were always rivals—on horseback, fishing, shooting, everything, yet nothing ever spoiled their friendship. I was a sort of go-between to see fair play, I suppose. We had some fine times together, I can tell you," he murmured reminiscently, a grin touching his mouth. And then, as if recalled to the seriousness of the moment, "Anyway, all went well until the year that Caro Manders came out—I swear that nothing could have come have come between them until they saw her. Then, nothing would do but for them to become rivals for her hand. They were safe from me, of course, for I had long since been bewitched by Lizzie." He smiled as he said it, but Sarah could see in his eyes just how much that infatuation had cost him. "I've often wondered what would have been the outcome had we all three been chasing her," he continued reflectively. "It always seemed to me, you see, that had two of us been disappointed in love together we'd probably have gone off together on some wild spree and there would have been an end to it. As it was, Miles won Caro, just as he had won my poor Lizzie's heart years before—you won't mind me saying that, I know, for you have seen how it is with her?"

Sarah only nodded.

"It seemed, with Miles's victory, that all rivalry must come to an end—Not so! Cranesby, you see, had never before been thwarted of anything he truly desired and, believe me, he wanted Caroline—she had made sure of that! No woman he'd liked had ever been able to resist him 'til then and he would not believe that Caro could. He simply would not give up his pursuit. And Miles did not care. After all, he had won her and it did not seem to occur to him that Cranesby might stoop to anything underhand, or that he had anything to fear from Caro. You see, Miles did not really understand Caroline!"

"Surely that can't be right, my lord?" questioned Sarah, puzzled, "Miles adored her, didn't he? Everyone says so."

"Adored her? Oh no, I think not!"

"But you are mistaken sir, for he has told me often and often how she was all the world to him!"

"How very sensitive of him, to be sure," he murmured, *sotto voce*. "Yes, and I really believe that he thinks she *was* all the world to him, that's the devil of it. Yet I would swear that if Cranesby had not wanted her, Miles wouldn't have either. As I say, they were always rivals. I have always believed it to be a matter of course that they should both have chased the most beautiful of women, just as they had chased the most wily foxes or tried to land the biggest salmon. To be honest, they were neither of them ready for marriage at all and that's the truth of it. When Miles won Caro, nothing would do but for him to start imagining her to be some kind of Helen of Troy, convincing himself that any woman he was to marry was worth a king's ransom. Unfortunately for him she proved herself only too costly, for it was through her that two men who had been dear to each other almost from birth became the deadliest of enemies. As for Caro, she loved it all!"

"But she was married to Miles!"

"Aye, so she was, but that kind of woman always has to have more than one man on leading strings," he replied bitterly.

"But Miles calls her his sainted Caro!"

"Sainted she wasn't, my dear, word of a gentleman, though it would be more than my life was worth to say so to Miles!"

"But what happened?" urged Sarah, "You still haven't told me."

"Well, next thing you know, she had married Miles—grandest wedding you could imagine, of course, and my poor little Lizzie eating her heart out. Not that that signifies, but it's what I recall most, as you may guess! Miles carried her off into the country for months—prolonged honeymoon, keeping her to himself and all that, while Cranesby kicked his heels in London, like a dog chafing on his leash! Terrible time for us all, I remember!"

Seeing his face turn grey with the memory, Sarah placed a hand over his, "If it hurts to think of it, I pray you not to go on."

One look at her pinched face was enough to make him continue, and, covering her hand with the other one of his, he continued, "Of course, the honeymoon could not last for ever and eventually they were back in town—Caro more beautiful than ever, while Miles looked even more like a dog guarding his marrow bone than before they went away. To Cranesby it was the biggest challenge of his life, especially as I, in the meantime, had been so fortunate," and here he gave a bitter laugh, "as to win Lizzie for myself. Caro, naturally, encouraged Cranesby to hanker after her for all she was worth—and not only him either. Lord, how she loved to set men at each others' throats. Yet all the time Miles could only see—or would only see—her as the best of wives."

He halted in the middle of his story and took a large gulp of rack punch as if unwilling to remember more, but Sarah's anxious face made him complete the tale.

"It was not long after I had married Lizzie, I remember, when things came to a head. We were all present at a grand ball being held at a mansion near Richmond. Lizzie and I were there, Caro and Miles, with Cranesby hanging around Caro like a dog on heat. Miles was still not jealous, you know? It was quite amazing, for everyone was prophesying disaster. But he trusted Caro completely—that's what I mean when I tell you he didn't really understand her, for when I say that she was without doubt the most faithless woman I have ever known. I do not exaggerate one whit!"

"You must be mistaken. Why, they were married such a short time!"

"Oh, I don't mean that she was physically unfaithful to Miles, though that would undoubtedly have followed in time—even that type of woman usually presents her husband with an heir first!—it was just that she couldn't look at a man without promising him the earth with her eyes. Eyes of the coldest blue she had. And believe me, men looked back! Cranesby, though, was not willing just to look. That night at Richmond he had a devil in him, and

Caro seemed determined to fan the flame of his jealousy ever more fiercely, so each time he was nearby she hung onto Miles's arm and held herself against him as if she could not bear to be away from him—not a very ladylike exhibition, but very effective as you might guess. I had more than enough on my plate keeping my poor Lizzie occupied to notice much of it, for it hurt her just as much as it did Cranesby and that, of course, made it even more exciting to Caro."

"She knew that Lizzie liked Miles?"

"Lord yes! It made the whole situation even more piquant for her. I never really knew the precise moment when things came to a head, for my real concern was to keep Lizzie apart from them, but Miles was forced to bring Freddy Middleton and later myself into it to help him hush it all up and keep his 'sainted' Caroline's name sacrosanct. I can tell you, it went hard with me to oblige him!"

"But what happened?" cried Sarah, unable to keep the impatience from her voice.

"Quite simply, my dear, Cranesby carried her off!"

Sarah stared at him blankly.

"Well may you look open-mouthed, but that is what happened. She went upstairs to tidy her hair and on the way downstairs he apparently met her as if by accident. Persuaded her to walk with him in the gardens and then took her off in his curricle—no-one knows to this day if he coerced her or if she went willingly, though Miles, of course, will never have it said but that he kidnapped her."

"What did Miles do?" whispered Sarah, vastly intrigued by this picture of Miles as wronged husband.

"As soon as he knew what had happened, naturally he chased after 'em, Freddy Middleton going too to try to calm him down—you may imagine what a good head Freddy has on him at such times. Miles guessed where Caro would be taken, of course, for Cranesby has a house near Hounslow which he sometimes uses when he is in London—well, if truth be told, we had often, all three, been there—Freddy too for that matter—for certain of those unsavoury little bachelor parties you ladies are right to despise so much. House was perfect for his purpose, secluded and quiet, only one or two servants. But he was rather stupid if he did not realise that Miles would guess straight off where they were heading—though it's always been my belief that he wanted Miles to follow. No point stealing his wife if he couldn't see how Miles would take it. You have found to your cost tonight, m'dear, that he is often hasty. Never weighs up the risks, just follows his instincts. Miles knew all the lanes leading to the house just as well as Rob did, just as we all did, indeed, so it could only have been a matter of time before Miles caught them up. In the event, it didn't matter much how long Miles took to find them, for on their way Cranesby overturned his curricle. Caro was killed outright!"

Sarah felt herself stiffen as he said it. She had heard Miles and Amabel talk of Caroline's accident any number of times, but never had she imagined anything like this. And surely Caroline had died at Beaumere?

"What did he do then—Miles, I mean?"

"He came up with Robert on the road—Freddy said that when they got there he was holding Caroline in his arms, weeping like a child." Lord Blissworth cleared his throat, embarrassed to report such unmanly behaviour. "Upshot of it was that Miles and Cranesby fought a duel—swords! That's how Cranesby got the scar on his cheek and that wasn't his only injury—deep wound to his chest as well. Freddy swears that Miles would have done for Cranesby if he hadn't intervened . . . That's about it, really. Freddy brought Cranesby to me and between us we managed to keep him hidden away until his wounds had healed . . . devil of a job keeping it from Lizzie, too, I can tell you. Only persuaded Miles to let him live by saying that Caro's name would be dragged through the mire if Miles killed him. We managed to keep her death secret for a few days and Miles went back to Beaumere. Put out the story that she had died on the estate while tooling a carriage round the grounds. Tongues wagged, of course—and they wagged even more when Cranesby came back to town some months later sporting that scar. They couldn't prove anything, though, so Caro's lilywhite reputation was saved. Even Amabel and Lizzie don't know the truth of it . . . Miles, of course, would never believe she was anything but innocent!" he paused significantly, "So now, my dear, you will understand why you shouldn't know Cranesby."

Seeing that Sarah was too shocked to speak, Lord Blissworth poured them each a glass of punch and bade her drink hers like a a a good girl. "You've gone as white as a sheet and no wonder, but you had to know some time."

She took her glass and sipped at the contents trying to make sense of all she had heard, then hesitated before asking him something which still puzzled her, but which he might find impertinent, "And did you indeed know that Lizzie loved Miles before you married her?"

He coloured, and looked down at his own glass, which he was now holding between both hands, "I regret to say that I did, my dear. Miles is not the only stupid one, you know: we all have a degree of self-deception, do we not, though in my case it did not last. Yes, I was foolish enough to think that I could win Lizzie from Miles when he married—might have done it, too, if it hadn't been for Caro's death." He turned his face eagerly towards Sarah's as if willing her to understand. "Fancy she had begun to turn to me, just a little. Just now and then it seemed that she had started to care for me—as a man, you know? No chance then, of course. All her hopes were raised again."

"But how could they be?" askd Sarah, naively, "She was your wife by then."

"Oh, I fancy she trusted to luck that something might happen. She has the true optimism of the selfish. Thinks the world is run to please her! She would not consciously wish me any harm, for she is fond of me in her way—but perhaps I might oblige her by contracting an incurable disease, or my horse might give me a toss in the park, something in that line. Of course, you have now dashed all her hopes again, for even Lizzie is not so sanguine as to expect two miracles."

Sarah was quite dazed by all she had heard. It did not seem possible that such dreadful things could have happened to people she knew and lived among. "Oh dear, my lord, what a terrible tale it is you have told me. No wonder Miles was furious with me, but if only he had had the sense to tell me about it himself, I would never have even wanted to know Cranesby. And you, my dear sir! What a good friend you have been to Miles in spite of all."

"Miles is the best of good fellows, you know, as good a fellow as ever lived. You must not blame him because

Elizabeth has him in her sway."

"And do you indeed think he is attracted to her now?" she asked anxiously.

"Can there be a doubt of it? You have seen my fine little Lizzie's determination. Can you imagine any man being able to refuse her? Forgive me, my dear, for I know how painful this must be to you."

"Certainly it is painful, my lord, but it is quite as painful to me to see you accepting it," replied Sarah unexpectedly and with a sudden new vigour which took Lord Blissworth by surprise. "Do not you think you should do something about it?"

He laughed shortly and said, "By all means. What do you suggest, Lady Wilberton? I suppose I could lock her up and put her on a diet of bread and water, but I doubt it would make her love me."

She appeared to consider his suggestion seriously. "Bread and water? No that would not do at all, my lord. I have something else in mind."

"Something tells me that I am going to regret asking this, Ma'am, but precisely what *do* you have in mind?"

Sarah took a deep breath and looked him squarely in the eye, "We must do our best to turn the tables on Lizzie and Miles, of course."

"And how do you propose to do that?" he asked, amused in spite of himself, "such a simple task as it is."

"Oh I do not say it will be simple, my lord, "She answered him, still serious, "nor that we will necessarily succeed. I think it is only right that you realise that much, for I would not wish you to be under any false illusion. It is just," she went on scoldingly, "that I thought you would think the effort as worthwhile as I."

Suitably chastened, he apologised and asked her to explain further.

"Well, has it never occurred to you that you are a very handsome man?"—he blushed—"Oh no, sir, do not colour up, I beg, for it is no more than the truth. Why any number of ladies would be delighted to attach you . . . and yet you allow yourself to languish at your wife's feet. Now I know I am not a beauty, but I am thought to be much improved of late," she said self-consciously, tugging at the

201

strings of her domino, head lowered to hide fiery cheeks.

"You are undoubtedly much improved," replied her gallant companion.

Her glowing face was raised once more to him, "Well then, why don't we join forces? I am said by my family to be quite obstinate, you know, and I never felt more so than in this. What you have told me about Caroline is truly dreadful, of course, but in a strange way it has given me new heart, for at a stroke it has removed one half of my problem. While I thought I was trying to replace the irreplaceable, the perfect wife, I was unable to think clearly about being rid of Lizzie—excuse me, won't you, if I put it that way! Now that I know that Caroline's perfections are a figment of my husband's imaginaton, that worry all but disappears. It seems to me, my lord, that together we might begin to make a push to dispose of the other difficulties if we are not always seen as underdogs. Freddy once said to me that I should never allow myself to appear at a disadvantage and he is always right you know."

He seemed taken aback at the thought of Freddy in such a new and startling light, but did not interrupt her flow.

"It can do our cause no good at all to be always at the beck and call of our spouses, as I'm sure Freddy would be the first to agree. You should begin to take notice of other ladies and," she added in a small voice, "I would be grateful if you would start with me!"

"I can assure you, Lady Wil . . ."

"Oh please call me Sarah, won't you, for then I may call you Jeremy! Our relationship makes it quite in order, doesn't it. And I am sure it will be much more effective!"

"Sarah, then. If I am to flirt with the ladies, I'd as lief begin with you as anyone," he assured her, amused by her exuberance, "but do you think it will serve?"

"Well, we will never know if we don't try, will we? It will at least stop *me* from feeling so ill-used and so should it you. I do not know how you have fitted yourself so neatly into the little niche Elizabeth has allowed you, so well-looking as you are and so . . . well . . . so nice! But it is time to break and away and show her that you are rather more that the complaisant husband she finds so convenient."

Lifting Sarah's hand to his lips, Lord Blissworth replied, "Madam, I find myself in complete agreement with you."

He would have said more, but at that moment two figures showed themselves at the low partition which surrounded their box and, before Sarah and Lord Blissworth had a chance to replace their masks, Amabel's irate voice was heard to say, "So there you are, Sarah. A fine chaperone you are. Why, we have been looking all over for . . ." She stopped suddenly in mid-sentence when she realised that Sarah's supper partner, who had sprung to his feet at their appearance, was more than half a head shorter than he should be and no longer had bright blonde hair. Seeing at once who it was who had taken Lord Cranesby's place, she cried out inelegantly, "Good Lord, Jeremy, is that you? What are you doing here? And where is Robert?"

Unwilling to wash her dirty linen in public, Sarah told a rambling tale of Lord Cranesby's sudden indisposition and how fortunate she had been to meet up with Lord Blissworth.

But Amabel and the Viscount were only half listening to Sarah's excuses, and before Sarah had even finished speaking, Amabel blurted out, "Heavens, Sarah, never mind all that, for we have something perfectly famous to tell you. You will laugh when you hear it, for Anstey and I are to be married! He is to speak to Miles tomorrow!"

CHAPTER 25

They did not return home by wherry, for, having lost Cranesby, and with all the excitement of the evening, Amabel did not think of it until they were almost back in Berkeley Square. Beyond saying, however, that she was sorry they had forgotten, she seemed not much put out and kept the Viscount, as well as Lord Blissworth, who had been so kind as to accompany them home, in the greatest glee at her high spirits. Always witty, tonight she was dazzling and the two gentlemen were hugely entertained. The Viscount was indeed scarcely able to believe his luck in securing her, once being moved to say to Sarah in a dazed voice, "Who'd have believed she'd have me? Why, she's a mile too good for me, you know?"

Privately Sarah thought so too and she wondered what Miles would say when Anstey went to ask his permission. He might well be angry that the Viscount had not applied first to him before paying his addresses to Amabel, but whether he would approve or disapprove the betrothal, she could not tell. Anstey was, after all, eligible enough: his fortune substantial and his birth impeccable. Was that sufficient to weigh with a gentleman who himself was willing to enter a marriage of convenience for the sake of an heir? And in truth, Sarah herself could not really find anything to say against him, other than that somehow she had expected Amabel to choose a man with rather more to him. Of course, if she loved him there was no more to be said, but Sarah had seen little sign of it. What was more, Sarah had a prickly feeling that Amabel's betrothal followed too hard on the heels of her quarrel with Freddy to be mere coincidence, a feeling which gave her little joy. She knew the misery which could result from a loveless marriage.

The more she thought about it, the more she began to

think it her duty to sound out Amabel, so when, having been dropped back at Berkeley Square with her sister-in-law, she found that Miles was still out, she took the opportunity and said to Amabel, "My love, I declare that I am all agog to hear the details of your betrothal. Are you too tired tonight? For if you are not, I would love a comfy cose with you when I have changed."

Amabel was delighted and when, a quarter of an hour later, Sarah entered her bedchamber, she was just tying a nightcap around her curls and dismissing Miss Bidmore.

"There you are, Sarah," she cried on seeing her. "Look, isn't this fun! I have had a pot of chocolate sent up and some cakes in case you are as famished as me. We can have a feast. See, Biddy has pulled this armchair by the bed, and there is a shawl in case you feel a draught. I'm getting into bed, if you do not mind, for my feet are frozen."

Since Sarah was dressed only in a silk nightgown and peignoir, she was grateful to be able to wrap herself in the shawl while Amabel snuggled down between the sheets, and they were soon sipping at their chocolate and nibbling macaroons, while Amabel explained to Sarah how her betrothal had come about.

"But how did he manage to find an opportunity to ask you, love?" asked Sarah puzzled, for that crush seemed to Sarah quite the last place in the world for a declaration.

"Well, it just happened really. It was quite droll actually," she said, pulling her knees up under her chin and bringing her arms round them tightly. "We were dancing, when we heard the bell for the Grand Cascade. Did you see it, by the way, or had Cranesby already begun to feel ill by then?" she asked innocently, unaware that Sarah's heart was thumping painfully at her question.

"Er, no . . . I'm afraid I didn't see it at all. I confess that I didn't even hear the bell," she said, hoping her voice sounded off-hand.

"What a shame, for it was vastly pretty I can tell you. When the bell stopped ringing, a curtain was drawn to one side to reveal the sweetest little miniature landscape. You would have loved it of all things. So true to life, with its waterfall, and in front the prettiest miller's house and windmill you ever saw and all of it lit by concealed lamps.

Well . . ." she paused dramatically, while she nibbled another macaroon and brushed some crumbs from the front of her nightgown. "It was then that he proposed . . . You see, I said to him that I would love to have a real house like the little miller's house—just funning, as you do. But you know how he takes one up so, and he said that if I would only marry him I might have anything I desired! I swear I was never more surprised, but it was so romantic I hadn't the heart to refuse, for he took my hand and pressed it and held it to his heart. It was all mightily affecting and I'm sure that anyone would have said yes. And he *is* nice, isn't he?" she asked, as if needing reassurance.

"Certainly he is nice, love," replied Sarah, carefully weighing her words, "It is just that, well, I had rather thought that you had a soft spot for Freddy!"

"Good heavens, Sarah, why must you be forever bringing Freddy Middleton into things?" cried Amabel crossly. "Freddy! As if I care for him."

"You are only saying so because you are annoyed with him, love."

"Well, I like that! *I'm* annoyed with *him*? A case of the pot calling the kettle black wouldn't you say, for if I remember correctly, he seemed a little put out with me. I should think you would be pleased that I have *not* got a 'soft spot' for him, as you put it, for you heard him yourself thank Heaven he was not one of my suitors!"

"You were both very angry and said things you didn't mean."

"You are mistaken. I meant every word. And now love, I really do begin to feel tired," she said, pretending to yawn, "and must sleep. Anstey calls for me early tomorrow."

Seeing that she had gone too far, Sarah was quick to say goodnight, giving her a peck on the cheek and remarking anxiously as she drew away, "I only want your happiness, dearest. You know that."

Amabel relented at once and sprang up in her bed, putting her arms round Sarah to hug her.

"Of course you do, silly goose, and how could I be otherwise than happy? Anstey is very good-natured, you know?"

If Sarah felt that a husband needed rather more solid virtues now did not seem the time to try to put Amabel right, so she left her, making her own way back to her room, feeling as she did so that the situation was hopeless. But hadn't Freddy always declared that he would remain a bachelor, so perhaps it was for the best that Ami did not think of him. It was only that lately she had once or twice surprised a look in Freddy's eyes when they rested on Amabel that had made her wonder if perhaps . . .? But it could come to nothing now that Amabel was so adamant. She might have felt rather more encouraged, however, had she been able to peep into Amabel's room a few minutes after she had left her, for she would then have seen her sitting up in bed, huddled against her pillows, crying as if her heart would break.

"What a mull you have made of things, you stupid fool," Amabel murmured to herself despairingly, as the tears ran down her face. "What a nonsensical thing to do! How do you expect to get out of this? It is not bad enough that you let your temper get the better of you and make Freddy despise you, oh no . . . But this! How can you possibly wriggle out of this? And harmless little Anstey, why bring *him* into it?"

At each thought her tears cascaded faster and she began to feel wretched indeed, whipping herself into despair until, eventually with exhaustion, came a certain optimism. Perhaps after all there was a glimmer of hope. "Suppose Miles won't let him have me! I shall be saved. Oh please God, don't let him say yes. I shall be so good if only you make Miles refuse him!" She continued to toss and turn as she tried to think her problem through, suddenly informing her Heavenly Father that she felt it might be safer after all to admit it all to Miles before Anstey called in the morning. "It won't be pleasant, for Miles will be furious with me for leading Anstey on, but it will have to be faced. Anything would be better than to have to marry Anstey. Yes . . . I shall see Miles first thing in the morning, that will be best. If only I don't have to tell him that I love Freddy . . ." and on that thought, and with a final prayer that all would be well, she began to drift towards sleep.

Her prayer was not answered.

So anxious was Anstey to win his bride, that he came

before breakfast to speak to Miles and before Amabel had even opened her eyes she had become a betrothed lady. Miles really had no reason to withhold his consent. If he had had other hopes for her, well, Anstey was her choice, so who was he to stand in her way? Heaven forbid that she should not be allowed to be happy. Did he now know himself where it might lead if one married where the affections were not engaged?

To Amabel's horror, therefore, the first words out of his mouth on seeing her at breakfast were affectionate ones of congratulations. Moreover, he called her a "crafty little puss" for keeping things to herself and not caring to share with her only brother such important news.

Amabel felt sick inside, for she would rather have died than admit her despair now that Miles had spoken with Anstey and all was agreed. But the thought of having to go through with her marriage made her feel physically ill and her mouth drooped pathetically when she thought no-one was watching her.

Sarah thought she knew how she felt. If only she had been able to see Miles before he had spoken to the Viscount she would have given him an idea of how she suspected things stood between Freddy and Amabel. He might then have withheld his consent, at least for a while, until they could be certain. But Miles was still keeping determinedly aloof from his wife and she had not caught sight of him at all the night before. Since their quarrel he had been punctiliously polite to her whenever they met, but he never sought her out or tried to be alone with her. And just how she was supposed to help him get an heir, as she had promised, was more than she could fathom in such circumstances, she told herself crossly.

So now, Sarah was forced to watch in silence as her sister-in-law played out her wretched charade. If Amabel looked less happy than might be expected in a prospective bride, her brother was too preoccupied with his own troubles to notice and he did not seem to see, either, that her face became deathly pale when he informed her that he had already sent a notice of her betrothal to the *Gazette*. Sarah saw it all and her heart went out to Amabel as she watched her trying courageously to hide her trembling lips in a smile.

Anstey, as may be supposed, spent much of the day with them in Berkeley Square, and made one of their carriage to Mrs. McBride's that evening, as if unwilling to leave his prospective bride for a moment longer than necessary, his affections hideous to her as he took advantage of his new position to offer such gallantries as had never been allowed before, though he had been strictly forbidden by her to breathe so much as a word of their betrothal to anyone. When he was finally persuaded to go home the strain was quite apparent in Amabel's face and Sarah, a victim herself of agitation until she had ascertained that Cranesby had absented himself from the party, longed to put her arms round her to comfort her. Really, men must be quite without feeling, she thought crossly, for Miles had obviously noticed nothing amiss, while Anstey obviously thought Amabel as much walking on air as he himself. All Amabel could think of was the notice which would appear the following day in the Gazette, to advertise her dreadful folly and finally cook her goose.

****

When Miles read out the notice to his wife and to his heavy-eyed sister the next morning, he seemed quite delighted. The news was seen in rather a different light, however, by a gentleman breakfasting at his comfortable lodgings in Duke Street, just off Pall Mall. Glancing idly down the column which would show him which of his friends had chosen to become tenants for life, his eye was arrested by a handsome announcement of the engagement of "Miss Amabel Rowena Lilian Greville, sister to the Right Hon. The Earl of Wilberton of Beaumere, Shropshire, to the Right Hon. the Viscount Stephen James Robert Anstey of Cornwalton, Dorset." an announcement which caused him to catch his breath. Without ceremony, he pushed back his chair, inadvertently knocking over his tankard, the contents of which splashed liberally not only over his newspaper, but also over the sleeve of his handsome silk dressing gown. He appeared not to notice, however, and instead of using the bell, called out to his manservant in a sharp voice unusual to him, "Perkins, I want you! Here! Now, man!"

Perkins, imperturbable as ever, entered the room at his

usual stately pace.

"I'm going out, Perkins! At once!"

"Indeed sir, and what might sir be wishful for me to put out for him to wear?"

It was then that Perkins received what, as he later said to his friends down at the Bull, he sincerely hoped would prove to be the shock of his lifetime, for his master said crossly, "Damn it, man, who cares what you put out? Anything will do. And see that Josh has my horses put to by the time I'm ready!"

Perkins toyed with the idea, for a few seconds, of giving in his notice there and then. It was, however, no more than a passing fancy, for he well knew that nowhere could he expect to find a gentleman so nice in his notions of dress as the Honourable Freddy Middleton, nor one so worthy of his ministrations. Moreover, he could use his peepers as well as any man and it was clear that his gentleman had received a leveller and it was up to Perkins to try to get him back on his feet for the next round. So, while Freddy was washing, he used his considerable artistry to select for him a costume·which many youngsters, intent on cutting a dash in society, would have swooned for. If he was surprised at the speed and lack of care with which Mr. Middleton tied his cravat, he comforted himself with the knowledge that the result was yet much neater than the gentleman his cronies served would manage to achieve if they spent a whole morning at it. He opened the front door for him, therefore, with only the slightest of misgivings, watching his master dash down the stairs and jump into his curricle in a scrambling sort of way, his many-caped drab coat half slipping from his shoulders and his high-crowned beaver held carelessly in his hand, a lapse which caused that superior gentleman's gentleman to give a little grimace of dismay, while hoping sincerely that whatever had occurred to put his master in a taking might be settled without delay.

By the time Freddy was driving his horses at a spanking pace across Piccadilly and up Dover Street towards Berkeley Square, Sarah and Amabel had moved with their embroidery into the drawing room where they always received morning callers. Miles was busy with his man of affairs in his study, but promised that he would sit with them as soon as he could send him away, for they must certainly all be available to accept good wishes from the flood of visitors expected when the ton read today's *Gazette*. Amabel's face was pale, yet composed, for she had a great deal of the Greville pride and was determined that no-one would guess that all was not well with her. Thank heaven Anstey would not be with them that morning, she thought to herself, for he too would undoubtedly be receiving a medley of well-wishers at his home. At least she would be spared the effort of showing the world that she cared for him, an effort which she guessed would prove extremely exacting.

Forced to watch all this silent suffering, Sarah felt almost as wretched as Amabel and she jumped very nearly as far off her chair as did that poor unfortunate girl when the front door was heard to ring for the first time that morning.

Sarah had time only to glance anxiously at her sister-in-law, who now exhibited a pathetically pinched look around her mouth, which she endeavoured to hide by lowering her head to her embroidery, before the door burst open. In place of the stately figure of Mitford there stood the Honourable Freddy Middleton, in almost his usual sartorial elegance, though still in his drab coat, which he had allowed Mitford no opportunity to remove.

Sarah jumped up immediately on seeing him, crying, "Oh Freddy, I am so pleased you are here!" but he walked straight past her without saying so much as a word, to where Amabel was sitting, her head once more bent to her embroidery, while she blushed a furious crimson. He stood over her until she was forced to look up at his face, and what she saw there made her heart leap.

"Well, Squab?" he asked gently, taking her embroidery from her and pulling her to her feet. "What is all this tomfoolery in the *Gazette*?" He continued drawing her hands upwards until they were resting against his chest. "Has no-one ever told you that it is very wrong to tell untruths? And you know full well that there was never a chance that I would allow you to marry anyone but me, don't you?"

As Sarah tiptoed from the room, she smiled to herself to hear Amabel reply meekly, "Yes Freddy, indeed I do."

CHAPTER 26

Only one person suffered from Amabel's *volte face*, and that was Viscount Anstey, though Sarah thought that never had he appeared so much to advantage as he did in his gracious way of accepting with fortitude the news which was to blight forever his hopes of her. Sarah had a sneaking suspicion that he was relieved not to have to become a bridegroom so soon, but whatever was the way of it, he agreed wholeheartedly to endorse Miles's public assertion that the announcement had arisen from a misunderstanding by his secretary, and that Amabel had all along chosen Freddy. Those few friends Anstey had already informed were soon sworn to secrecy and all could be comfortable once more.

Never could news of an engagement have been received with more joy, for Sarah thought no-one could be more worthy of her dearest Amabel than her equally dear Freddy, and Miles confessed that he had hoped for Freddy as his brother-in-law for as long as he could remember.

Even Aunt Almeria found it difficult to disguise her delight in the match, and contented herself with saying only that she was sure that such a 'chuckle-headed pair' would deal delightfully together, but that she would be glad when the knot was safely tied, for then the family might stop smelling of April and May.

No-one could doubt Amabel's pure happiness, for, beautiful as she had always been, her eyes now took on a softer gleam which deepened whenever her eyes chanced to fall on her betrothed. They were to marry at the end of the Season, and as if even Nature was determined that the weeks leading up to their wedding should be halcyon, the sun smiled kindly on them, making it a time of enchantment that they would always remember.

Happy as Sarah was to see their joy, she could not help feeling envious, for things were no better between her and Miles. He continued polite towards her as ever, of course, but never did he seek the comfort of her bed now, and she began to wonder how much longer she could endure living with him under such circumstances.

Had it not been for Lord Blissworth she would have found herself in pretty poor pass, but, true to his word, he had taken steps to attach himself to her firmly, eager as she was to try if it might not answer. Sarah was grateful to have found such an amusing companion and valued confidant, for Amabel was much occupied elsewhere, and as a result of their enforced intimacy, Sarah's friendship with Lord Blissworth blossomed.

He had called in at Berkeley Square a day or two after Amabel's betrothal to ask Sarah to take a turn in the park in his high-perch phaeton, and he followed this up in grand style by escorting her to the Theatre Royal where they agreed so well together that it was no hardship at all to arrange other outings together. By the time Miles had begun to suspect that their relationship might be more than the casual acquaintance of family friends, they had become very comfortable together indeed, and it was usual for them to meet almost every day. Truth to tell, Sarah and Lord Blissworth had almost given up hope of eliciting any jealous response from their respective spouses, but, as they continued happy in each other's company, there had seemed no reason why they should not go on as they were.

At first, Miles had greeted Sarah's friendship with Lord Blissworth with something like relief. Jeremy was, after all, one of his greatest friends and was, besides, one of the family. Nobody could suspect that Sarah was overstepping the mark when she was with Jer, and if she was with him, she could not possibly be with Cranesby. Miles might never have had cause to reconsider his comforting thoughts on the subject had the matter not been brought to his attention one afternoon when he was enjoying a hand of piquet with Lord Mountjoy at White's. Miles had just taken the last trick and Lord Mountjoy ruefully said that he should get off home.

"But it's only five," protested Miles, faintly surprised. "Aren't you well, old man?"

"Never better, but m'wife plays havoc if I'm not home in plenty of time to dress for dinner."

"No? Does she indeed? Well, who'd have thought it? Rather imagined you had an amicable arrangement there. Can't think what I should do if Sarah rang a peal over me."

Nettled at Miles's self-congratulatory tone, Lord Mountjoy was moved to reply, "Well, it's not likely to happen in your case, is it? I can't say how much I wish I had a friend like Blissworth to keep *my* wife out of mischief."

Miles rose to his feet, his face a polite mask, though his thoughts were seething. "Perhaps you would care to explain what you mean by that?"

"Didn't mean anything by it, Miles old chap, so no need to get on your high ropes," he replied, disagreeably aware that he had tapped a spring of discontent, and unwilling to risk a flood. "Nothing wrong in your wife going about with Blissworth. Family, aint he? So don't go making a cake of yourself. You know me well enough to know that I don't go round making mischief."

Miles knew precisely that and recollected in time the impropriety of forcing a quarrel on an old friend for no reason. And of course, there *was* no reason, of that he was sure. As Mountjoy said, Blissworth was just family.

When he arrived home only a little later, however, and found his wife practising duets with Blissworth in the music room, he received a nasty jolt and when he heard at dinner that Blissworth was to return later to collect Sarah and take her to a benefit night for Madame Camporese at the King's Theatre, he began to wonder if Lizzie's husband was not playing a deep game.

He determined to try if he could not re-establish some measure of his previous good understanding with Sarah and wean her from Blissworth's company, and next morning at breakfast asked her if she would care to go with him to see the spring flowers in Richmond Park.

"Why, Miles," she replied with pleasure. "How very kind of you to ask me, but you do not need to trouble yourself, for Jeremy is calling later to take me up with him in his phaeton." She gave a little giggle, "He lets me tool the ribbons, which I am quite sure you never could be persuaded to do."

"You know, my dear," he replied thoughtfully, "I was once foolish enough to consider myself top-of-the-trees, but so much for my pretensions, for I am sure you make me feel the veriest flat!"

"How absurd you are, Miles," protested his wife, blushing fiercely, "You know you do not think any such thing. Why, any lady must be happy to have your escort!"

"Almost you unman me, my dear, with your flattery. It occurs to me, however, that perhaps it is less true than once I thought, since my wife apparently prefers almost any escort to mine. After all, did we not first have Freddy, and then Cranesby? Now we have Blissworth—Oh no, it is Jeremy, is it not? It is all very intriguing."

"You cannot object to my calling Lord Blissworth Jeremy? Why, I call his wife Elizabeth, and you have never objected. And surely it is folly to be so formal with a cousin."

"As you say, my dear, folly! But I would ask you to remember that I am not as foolish as perhaps you think."

"I think you must have had a bad night," said Sarah briskly, "for you have certainly woken up in a very peculiar mood. But if you wish it I shall certainly send a message to Jer . . . to Lord Blissworth, to say that I cannot go with him."

"But who *will* you get to take his place, my love?" he asked with derision, "Lord Cranesby?"

Swiftly the colour flew to Sarah's cheeks, as she stammered and said "N-no, my lord, I do not ride with Lord Cranesby nor do I meet him anywhere else since I have understood how strong is your aversion."

"Perhaps Freddy then, or is his newly engaged state sufficient to make even you consider him as beyond the pale?"

"It seems you mean to be insulting this morning, sir, but since I can see no reason why I should have to listen to you, I think I will leave you to finish your breakfast in peace and see if Amabel is about yet. Oh, and if you decide that I must cancel my drive with Lord Blissworth," she called back over her shoulder, "I beg that you will send up to tell me!"

****

215

Since no message to the contrary arrived from Miles, she was able to tell Lord Blissworth in person of her conversation with Miles, while they were out driving through Richmond Park later that day, Sarah holding the reins of the dangerous-looking vehicle.

"So, I'm to expect him to plant me a facer any time now, am I?" he asked grinning.

"How can you be so foolish, Jeremy? Miles is far too fond of you to do any such thing. At least," she amended cheekily, "we must certainly hope so."

"Indeed we must. I bruise very easily."

"But aren't you just a little pleased that we have made some progress?" asked Sarah, giving the leader an expert flick to encourage the team to trot faster, "I must say I find it delightful to think that someone suspects me of being naughty enough to have a liaison."

"Sarah!" cried her friend, pretending to be shocked. "You are completely incorrigible."

"I rather think I must be, Jeremy, and it is the greatest fun I must say. But you disappoint me today, for I was sure you would be as pleased as I am that we have shaken Miles's composure."

"Of course I'm pleased, but I'd like to have made some impression on my wife as well."

"I am confident that will follow, but in the meantime we must persevere. You won't forget, will you, that you are engaged tonight for Lady Mountjoy's ball. You are promised to me for two waltzes, so don't be late! Oh, and try if you can to take me to supper! I cannot think of anything which would make Miles more cross!"

"You will undoubtedly get me strangled," replied her intrepid champion, giving the phaeton's rein a slight tug to ensure that they avoided collision with an oncoming vehicle, "and I feel quite certain that a wise man would decamp here and now while his skin was still whole. But I was always thought to be a fool, so I suppose I will go on with it."

* * * * * * * * *

Lady Mountjoy was determined that her ball would rank

among the successes of the Season. No trouble or expense had been spared in her preparations and sufficient people had been invited to ensure that the ball would earn the agreeable distinction of being called a "shocking squeeze". For days the house in Hanover Square had been in a turmoil as housemaids polished chandeliers and mirrors, cleaned silver and washed glasses, moved furniture and scrubbed floors, until the house gleamed.

Gunter's had been called in to organise refreshments, which promised to be something out of the ordinary, and Lord Mountjoy's supplies of the best champagne became fiercely depleted as his cellars were callously attacked by his lady's butler to ensure that only the very best was brought up on the night of the ball.

Lady Mountjoy could not help but feel that her exertions had been worthwhile and her plump bosom swelled with pride, as she stood at the head of the stairs and saw very nearly all of her invited guests making their way up her fine staircase to the strains of music being played by the excellent orchestra she had engaged for the evening.

Sarah's party did not arrive until after midnight for they had called in first at a very dull affair being given by Miles's godmother which they felt obliged to give at least the courtesy of a brief visit, but there was still a crowd of people climbing upwards, and Sarah was forced to take care to prevent her gown from being crushed as they made their way to the ballroom. She had chosen a robe of palest blue crape, ornamented with knots of blue ribbon, sapphires and pearls, that evening, and around her neck wore the necklace her husband had bought her as his betrothal gift. Miles thought she had never looked better, and many men in the crowd gave her more than a passing glance. Sarah herself thought she looked rather well and was feeling complaisant until, looking up, she saw Lord Blissworth, on his arm a vision to stun the senses!

CHAPTER 27

Seeing how her chin had fallen when she had caught sight of Lizzie, Lord Blissworth gallantly solicited Sarah's hand for the two waltzes just starting up, and her husband watched frowningly as they danced elegantly away on the floor, leaving him alone with Lizzie, for Freddy and Amabel had been captured on their way in by their lionizing hostess as a legitimate prize to be exhibited about the ballroom in their newly betrothed state.

"Well, Miles dearest," said Lizzie, flirtatiously, peeping shamelessly up at him from beneath her lashes, "Aren't you pleased to see me?"

"What? Oh . . . yes, of course I am," replied Miles absently, as he searched for a sight of his wife through the crowd.

Lizzie pouted crossly. She had had no chance to see him privately since that night at the opera when he had suddenly become so furious and she wasn't going to let another evening pass without getting him to herself. She placed her hand on his arm and leaned towards him, so that she was as close as it was possible to be, forcing him to look down at her, "You don't *seem* very pleased to see me, Miles. Why, you haven't even asked me to dance. It is a great deal too bad of you to turn me into a wallflower."

Miles exploded into laughter at the ludicrous suggestion that Lizzie might ever be among the drooping band of plain girls at the side of any ballroom.

"Lizzie, you are preposterous! You know there are about twenty men all around me ready to stick a knife in my back only for the privilege of being allowed to stand here in this very advantageous position and survey your stunningly ample charms. And that does not include those who would pay a king's ransom if they could get their wives to turn a blind eye while they danced with you, you wretch!"

Lady Blissworth was moved to bestow on him her gayest smile.

"But your wife cannot possibly be one of those who would object if you danced with me, can she, for she is dancing with Jer at this very moment, so you can have no possible excuse for refusing to take the floor with me. We ladies demand fairness in all. If she steals my husband, I am entitled to borrow her's."

As soon as she saw his face, she knew that she had said the wrong thing. "What is it, love?" she asked, confused. "What have I said?"

"Come and dance, Lizzie," he replied gruffly, "It is nothing you have said," and he whisked her onto the floor before she could question him further.

Out on the floor, Sarah was determined to enjoy herself. It was no use allowing herself to be put off by Lizzie's brilliance and anyway, Jeremy was a divine dancer, so why should she not make the best of things? Here she was at a ton party, in a pretty gown, and with a handsome partner. A few months ago, such would have been the zenith of her dreams. If now she was not so easily satisfied, why then the fault must be with her! When Miles and Lizzie caught up with them in the waltz, therefore, Miles was in time to see her laughing up at Lord Blissworth as he leaned down to hear something she was saying, and to follow in their wake as they twirled round and round, their steps in perfect unison, as if they had been used to dance together for ever. Miles was furious to see them there, apparently so happy in each other's company.

In retaliation, he began to flirt dangerously with Lizzie, paying her the most extravagant of compliments and holding her so close to him that many of the chaperones sitting to one side of the room began to watch them very intently indeed. When they noticed, too, how comfortable Sarah looked in Lord Blissworth's arms, they began to wonder if the quartet had not come to the type of amicable arrangement common among the ton, and tongues began to wag in earnest.

Miles was determined to claim his wife for the two country dances to follow and keep her out of mischief, but

Lizzie managed to keep him so long at her side that, when eventually he found Sarah, she was already being solicited for them by Freddy, so he made his way over to where the refreshments had been placed, and was liberally helped to some of Lord Mountjoy's excellent champagne, ignoring the sideways look of some of the ladies sitting out, after which he leaned against the wall with his arms folded watching his wife perform her steps with Freddy.

Just at that moment, Lord Mountjoy came up to him, leading an insipid young damsel by the arm. Too late Miles realised that he had made a tactical error in remaining in the ballroom instead of seeking the safety of the card room, for Lord Mounjoy took the opportunity offered to introduce Miss McFarlane to him as an eligible partner and there was nothing for it but for Miles to accept the inevitable and join one of the sets with her. She was a very young, plain girl, obviously not very certain of her steps, and at any other time Miles's natural good breeding, coupled with his experience, would have ensured that he led her comfortably through the dance. As it was, he was too concerned to keep a note of his wife's behaviour to trouble himself with the poor girl and she endured a half-hour of the utmost misery as Miles constantly upset the dance by moving negligently up his own set, while keeping an eye on one at the other end of the room. It was debatable whether Miles or Miss McFarlane was best pleased when the dance was complete. What is certain, however, is that they parted with an alacrity which left no-one uncertain of how much pleasure each had obtained from it. Now Miles went hurrying over to where he had last set eyes on his wife, only to see her being led by Lord Blissworth towards the supper room next to the ballroom. Furiously looking about him, his eye fell on his cousin Lizzie, who was being earnestly solicited by a handsome young ensign to be allowed to take her into supper.

"Ah, there you are, Liz," he said audaciously, taking hold of her arm, "You are promised to me for supper, I think?"

In reply, Lady Blissworth gave him a glittering smile, and they entered the supper room hard on their spouses' heels. Miles had hoped to get a seat near his wife so that he could keep an eye on her, but one look at the crowd was enough to show him that there was not a single seat to be had by her and they were forced to go to quite the opposite side of the room to find a table.

Sarah gave a little squeak of dismay when she looked over and saw them together, but far from showing her distress, for the next half-hour she treated Miles to such a brilliant show of flirtatious behaviour with his long-time friend that it alarmed Blissworth almost as much as Miles. He whispered anxiously to her under his breath, "For the Lord's sake, Sarah, have a care. He'll kill me in a minute!"

"Oh stuff!" she declared furiously, for she had just seen her husband gazing, she was sure, directly down at his cousin's bosom, "If he wants to play games, so will we," and she leaned forward, presenting her own pretty, though admittedly more modest bosom toward a horrified Lord Blissworth, and taking the hand which held his glass, sipped from it, holding her own glass in turn towards him. Disinclined though he was to accept it—he was, after all, no hero!—she held it so close to his lips that he had little choice and he sipped self-consciously, keeping one eye on Miles.

When he saw what was happening, Miles choked with fury on the sandwich he was eating. Then he took Lizzie's hand and began to play a complicated little finger game with the delighted lady, which seemed to an incensed Sarah, to consist largely of his kissing each of Lizzie's fingers in turn and ended up with him kissing her palm!

The gossips were in transports, and were all sitting declaring to each other that it was a scandal not to be borne, while each was secretly thanking heaven that they had not chosen to go instead to a rival ball being given that evening by the Dowager Viscountess Clavering, and so miss all the fun.

Just then Miles had his view blocked completely, for Mr. and Mrs. McBride had seen them and made their way over, standing before them, since no seat offered itself, and so preventing Miles from watching Sarah at all. He was obliged to endure ten minutes of small talk before it became apparent, even to the McBrides, that he was answering them perfunctorily, and they frostily took their leave, allowing Miles liberty to look around him again. But they had remained too long, for Sarah was no longer anywhere to be seen in the supper room: nor, indeed, was Blissworth.

Miles rose to his feet, giving a bewildered Lizzie no time to finish her glass of ratafia before he dragged her by the arm, more swiftly than elegantly, from the supper room and back into the ballroom. There he redeposited her, without compunction, with her besotted ensign and began to make his way rapidly round the ballroom in search of Sarah.

Seeing Freddy ambling by, he asked him at once if he had seen Sarah.

"Can't say I have, old man," he replied, wondering just what had brought that black look to his cousin's face. "Anything amiss? Something I can do?"

"Anything that needs to be done will be done by me, I promise you," was the less than reassuring reply and Freddy was glad that the fury which had sounded in Miles's voice was directed at someone other than himself.

"Remember that it's a ball, old man," he warned doubtfully, "Can't go upsetting a ball, you know—dashed bad ton!"

"Oh, go to blazes, Freddy!" replied Miles, in a tone which, as Freddy later told Amabel, boded no good to some unlucky person.

Having determined to his satisfaction that Sarah and Jeremy were no longer in the ballroom, Miles decided that they must have gone into the garden. He ground his teeth at the thought of them together in some shady little grove and set off to find them without delay. But the garden was larger than he had imagined a town garden could be and seemed specifically designed for lovers to lose themselves in. Here were covered walkways and arbours in plenty, as well as a temple, which gave seclusion to those who wished to avoid company. By the time Miles had completed a circuit of the garden to no avail, and had examined the temple to make sure the truants were not hiding there, he was feeling completely incensed, and when he heard his cousin Lizzie's voice calling to him from the shadows, his fury was ready to overflow.

"Miles, dearest," she whispered, as he was striding past, "I've been looking everywhere for you. What a naughty man you are to leave me with that silly child."

"Oh, so it's you, is it Lizzie," he asked, faintly aggrieved, joining her in the shadows, "Suppose you don't know where that precious husband of yours is, do you?"

"Jer? No, why should I?" she replied, languidly wafting her fan to and fro.

"Well, he is your husband, you know? It doesn't seem altogether too much to expect you to have an idea where he is."

Lizzie gave a tinkling laugh, as if she found the notion amusing. "Whyever would I want to know where Jer is, my dear, just so long as he is not here."

"Lord, Lizzie, but you're a cool one, I'll say that for you," said Miles, noticing for the first time the hardness in her voice.

She moved quickly toward him and placed her hands on the lapels of his dress coat. "Oh no, Miles, I assure you that I am not. And so you would find out if you would only allow yourself a chance."

"You forget, Ma'am," said Miles in a freezing voice, forcibly removing her hands from his person and pushing her away, "that we are both of us married."

"Forget? When do you ever allow me to?"

"Perhaps we have both forgotten only too often, Liz," he wondered ruefully, suddenly realising how frequently he had flirted with her and reflecting, for the first time, on how it might have appeared to Blissworth, one of his best friends for so many years.

"Really, Miles," she replied, moving confidently back towards him again, "Don't pretend, after tonight, that you don't like my attentions, for I'll not believe you."

"If we are speaking of attentions, my girl," he said tartly, aware that she perhaps had good reason to be so confident, "maybe it is time you gave more to your husband, for then he might not feel a need to spend so much time with my wife!"

Elizabeth was halted for barely a moment. "And what is that supposed to mean? Do you really expect me to be worried? What could Jer see in such a grey little thing as Sarah?" she was stung to reply, surprise making her less than careful in her choice of words.

Suddenly she knew a moment's fear, for his face clouded and he clenched his fists in an effort to keep his temper in check.

"Have you looked at my wife lately, you little fool? Are you really so conceited that you can possibly have failed to notice the change in *her*? Failed to notice that she has every Bond Street puppy hanging around her skirts every minute of the day? Your husband's been dangling after my wife for weeks and you are so busy looking into your mirror that you fail even to notice!"

"It's not true, Miles," said Elizabeth, her mouth trembling as she tried to smile. "I don't believe a word you say. Bliss loves me! He always has! He would never go off with anyone else."

Realising that he had dealt her a damaging blow, Miles put one finger under her chin. "Poor Liz. You really haven't noticed, have you?" he said in sudden sympathy. "The man is only human, you know, and you haven't given him much to hope for."

"I don't believe you, Miles. Bliss is perfectly happy. You are just trying to make me cross."

"No love, I'm not trying to make you anything. I think we have both of us been rather childish, do not you? But I, for one, am determined to see if I cannot make things right."

"I shall go and find Bliss now. Just to prove to you that you are being silly. Sarah can be nothing at all to him. It's me he loves. He has always loved me. He says so!"

"Don't we all say things to suit our ends? Didn't you when you married him?"

"That's not the same at all," she replied confused. "He loves me. He does!"

"Why, Lizzie. I do believe you care for him after all."

"Don't be foolish," she snapped, "But he's mine and I dare Sarah to try to take him from me. She would find it not so easy!"

"I believe you! Only go to Bliss and convince him, and then perhaps we may all lie easy in our beds."

Without a word, Lizzie left his side and hurried away up the garden towards the lights.

Miles made his own way back into the ballroom, smiling ruefully and feeling, with Lizzie's departure, about a hundred years younger. Until he looked across the ballroom to see his wife in serious conversation with Robert Cranesby . . .

Miles would have found little in their conversation to concern him. Cranesby had come upon her unawares, bowed penitently over her hand, as if to acknowledge his previous fault, and asked her to dance. Truth to tell, he had been in a living hell since the night at Vauxhall, for it had gradually been borne upon him that the feelings he entertained for the new Countess of Wilberton were not simply such as he had imagined them. He had taken her to Vauxhall to get back at Miles, but now, each time he remembered her pale face when she had begged him not to kiss her, he felt sick. Ludicrous as it was, he had fallen for Miles's little Countess, and as he stood before her, he wanted nothing more than to be her friend. At the anger in her face, he flinched.

"Oh no, my lord. I think not indeed! You and I can have nothing more to say to each other."

"Come Sarah, you cannot be so cruel."

"I am not cruel at all, and my name," she said haughtily, drawing herself up to her full height, "is Lady Wilberton."

"So be it, Ma'am," he laughed delightedly, "and as such, Lady Wilberton," (heavily underlined), "I only beg for the liberty of one little dance."

"Ah, but my lord, I feel that any liberties to which you may have been entitled have been used up by you already. It is what I am always telling my brothers, you know, greed has to be paid for in the end," and she stormed away from him across the ballroom, making her way to where she had spotted Freddy and Amabel, leaving him looking after her thoughtfully.

It required some patience to steer a path through the crowded ballroom, and Sarah had not quite reached her destination when she felt her hand being urgently tugged and found herself being pulled bodily into a curtained-off recess to one side of the ballroom. Amazed, she turned round to confront her husband.

"So, my lady," he thundered, "at last I've found you. I

declare you are as slippery as an eel."

But Sarah had seen him with Lizzie and was in no mood to be harangued. "As to that, sir, you are not so easily come by yourself," she said nonchalantly, snapping open her fan and wafting it before her.

"Well I'm here now, so perhaps you will explain to me what you were doing just now with Cranesby."

Aware of her unassailably virtuous position, she replied tartly, "I was telling him that I could not dance with him, my lord, following your instructions!"

Miles was nonplussed for no more than a moment. "And what about Blissworth? I suppose you will tell me you were refusing him too?"

"If we are to conduct a detailed examination of all my partners, my lord, this conversation may take some time," she returned crossly, folding her arms before her and tapping her foot. "I have danced with Lord Blissworth, have had the temerity to take the floor with Freddy Middleton, and am promised to at least four other partners. Would you wish me to furnish you with their names and titles now, or may we leave it until later, when you may rant at me 'til your heart is content?"

"It is of no concern to me, Sarah, with whom you dance, but the particular nature of your relationship with Lord Blissworth is becoming the subject of considerable speculation among the ton, and I will not stand for it!"

"Speculation among the ton?" she said with a brittle smile. "Of course there is speculation. Your behaviour with your cousin has been the subject of gossip for years!" and without a further glance at him, she wrenched the curtain aside and dashed back into the ballroom in undignified haste.

He made to follow, then recollecting the impropriety of causing a scene, stepped quietly back into the recess, drawing the curtains on himself. He needed some air and opened the long window which led from the recess out to a balcony overlooking the gardens. Flicking back his coat tails, he flopped heavily onto a bench placed there, and took out a silver case from which he extracted a cigarillo. A few moments later, Freddy found him puffing at it abstractedly, looking down at the garden beneath him.

"Mind if I join you? Dashed hot in there," he said, taking the seat next to Miles and placing on a small table a bottle of champagne and two glasses. Wordlessly Miles handed him his case and with his own cigarillo lit the one Freddy extracted from it. They both helped themselves liberally to some champagne. After a long pause, Miles said, puzzled:

"Do you understand women, Freddy?"

"No," said Freddy blandly.

"No more do I."

These simple statements seemed to give great satisfaction. They continued to sit in companionable silence smoking and drinking deeply.

Eventually Miles said, "Where's Ami?"

"Dancing with Bliss, last I saw." said Freddy comfortably.

"Fellow ought to be shot!" came the unexpected reply.

"Bliss? Surely not! Got the wrong fellow, Miles. Must have."

"Haven't," he replied simply.

"Must have! Stands to reason. Bliss, best of good fellows."

"Wouldn't say so if he was chasing your wife."

"True," said Freddy fairly. "Wouldn't like anyone to chase Ami."

"There you are then," replied Miles satisfied.

Five minutes later Freddy said thoughtfully,

"Bliss chasing someone's wife, Miles? I didn't know that."

"Mine!" he replied tersely, banging his glass down on the table.

"Too much champers, old fellow! Either that or you've got the wrong chap. Bliss's too busy chasing his own wife to have time for anyone else's."

"Well, so I would have thought," replied Miles fairly, "but he lives in Sarah's pocket these days. Stands to reason what's going on. You must have seen them tonight!"

"Sorry, old chap. Too busy noticing you and Liz. Even Ami thought you'd crossed the line tonight, and you know how she worships you."

"Liz! What has she to do with it?"

Freddy coughed deprecatingly. "No business of mine, old chap, but you must know what people think."

Miles's head cleared in a trice.

"No, Freddy, I may be the most dunderheaded fool in London, but I do *not* know. Perhaps you should tell me."

Freddy's head was suddenly clear too.

"Not going to like it, old fellow, but perhaps I should. Thought about it often before. Not going to shirk it this time. Gossips been pointing the finger at you and Liz for years. Pointing out Bliss as figure of fun, too!"

"No! You know I'd never cross Bliss."

"*I* know it, old man. Trouble is, other people don't. Liz not very discreet, is she?"

"There's nothing to be discreet about! We flirt, that's all. Same as anyone else."

"Trouble is, people don't *know* that, do they? You must admit that you and Liz seem pretty chummy, and there aren't many men who'd refuse her."

"You would!"

"Yes, I would, but that's not to say anything. Not my type. Don't like overblown women. Make me uncomfortable. Don't like making passes at other men's wives, either."

Miles was silent. Taking a deep breath Freddy forced himself on.

"Not going to like this either, old fellow, but think you should know that Sarah saw you kissing Liz in Aunt Stanham's library that first night you were in London. I was with her. We both saw you."

Miles groaned, and buried his head in his hands.

"So that's it! No wonder Sarah's as prickly as a pincushion when Liz is about. But it wasn't how it looked. Dashed girl threw herself at me before I knew what she was about. I was just trying to get out of it without hurting Lizzie's feelings."

"Should have tried a bit harder! . . . Good little thing, Sarah! Kind of wife anyone might be proud of," said Freddy, feeling his way. "I'd have thought you could have made a go of it."

"Nothing I'd like more," said Miles, nettled by the faintly scolding tenor of Freddy's discourse, "but when I try to get near to her she keeps me at arms' length. When I met her, didn't seem to be any reason why we shouldn't get on as well as any of our friends do. It just hasn't worked out that way."

"Not surprising, old fellow. Why, even at Beaumere Liz led her a merry dance, but you were too full of yourself to notice. Damage done then. Can't think what a state she was in when she caught you together at Stanham House. Seemed to bear out all her fears. Crying her eyes out, poor little sweet. That's why I helped to get her togged out. Seemed the least I could do." He looked down at his hands. "Only time in my life I've ever been ashamed for you, Miles."

Instinctively Miles clenched his fists, but relaxed them again as he acknowledged the truth of Freddy's words.

"Damn it, Freddy! What a mess I've made of it. But it's too late for us now."

Freddy stared stolidly at his glass. "You never know, old fellow."

CHAPTER 28

Unlike Lord Mountjoy, Miles was little troubled by any of the arrangements for the ball to be held in *his* house to announce Amabel's betrothal, for Sarah was too good an organiser to need to trouble him, and besides, Amabel had been for so long in charge of such arrangements for her brother that the two ladies found it a matter only of routine to decide things to their entire satisfaction.

Their most taxing problem was in deciding what to wear and Amabel solved her dilemma by appearing in an elegant white lace dress worn over a white slip, its hem trimmed with a drapery of white lace entwined with pearls and ornamented with rosebuds. She completed her ensemble with white kid gloves and, to one side of her silvery curls, wore a rakishly daring white satin toque. Round her neck hung a string of fine pearls, Freddy's betrothal gift to her, and, as she walked downstairs, Freddy's small nod of approval told her quite as well as the most extravagant of compliments that she looked very well.

Sarah would have loved to have been able to wear such an outfit, and white was so pretty for a ball, but she gave it only a passing thought, for she was not foolish enough to chance it. Instead, she contented herself with an open robe of apple-green satin, over a white slip. Her headdress was a half-garland of tiny flowers, and white kid gloves and corded silk shoes completed the rest.

When he saw her walking down the staircase to where he and Freddy waited, Miles thought she looked lovely, but they hadn't spoken anything but commonplaces to each other since the night of the Mountjoy ball, so he couldn't tell her so. Sarah went miserably to meet their guests wondering why she had spent so long in getting ready and thinking him the most unfeeling man in the world.

The family and a few intimate friends had been invited to dine at Wilberton House before the ball, and Sarah had her usual qualms as she saw Elizabeth making her way upstairs towards them. For once, however, she seemed not at all interested in Miles: in fact she was far more watchful of Sarah as she and her husband made their way along the receiving line, drawing herself up to her full height in quite an alarming way as her husband took Sarah's hand. Since Miles had kissed Lizzie on the cheek as a cousinly tribute, Sarah thought it no more than fair that she do the same with Jeremy, and, though he made every attempt to hide his smile, he could not prevent his eyes from crinkling at the corners as, following Sarah's boldness, his wife put her arm possessively through his and moved along.

Sarah had placed Jeremy to her own right at the large dining table, and his wife at Miles's right at the other end of the table. It proved to be a very unsatisfactory arrangement, since Miles and Lizzie spoke hardly half a dozen words to each other throughout the meal and eyed their spouses suspiciously.

Lord Blissworth was, of course, in seventh heaven, but as much in the dark as to the cause of his wife's *volte face* as Sarah. He only knew that Lizzie had not allowed him out of her sight since the Mountjoy ball, so that he had been unable to keep his fellow conspirator informed as to this strange new turn of events. Now that he was free to do so, Sarah too was unable to account for it, however delighted she felt for him. She was less delighted to hear him voice his regret that their own friendship must now be at an end, and hissed urgently, dismay preventing her from being as tactful as usual,

"Good heavens, Jeremy, that is the very last thing you must think of. With someone like Lizzie the only way to keep her in check is to have some hold on her."

"Devil take it, Sarah," he replied stiffly, "You are speaking about my wife, you know?"

"Well, indeed I am," bristled his dinner partner, "so there is no need to lower your brows at me. I know only too well how long it has taken for us to bring her round your thumb. You surely cannot wish to spoil all our efforts? And besides, we still have to try to work on Miles, though I am the first to say *that* seems an impossible task."

Lord Blissworth was immediately contrite. "I fear I shall never be as good at this as you are my dear, so of course I will continue to be guided. And at least I shan't have to lose your friendship, which, have I told you, I value very much?"

Lady Stanham could not fail to notice how often her great-nephew's eyes were drawn to the other end of the table, and how he glowered when Sarah laughed with Lord Blissworth. She whistled under her breath. "Sits the wind in that corner now? Well done, my girl, well done!"

The ball was a resounding success. No-one doubted that it would be, for there must be few indeed who would refuse an invitation to Wilberton House at any time, and many considered it quite the most important function of the season, thus rendering Berkeley Square chaotic as the night air echoed with sounds of carriages arriving and departing, an atmosphere of hubble and noise creating an arc of excitement which enlivened the whole square.

It was Lord Mountjoy who had the felicity of taking Sarah into supper, but they had been sampling the delicacies provided by Miles's French chef for no more than a few minutes when one of the extra footmen hired for the evening came up to her respectfully and leaned down to whisper that she was wanted in the library.

Surprised, she excused herself and made her way quickly to the library. As she pushed open the door and saw no-one there, she became aware of a vague feeling of unease. Going further into the room, she made her way over towards the window leading on to the balcony, but spun round quickly as she heard the door close behind her . . . and found herself face to face with Lord Cranesby.

"You!" she cried aghast. "How did you get in? Miles will kill you if he finds you here."

He came towards her, his usual carefree manner not deserting him for as much as a moment, and, lifting her hand to his lips, he murmured smoothly, "How kind of you to be concerned for me, Ma'am. I knew that we would be friends again when you had had time to cool down."

Sarah snatched away her hand. "You are mistaken. Friendship is something which we can never share, as well you know! And after what you did with Caro, it shocks me that you could even think of it."

A look of resentment snapped across Lord Cranesby's face, which he was quick to disguise with a grin.

"Ah, so he has told you about that, has he? How wise, how very wise of him to tell you Caro's little secret."

"It wasn't Miles who told me, but Lord Blissworth. Miles is rather more of a gentleman than you are and wouldn't besmirch Caroline's good name!"

"Good name?" Cranesby laughed incredulously. "Really, my dear, that's coming it rather too strong, wouldn't you say?"

Sarah, reluctantly forced to admit the justice of his remark, remained silent.

"Exactly, my dear. Your sense of fair play compels admiration. It palls after a while to be considered a villain when you know full well you aren't one. It may surprise you to know that Caroline was quite as eager to come away with me as I was to have her. And I was certainly eager to have her! She was quite beautiful, you know, and had led me along shockingly by the nose."

Considering this for a moment, Sarah thought that there was probably much in what he said. After all, hadn't Lord Blissworth more or less admitted as much?

"But why have you come here?" she asked him then, her voice several degrees less frosty. "You know that too much has passed between you and Miles to let you have the run of the house. And anyway, how on earth *did* you get in?"

"Oh that was easy," he replied, a charming grin lighting up his features as he sensed Sarah's thawing, "I came in through the garden entrance. I know the house well so it was no trouble at all getting in that way. I climbed up the old chestnut tree—just as Miles and I always did when we were boys—and dropped onto the dining room balcony. There is no way of getting up to this one—nothing to hang on to you see? It was a bit of a risk, I suppose, because the servants know me of old, but I guessed you'd have to have a lot of extra help tonight and that the usual servants would be too busy to notice me. I simply trusted to my usual run of luck that I should be able to avoid the ones who knew me and, as you see, I've been fortunate."

Almost Sarah laughed: he was so like her brothers crowing when they had successfully played a trick on someone, that it was difficult to consider him dangerous.

"I managed to get into here without coming up against any of the family and since only they know that I've been denied entry, no-one thought it at all odd to see me in the house tonight. Chose one of the temporary footmen to deliver my message and that was the whole thing, sweet as you like. Only one nasty moment to speak of. Viscount Anstey gave me a knowing look, but since I'm pretty certain he isn't in on the story, I think I'm on solid turf right enough."

"Well, you certainly have taken some chances, I'll say that for you," said Sarah, with reluctant admiration and quite off her guard, "but what on earth for?"

She was to know only too soon, for to her dismay he came towards her, his arms outstretched. The speed at which he covered the distance between them took her by surprise and prevented her from avoiding his embrace and she found herself tightly clasped, her arms held tight to her sides, as he brought his face close to hers.

"You must know what it is I want by now, Sarah," he murmured trying to kiss her throat, while Sarah wriggled to be free.

"Don't be so foolish. I've told you that I want nothing to do with you, and I meant it."

As she saw the darkling look which now spread itself across his face, Sarah knew real fear.

"But I must have you, you see, my dear," he explained, his voice almost conversational, "Miles cannot be allowed all the sweets."

"You are mad," she whispered, "Quite mad."

"No, not mad. Unless it be with love for you."

"This is not love. I think, my lord, that you will never understand what love is."

If she hoped to nettle him, she was disappointed, for he showed no anger, saying matter-of-factly, "Well, as to that, it may be. But whatever is the right of it, Sarah, my love, you must come with me now."

"But I shall not," cried Sarah, "You cannot make me go, for I shall scream and scream loudly, I warn you."

"Why, so you would, little firebrand, I thought you

might," he laughed. Then his voice changed to become oddly flat and he went on, "And so I was forced, my dear, to take certain precautions." He looked towards the balcony curtains, just behind her,

"Hardy! Now, if you please," and before Sarah had even time to turn her head or call out, she felt a hand clasped over her mouth and another around her person.

"Forgive me, my dear," said Cranesby, now towering over her as his henchman held her fast, "You will not be uncomfortable for long. Only until I get you safely away," and he began, workmanlike, to tie her hands behind her back with a neat length of cord which he took from his pocket. Next, using a handkerchief he had also brought with him, he bound her mouth securely.

"Now Sarah, we have to let you down from this window. No chance of getting you out any other way without being seen. Hardy will get down first and I will lower you down to him. I must warn you, Sarah, that if you struggle I will probably drop you and you may break your neck, so it is in your own interest to be still . . ."

CHAPTER 29

"Well, my boy," said Lady Stanham, as her great nephew took his place beside her on the small sofa from which she had regally held court all evening. "You are looking mightily fussed."

"Am I, Aunt?" he replied, for once not smiling at her presumption. "I wonder what should cause that?"

"Hmph. Wonder, indeed? No need to case dice with me, m'boy. I am more than seven, you know?"

"No! Well, I must congratulate you on how well you hold your years, for it don't show, word of honour!"

"Don't try flummery with me, m'lad. I'm more than a match for you," she replied tartly, "always was. Expect to be 'til m'dying day."

"No doubt of that, Ma'am, at all," soothed Miles, "But I haven't thanked you yet, Aunt, for gracing the evening with your presence. It's good of you to come, for I know how such evenings bore you, and good of you to stay so late too, for I'll be bound you must be worn to a cinder . . ."

"Ha! The day that I can't outpace this mamby-pamby generation, m'boy', 'll be the time I'm ready to cut stick. And anyway, I wouldn't deny myself the pleasure of seeing Ami betrothed. Never thought to see her choose so wisely either. I must say, there's precious little to give me pleasure at my time of life, but it warms m'heart to see you both so well settled. Hope you like the match, Miles, for I'm of the opinion that Freddy's one of the best of the bunch. Not the greatest intellect, but a good deal of bottom."

"Indeed, Ma'am," replied Miles with enthusiasm, "he's one of the best, as you say. And Sarah will have it that he has a great deal of what she calls 'true wisdom'."

"Sarah says so too, does she? Well, good for her. And it's glad I am to hear that her opinion has such weight with you, m'boy. I'll tell you now, that I was afraid for your girl at first. Afraid she wasn't up to snuff, as they say. Relieves m'mind that she's cleared her fences so well. Hear nothing but good of her wherever I go. Just a pity you two are still squaring up."

"Precious little escapes you, Ma'am, does it?" said Miles dropping a kiss on her forehead.

"It's just as well for this family it don't," she muttered curtly, secretly delighted by this tribute. "And speaking of this family, as head of it I'd like to see you setting up your nursery soon."

Her bluntness took the wind from his sails for only a moment.

"Well, in all modesty, I can only say, Aunt, that I mean to do my possible!" he said, failing to school his features into serious lines.

"Wretch! Just you see you do. Not much time left for me, you know, and I'd as lief see a new generation hatched before I do."

"If that's all that's worrying you Aunt, there's no need for me to cram my fences at all, since you'll undoubtedly outlive us all!"

She was saved the trouble of a further retort, for just then they were joined by Viscount Anstey, exhibiting a mildly troubled expression.

"I say, Wilberton old chap. Was I seeing things or was that Cranesby in the house just now? Thought you and he were at odds drawn and all that?" he asked hesitantly.

"Must be deeper into your cups than you think, Stephen," said Miles unperturbed, "Fellow couldn't get past Mitford for love nor money."

"Well, so I thought, old man, so I thought! Dashed strong stuff this champagne of yours. Stick to blue ruin in future. Know where you are with it. Fine ball, though. Dashed fine. Enjoyed m'self and no hard feelings."

"You're a good fellow, Stephen, so you are," replied Miles sentimentally, but with perfect truth, for few men would have accepted so coolly being jilted. "By the by, have you seen my wife on your travels? She's promised to me for the next dance."

"Last I saw of her, old man, she was with Mountjoy in the supper room."

Excusing himself to his Great Aunt, Miles went off in that direction, hoping to take advantage of such a joyous occasion to ease the constraint between him and his wife. Spotting Lord Mountjoy with Amabel and Freddy, to one side of the supper room, he made his way over to them.

"There you are, Mountjoy," he began pleasantly, patting him on the shoulder, "I hear you've been running off with my wife. Any idea where she is now?"

"None at all. One of the footmen brought a message from someone for Sarah to meet him in the library. Said something like . . . er . . . a fellow . . . er, something to discuss with her, or some such thing. Sounded like a dashed hoax to me."

Miles experienced a distinct twinge of unease and recalled very clearly Anstey's warning that Cranesby had been in the house. "Don't suppose you recognise the chap who brought the message, old man. Think I'll play a trick of my own."

"Be reasonable, Miles dear old fellow. Wasn't paying attention. Doubt if I'd recognise him from Adam . . . Wait though, I wonder if it wasn't that chap over there, now I come to think of it, the tall one. Can't say I'm sure, but wouldn't be surprised. Ask him if you like?"

"It's alright, old chap, don't put yourself out," said Miles in a steady voice, while his mind repeated a single phrase. "Not Sarah! Please not Sarah!"

He moved over to where a footman was handing round glasses of champagne from a silver tray, and all the time the same words monotonously intoning in his furiously working brain.

A few seconds' questioning were enough to convince him that the man in the library had been Cranesby, and as his sister and Freddy joined him some moments later, not deceived by his heavily casual air, his face told its own story.

"Something's happened, Miles?" whispered Ami, achingly afraid at his pallor. "What is it?"

238

"Cranesby," he breathed through clenched teeth. "Sarah's gone with him. This time I'll kill him!"

Freddy was moved to intervene. "Not so furious, old chap. Not so furious. We know nothing yet. No need to hand it to the gossips on a plate. Keep smiling. That's it. Chin up 'til we get outside, then we can see what's to do," as he propelled Miles out of the ballroom and into the corridor, moving swiftly from there along to the library, mercifully still empty.

Freddy's first reaction, when he heard Miles's reasons for fear, was one of incredulity.

"He couldn't do it, old man. You haven't thought. How could he get in?"

"That's what I mean to find out," replied Miles in a constrained voice. "Come Freddy, nothing to be seen here. We'll go outside and have a look. He can't have got far with her yet, and I'll be damned if I mean to allow him a chance to do so."

"Surely we have to make sure that she has really gone before we do anything. We need to search the ballroom and the other rooms first, and Ami, go to Sarah's apartments to see if she is there."

A thorough search failed to locate her, and Miles was, by that time, grey with anxiety.

"Let us lose no more time. See if we can find anything in the grounds," he said curtly.

"What shall I do, Miles?" asked Ami, trembling, blaming herself for allowing Sarah ever to meet ·Cranesby.

"You must bear up like a good girl," said Freddy, with his usual good sense, clasping her close to him. "No-one outside the family must suspect anything, d'you hear, my love? And it's on your shoulders to make sure they don't. Keep smiling and thank God there's still a crowd here, for with luck no-one will realise we've gone. You have to make some excuse for Sarah, for she may be promised for some dances. Say that she's had to lie down with a headache, or . . . anything, only keep any hint of scandal out of court."

Within a few moments, Freddy and Miles were standing underneath the library window, holding a lantern by which to see.

'Look Miles," whispered Freddy, noticing that the earth was disturbed, "there are recent footprints here."

"So that's how he did it. Through the window and over the balcony. Just as we did as boys. God help me, but if he's hurt one hair of her head I'll flay him alive! I've been the most ridiculous fool to send her rushing off to a man like Cranesby."

Freddy looked up in surprise. "Rushing off? You're mad if you think that Sarah's gone willingly. You're also the worst judge of character I've ever met!"

The anguish in his cousin's face prevented him from saying more.

"Why shouldn't she go with him?" said Miles, staring unseeing into the gardens. "You don't know anything about it. It's damnable, but I've never even told her I love her. Didn't even realise it until just now." He pinched his forehead in his fingers. "All this time she's been my wife and I've never told her I love her. But the thought of her with someone else burns like a physical pain. I can't do without her. And if she's been persuaded to compromise her own and her family's good name because I made her life impossible, how can I bear it?"

"You don't *have* to. She'd never go off with him from choice. She always loved you. Always! Even when you hurt her beyond what was permissible. There were times when it wrung my heart to see how much."

Miles groaned, wanting to believe him, but could not be satisfied that Freddy spoke the truth. He had only one thought in his mind. "If he's touched so much as the lace on her gown, he'll die."

"Hush, dear boy, not so loud. Do you want everyone to hear?" hissed Freddy, giving up the struggle to convince him to concentrate on more urgent tasks. "Have some sense. The chances are that he hasn't yet managed to get her away. You've a man on the main entrance, haven't you?

"Lord, yes," said Miles, glad to have his immediate actions decided for him. "Why didn't I think of that? They must still be in the grounds. Quick Freddy, this way."

His hopes died almost immediately, however, for when he reached the wall which encircled the back garden and found the door which led through to the mews behind the house, there was no sign of any manservant. A swift examination was enough to reveal a man's form, partially hidden by some bushes, a figure which proved to be one of the temporary footmen hired for the evening. Though he was unconscious when they dragged him out, it took Miles only a few moments to bring him round and to hear how he'd allowed a gentleman to come in by the back way without a card, because he was "obviously a flash cove", and how he'd been speaking to him "friendly like" when, suddenly, everything went black.

"So there must have been an accomplice to hit him from behind," murmured Miles to Freddy, "God knows how long he's been unconscious. I must go at once. I'm pretty sure he'll make for the house at Hounslow—that's where he was taking Caro—it'll be his idea of a rum joke. But, as God is my witness, he won't think it much of a joke when I get at him!"

"Look Miles," said Freddy, restraining him by the arm, "best let me come too, don't you think?"

"Not this time, Freddy," replied Miles, "I need you here to make sure that not a breath of scandal soils Sarah's reputation. Caro . . . well, maybe Caro didn't deserve such attention, but you know Sarah almost as well as I do, and I trust to you to make all well for her."

"You know I'll do my possible, but . . ."

"I said *No*, Freddy! This is a matter only for him and me to settle. He'll not have your protection this time. Go back inside and look after Ami. God willing, I'll bring Sarah back before morning," and with that, Miles walked swiftly out through the garden entrance and into the mews behind, where he woke his groom from his make-shift bed in the straw and demanded that he prepare his racing curricle.

"What, now, m'lord? You mean this minute?" stammered the drowsy groom.

"I mean exactly that. I'll be back within ten minutes, so see it done," replied Miles curtly, in a tone so unlike his own as to make the groom wonder if his lordship hadn't imbibed too much of his own champagne.. While Miles was waiting for his Greys to be harnessed, he quickly walked back through the gardens and into the house, making his way to his study, where he rang a bell to summon Jepson to him. Jepson arrived in seconds, at his usual stately pace.

"Ah Jepson, I am going out," said Miles, his face an expressionless mask. Jepson betrayed no sign of curiosity.

"Certainly sir. Now sir?"

"Now."

"You will require your outer garments then sir," he replied and he left the room unhurriedly, to fetch Miles's many-caped drab coat and beaver.

Left to himself, Miles went over to the mahogany bureau which stood in front of a large window, and slid open one of its drawers. From the drawer he extracted a beautiful papier-mâché box, the lid of which he flicked open to reveal two magnificent matched duelling pistols. Quite deliberately, he began to clean and load them . . .

****

Sarah was beginning to feel very cold now. On leaving the outskirts of Town, at Hyde Park Corner, they had circled the Park to reach the village of Knightsbridge and then continued on towards the remoter settlement of Kensington Gore, where they were forced to negotiate the Halfpenny Hatch turnpike gate. Taking no chances, Lord Cranesby had kept a hand securely over Sarah's already bound mouth, while his man was paying the toll. Beyond Kensington all was country until they reached Hammersmith and it was during this stage of their journey that her kidnapper had loosed Sarah's bonds.

At first he was inclined to be familiar, but Sarah's frigid reception of his advances, together with the joltings and bouncings of the vehicle, had shown Cranesby the wisdom of waiting for such delights until they reached their journey's end, so Sarah was left in comparative peace to sit in one corner of the coach as far away from him as she could possibly get.

At Hammersmith, my lord's coach had pulled in at a wayside inn, which boasted a high red-tiled roof and vast, if run-down stabling. Now was Sarah's chance to make a move for freedom, and as Lord Cranesby's servant let down the steps and handed her down, she had kicked him as hard in the shins as her little evening shoes would allow, and bolted, in search of a saviour, towards a door which seemed to be the entrance to a brightly-lit tap room. She had gone no more than a few feet, however, before she felt her arm caught in a harsh grip and then drawn up behind her back, and she found herself being roughly manhandled back towards her captor, still lounging at his ease within the coach. Slowly, his face like thunder, he had descended the steps, to stand before her, lifting a hand to pinch her chin hard between two of his fingers and force her to look up at him. "My dear . . . my very dear Sarah, what a singularly foolish thing to try, and what an unfriendly way to begin what is to be, I trust, a long and mutually satisfying adventure together. Do you seriously think that I would allow you to descend willy-nilly if there was the slightest chance that you would escape me? Come, my little bird, you must know me better by now."

She had deigned no reply, and his mocking voice continued, "Just in case you are thinking of making another run for it, I think it only fair to mention the name of this tavern. Really, it is quite well-known, I am sure, even to such well brought up ladies as yourself. The Red Cow—have you heard of it? And the landlord is a particular friend of mine. Known him forever, and I have no hesitation in telling you that, should you try to leave my . . . er . . . protection, he will return you to me with all speed. I have the money to pay for you, you see. Really your interests will be best served if you sit quietly. Try another run for it by all means, of course, my dear, but I must warn you that I shall be far less lenient with you when you are brought back again. Oh, and if you are really thinking of applying to any of the good people in the tap room for assistance, I regret that you will find most of them to be 'cly-fakers'—or is the word unfamiliar? Footpads may convey more to you? The landlord is a most generous creature and lets them gather here before they begin their honest night's toil on the Heath . . . for a consideration, of course."

"Don't worry, he continued silkily, as she shivered at his words, "for we will be here for no more than a few minutes, and anyway, they know better than to try their tricks on me. The fact is, my love, that, comfortable as is my carriage, it is rather cumbersome and, unless we transfer to a faster vehicle, we may find ourselves overtaken. But fear not! My men, you see, have had my curricle and my bays brought here and you and I are to go on in that, while they see to it that our tracks are hidden. It will be a trifle chilly, but that cannot be helped. And I promise to warm you well when we reach our destination."

As he spoke, his curricle, drawn by his famous bays, was driven round from its hiding place behind the stables, an arc of light being given off by each of its lanterns, and while two of his grooms began to harness the town coach, another drove the curricle onto the roadway.

Cranesby had a few last orders for his men before lifting Sarah up into the curricle and exchanging places with his groom on the seat beside her. So, she was to travel alone with him now! No point, then, in wasting any more strength in escape bids until the odds were better. Time enough when Cranesby had put some distance between them and the inn, for it must surely be easier to outwit one man than a group. Not that it would be easy, in any case, she told herself, for even she had by now realised that they must be making towards Hounslow Heath. If Cranesby had not bothered to enlighten her as to the name of the inn at which they had stopped, the eerie landscape would have told its own story. At the thought of all the tales of robbery and murder she had heard about the place her blood chilled.

Cranesby placed a heavy cloak around her shoulders when he had her safely stowed beside him in the open vehicle, but her ballgown was flimsy and the night air cold. She shivered as she felt the wind whipping through her hair and pulling at her clothing, so fast as they were travelling, and she tried to pull the cloak more closely to her to keep as much warmth around her as she could. The trees they passed were twisted and eerie, like supernatural beings, with long flailing arms, and she shuddered each time a bough brushed against her hair when Cranesby creased the edge of the roadside.

"Cold, Sarah?" he asked anxiously, as he caught the movement from the corner of his eye. "Snuggle close to me, my love, and you'll be warmer."

"I'd rather freeze, thank you," she replied at once, moving deliberately away and taking care to keep as much distance between them as she could.

He laughed delightedly, "By the heavens, but you've enough spirit for any man. Game as a pebble, ain't you, even now, when you know you are completely in my hands? It's what I've liked about you from the start!"

Sarah refused to answer: she was too busy thinking. There was a full moon, but the night was overcast and clouds kept scudding across the sky and blocking off the precious light. Driving would have been hazardous enough on any such night, but at the speed he was pushing his horses, it was positively deadly. And now, he was forced to avoid the Turnpike Roads too, since they were travelling in the open vehicle, and he could not chance Sarah's co-operation while the gates were opened. At Turnham Green, therefore, he came off the main road, using lanes and tracks to enable him to skirt the Hounslow turnpike, always choked by traffic, day and night. But he'd had many a lark up there on the heath with his friends when they had all been young bucks, and he knew precisely the best way to go to avoid going through it—why, it had been one of their favourite pastimes, avoiding paying the toll, and there was an excellent short-cut they had all used, which would rejoin the road further along.

Even in her dilemma, Sarah's reluctant admiration was aroused by the consummate skill with which he manoeuvred his curricle along the unlit country tracks and lanes between villages, for, even when the moon came from behind the clouds, she was unsure where the road ended and the hedges and ditches began. Yet he never seemed to falter or even to slow down. How was she to suspect that he knew every inch of these lanes from madcap races he had had with Miles and Jeremy in their youth?

Sarah had no idea where he was taking her and how far was their destination, but common sense told her that they could not have very much further to travel, since he had chosen to use his curricle. She remembered Jeremy telling her of the house Cranesby owned near the Heath, and to which he had been taking Caro. Surely he could not be so foolhardy as to choose the same place for a second kidnap?

Or could he? She knew herself, only too well, how impulsive he was, and it just might be that he was so foolish as to take her there, at least for the night. If it was indeed so, surely Miles would come for her? He must know Cranesby well enough to guess what he would do, mustn't he?

Commonsense told her she could not rely on it: if she was to save herself she must think of a plan of her own in case Miles did not reach her. Try as she could she could think of nothing else: as far as she could see, there was only one thing possible. As soon as the curricle slowed down, she must take a chance and jump for it. She knew full well that it would be risky, for if she hurt herself she would be more at his mercy than ever, and if he managed to rein in his horses very quickly after she jumped, it might well be that she would have no time to hide before he recaptured her again. That there was a third disastrous possibility and she might kill herself did cross her mind, but it was pointless to dwell on that. Since nothing better offered itself to her usually fertile brain, what else was there to do? She must take her fate securely in both hands and chance it—but, would the man never feel the need to slow down?

Some miles later, she was still asking herself the same question and her heart was thudding painfully, for surely they would soon be at the end of their journey? They were travelling along a wider road now, and she suspected that they were on the Heath itself, so desolate was it. All around, she caught glimpses of furze bushes and swampy gravel-pits, which the ghostly light picked out as they passed. At night, she knew that the whole swarmed with footpads and highwaymen, and she swallowed hard as she saw Cranesby take a pistol from the pocket of his great-coat and cock it in readiness, holding his whip and the reins quite steadily with only one hand.

Thankfully, she soon noticed that they were coming to the outskirts of a small hamlet, for they were passing a straggling ribbon of buildings beside the road, and she offered up silent prayers that they had at least safely skirted the Heath. Just at that moment, the moon chose to hide itself again, and fingers of blackness spread themselves across the surrounding fields. Still Cranesby didn't falter, until, suddenly as they took a bend, they found coming towards them, as if from nowhere, a stage coach, lanterns blazing from the darkness. Sharply he pulled on the reins. Sarah had time only to see him flinch at the unaccustomed glare, before she jumped . . .

* * * * * * * * *

Not more than twenty minutes later, Sarah's husband was passing the same thread of buildings she had noticed just before her jump, and which, had she known, signified the outskirts of Cranford. Unerringly, Miles had followed their route, guessing that, with a prisoner in tow, Cranesby would be forced off the Turnpikes, for he could never negotiate the busy Hounslow toll gate and keep Sarah hidden. Blessing the fact that his past companionship with the man had given him a knowledge of all the lanes leading to his love-nest, he in turn left the turnpike road at Turnham, thankful that he knew enough not to have been led into joining a queue of traffic which would have held him up far too long. He prayed now that he had read the man's mind correctly and that he had brought Sarah to Hounslow, for he was honest enought to admit that if he didn't find her there he had no idea where else to look.

He knew a sudden thrill of elation now, as he saw the outline of a coach ahead, blocking the road, but any elation quickly turned to fear when he realised that it was a common stage which was barring the way, and that just behind it lay the tangled outline of an overturned vehicle, a small crowd all around. His mind went back, then, reliving a night not unlike this one, when another lady had been stolen from his side and he had found her, no longer breathing, in just such a tangle.

"Not Sarah, Lord," he whispered as before. "Please not Sarah!" and almost before his horses had halted, he had let go the reins and was jumping from his curricle, and then running towards the little knot of people who had gathered from the village, awoken by the noise of the crash. Quickly he went towards the overturned vehicle, which was lying at a dangerous angle on its side, as though ready to tip right over. To one side of the road he could just see that one of Cranesby's beautiful bays lay dead, while the others were being held in check, with some difficulty, by some of the men in the crowd. As he moved onward, a large burly individual blocked his path and held up a hand before him as if to bar his way.

"I shouldn't go any furver, sir, if I was you," he advised respectfully, "No' a sigh' you'd be wishful to see, if you take m'meaning. And the poor 'orse 'aving ter be sho' too—broken fetlock!"

The horror in the man's voice effectively halted Miles. He couldn't face seeing Sarah crumpled up and broken as he had once seen Caroline. "The lady?" he whispered, fearfully, "The lady?"

"Oh no, sir," replied his informant, reassuringly, "Weren't no lady, just the pore gent. And 'im not long fer this world, as yer might say. The sawbones is wiv 'im nah, sir."

Swiftly Miles pushed the man aside and walked around the curricle. The colour drained from his face at the sight which met his eyes there, for lying in a pool of blood, was his old protagonist, a man kneeling above him trying in vain to staunch the flow from numerous lacerations. To one side could be seen the huge bulk of the bay, half in and half out of the ditch which had caused Lord Cranesby's downfall, its life blood running in a long sticky river across the road, from a wound made by a bullet obviously clumsily administered and which had shattered half its head.

Forcing his eyes away from the gory sight and back to his one-time friend, Miles saw his eyes, once piercing, now opaque, open, a flicker of recognition in them as Miles's face came into view. Cranesby's lips were moving as if he wished to speak and Miles went down on one knee beside him to try to catch his words. As he got nearer, he saw, to his horror, that the front of Cranesby's shirt was soaked in blood and that splinters of glass were sticking through it.

The doctor turned as Miles knelt beside him, "A bad business, sir," he murmured, "A bad business. Curricle overturned and this unfortunate fellow impaled on the glass from the lantern. Mostly small wounds, but one or two very deep, and to the heart. No chance at all to stop the bleeding. Only a matter of minutes I should think."

"May I speak to him, doctor?" asked Miles urgently,

unable to keep his fears for Sarah's safety from his mind. "We are old acquaintances."

"Oh, I see, sir . . . well . . . I suppose there's no harm. Won't make any difference one way or t'other to him. Can't say if he'll be able to answer you though," and he moved a few paces off.

By now, Cranesby's eyes had closed again. "Rob," whispered Miles urgently, "Rob, wake up! It's me, Miles. Wake up, old man."

The watery blue eyes flickered open again and, as if he was speaking from a long way off, his thin, whispered voice murmured, "Oh . . . it's you, Miles. Sorry to greet you like this. Trifle out of sorts . . ." His eyelids fell.

"Rob . . . listen . . . Sarah? What have you done with her?" cried Miles urgently.

For a few seconds Miles thought it was too late and that he was dead, then he heard him chuckle, very softly, and saw a wistful expression settle near his mouth, his eyes still closed. Agonizingly slowly, and breathing heavily almost between every word, he said,

"Boot's on—other—foot. Done for me. Game as—pebble."

"Yes, I know, old man," interrupted Miles impatiently, "but what has happened to her?"

"Jumped!—Just as we—saw—coach. I forced her to come. She—struggled. Game as—" At that he let out a terrible groan and his eyes opened wide to meet Miles's.

"Caro—wasn't worth . . . Sarah—good little th . . ." and with his lips still mouthing the word, he died.

Miles's mouth twisted then, as if he had himself received injury and it seemed an added hurt to remember the duelling pistols still resting in their case in his curricle. What fools they had been to allow their friendship to end this way over someone as worthless as Caroline . . . And even now, he could take no time to mourn for him. He must find Sarah, since in all this she was the one innocent.

Pausing only to close Cranesby's eyes and to say a few words to the doctor, Miles hurried back to his curricle, expertly turning it to retrace his steps. Cranesby had said she had jumped only just before they'd seen the coach, so she couldn't have gone far—not already, not in the thin things she was wearing. He drove his curricle slowly and carefully along the road, his horses chaffing at the speed they were being forced to travel. He was afraid that she might be lying injured there and began calling her name every few yards in the hope that she might realise that he had come for her. Things were made very much more difficult, then, for the clouds now completely hid the moon and the only lights to be seen were those given off by the lanterns on his vehicle. He had gone some quarter of a mile in this fashion and was beginning to feel desperate, when the moon suddenly showed itself scudding between clouds, as it continued its stately progress across the heavens. As a silvery light spread slowly over the landscape, he could see a small figure running furiously along the side of a field, away from the road, obviously trying to reach, for safety, a large clump of furze bushes some few hundred yards further along.

"Sarah," he shouted, as he brought his team to a sudden halt. "Sarah, don't run. It's me!"

She ran, if anything, faster than ever and he began cursing to himself as he realised that she thought it was Cranesby after her.

"Sarah, don't run. It's Miles," he called then, and this time, to his relief, she stopped in her tracks.

He reached her in a few seconds, intending to take her into his arms, but when he came up to her, she had become entangled in a bramble and was trying to free herself.

"Thank heaven you've come, Miles," she said, head bent, face creased in concentration as she wrestled with the prickly branch. "This wretched thing has caught me."

After the impassioned scene he had envisaged, the anti-climax was too much for him and a shout of laughter sounded from him. "Sarah, you're a pearl beyond price!"

After all she'd been through, Sarah was incensed. "I might have known you would find this funny, Miles Wilburton!" she blurted, as he freed her. "I suppose I should be grateful that you have dragged yourself away from Lady Blissworth for long enough even to come after me!"

She was a poor, dejected-looking figure, her hair half down and her face and dress streaked with mud, while her slippers and hem were soaked from running over the marshy ground, and at the tremor which had sounded in her voice, he was at once contrite.

"But I did drag myself away, Lady Wilburton, didn't I?" he said gently, taking both her hands. "Foolish girl. Did you really think I would let someone steal what is most precious to me?"

She looked up at him in doubt, and his heart berated him at her uncertainty.

"Am I that to you?" she asked seriously, searching his face for confirmation.

"You are!" he said, drawing her towards him. "Fool that I am, it took Robert Cranesby to teach me that lesson. He can't trouble you again, but I won't forget that he showed me what I was in danger of losing."

Sarah was afraid to listen to his words. He offered joy—yet surely they were still divided?

"Lizzie?" was all she said. His answering groan threatened her happiness for only a moment, since he held her more tightly than ever.

"You *must* know that my cousin means nothing to me at all? She's my cousin, that is all, and I never . . . never . . . thought of her as anything else," he said, interspersing his words with kisses, promissory of the future.

His lips moved down towards her shoulder distractingly, but, being Sarah, all her fears must be pursued. She tugged herself out of his grasp, and moved away.

"And what of Caro, Miles? Does she still hold you? Can you still only promise me what you did once before? 'A degree of affection'?"

Appalled to have his words thrust back at him, he pulled her ruthlessly into his arms once again, to quieten her doubts so fulsomely that when he presently declared himself shocked that she had cared to marry such a numbskull, she was enough secure to reply teasingly.

"But I was quite sure that I was shrewish enough to bring you to heel if kindness did not answer."

"Thank heaven you have," he said, hugging her to him.

"Strange, but until I saw you that night at the opera with Cranesby, I had never questioned my love for Caroline. After that, somehow I found myself always comparing you and it was always Caroline who was found wanting. She was a menace, a . . . a doxy! I made her a heroine."

Sarah laughed delightedly into his chest. "Oh Miles, you are a funny one! What a marvellous old-fashioned word . . . a doxy!"

"But that's just what she was, and I too stupid to see it. When you are young, it is very easy to deceive yourself. I've always pretended that she was an angel because I could not bear the truth." He kissed her contentedly on the mouth. "It wasn't until I was married to you that I realised what an angel was."

At that, Sarah pulled free again, and stood away from him, her hair tumbling wildly in ringlets around her shoulders. "What a fibster you are," she laughed, her eyes wide in disbelief. "You can never have thought me an angel in your life!"

Ruefully Miles tugged at her curls. "Madam wife, for once I find myself in complete agreement with you! And when I think of the merry dance you have been leading me with poor Bliss, I don't know how you have dared to rail at me about Lizzie. I'm by no means certain that you are not a little in love with him."

"Oh well, of course," said Sarah sweetly, "how could anyone not be, so gentlemanly as he is?"

"You really are a wretch, do you know it," he replied through clenched teeth, threading his fingers roughly through her hair and pulling her face close to his own. "I should warn you, my little dove, that there is at least one man who will not allow his wife to be in love with Bliss, and so you would do well to remember! I think perhaps I should beat you at least once a day to remind you of it."

"How you do jump, Miles," she laughed, but her laugh quivered as she realised suddenly how cold she was, even in his arms. "Thank heaven you found me, my love," she said between trembling lips. "But in my heart I knew you would."

He felt her shiver and was called back to practicalities at once. Taking off his drab coat, he draped it around her shoulders and fastened it at the neck, saying matter-of-factly as he did so, "Of course you did, my darling. How should it be otherwise when I have received strict instructions from Great Aunt Almeria only this evening that we are to set up our nursery?"

"Oh no," gurgled Sarah, her teeth refusing to stop chattering but diverted in spite of herself. "Did she indeed say so? And what did *you* say?"

"What could I say, love?" he replied, carrying her to his curricle, removing her wet slippers and wrapping a warm rug round her, "for you know what a termagant she is. Naturally, I said I would do my possible. Nothing else for it!"

He jumped up beside her and hugged her to him to warm her.

"And will you?" she whispered, feeling very much better.

"Well, not at the moment," he replied seriously, gazing intently at her, "for you look a positive fright, you know, besides being covered in mud. Quite like King Cophetua's beggar maid. Well—probably even worse!"

"Oh you . . . you . . . wretch!" cried Sarah, removing herself from his arms, bosom heaving alarmingly.

"And you say *I* jump?" laughed Miles, bringing her once more into the circle of his arms. She hugged him tightly, leaning against his shoulder, "But I would *like* to have children, Miles, would not you?" she asked tremulously, her misty grey eyes raised to his face.

"Oh, I think I can safely promise you that you will, my little love," said Miles urbanely, as his horses moved smoothly off. "I think I can safely promise you will . . ."